ON THE WILD SIDE

THE WILDS OF MONTANA

KRISTEN PROBY

Ampersand Publishing, Inc.

On the Wild Side

A Wilds of Montana Novel

By

Kristen Proby

ON THE WILD SIDE

A Wilds of Montana Novel

Kristen Proby

A NOTE TO THE READER

I don't usually offer trigger warnings in my books because I don't feel like I typically need them, but I am going to warn you of a couple of things here, just in case. In *On the Wild Side*, you will see the death of a spouse and sexual and physical abuse of a minor, all off page. You will also see graphic nightmares due to the trauma mentioned above.

Kristen

PROLOGUE

ABBI

Five Years Ago

"What am I supposed to do without you?" I can't stop the tears that fall onto my cheeks. Nate has been in and out of sleep, and they tell me that he'll likely slip into a coma soon, so I should say everything that I want to say now, while he can still hear me.

He's on a ventilator, but he's watching me with those big, brown eyes, and his hand tightens on mine.

"I'm so sorry this happened," I continue and lean in to kiss his cheek. "It's not fair. It's not right."

He squeezes me again, comforting me.

Nate is the *sweetest* man on the planet. He's good and generous, and he doesn't deserve this.

"I'll take care of Daisy. Don't worry about us. I promise we'll be okay."

His eyes suddenly look panicked, and I brush my fingers through his hair, doing my best to calm him.

"I won't let her near our baby, Nathan. I will *not.*" He blinks, and I can see that he wants to talk, but he can't.

"I know," I continue. "We already talked about this, and everything is in place, so she can't touch us. I'll make sure of it. And I'll make sure that Daisy always knows you. She's still so little."

Not even two years. Nate didn't even have two whole years with his daughter before he caught pneumonia that devolved into a systemic infection, causing his organs to fail.

He isn't going to get better. He isn't going to leave this hospital.

And I want to wail at the injustice of it.

"I love you." His eyes droop, and I can see that he's so, so tired. "Thank you for five wonderful years. Thank you for being my best friend and such an awesome dad to our baby girl."

He squeezes my hand once more, and then he's asleep again, and all I can do is lay my head on the bed next to him and cry.

CHAPTER ONE

BRADY

"Come on, girls, it's going to be a bitch of a winter." I crack my whip and maneuver my horse through the snowy pasture, herding our cattle to a meadow closer to the barn, where we can keep an eye on these ladies during the coldest months of the year. Winter in Bitterroot Valley, Montana is a bitch, and it's only early December, which means we haven't even hit the solstice yet. We've already seen record snowfall this year, which tells us that it's going to be a long, cold season.

And we need to make sure these girls make it through calving season in a few months.

"Storm's moving in," my oldest brother, Remington, yells out to me, and I tip my head back to look up at the sky. The wind has picked up, and the clouds have dropped and grown darker.

"Fuck," I mutter and crack the whip again before I call back to him. "We'll be down this hill in an hour!"

"Let's hope the blizzard holds out that long," Lucky, our senior ranch hand, replies. He's got to be ninety if he's a day. I swear, there's never been a time when Lucky wasn't old as fuck. And no one on this ranch knows what they're doing better than him.

Which is saying something, because my family has owned this land for well over a hundred years. My father, leading us all up ahead, passed the reins on to Remington a few years ago. Ranching, *cattle* ranching, is in our blood. It's who we are.

It's what we do.

But shit, I think Lucky worked for my *grandfather* once upon a time.

I wonder if he's a goddamn vampire.

When we're about a mile from the pasture that the cattle will spend the winter in, the snow starts to blow harder. None of us, the humans or the animals, want to be out here in this, but it reinforces that it's the right time to move the herd.

We might not be able to get to them in a few days, and they'll have a better chance of survival if we can watch them.

With our heads down and our minds on the work, we get everyone safely into the fenced field in less than the hour that I predicted.

"I'll get the water," Bruiser, another of our men, shouts as he swings off his horse and hurries to the troughs to fill them with fresh drinking water for our cows.

Despite the troughs being heated to keep them from

freezing, we'll have to come out here several times a day to break up ice that'll form on the top.

Montana is fucking brutal.

But damn if I don't love her.

We work as a team to spread hay, and when everyone is settled into their new home, we lead the horses into the barn so they can warm up and rest. We all put in one hell of a day.

I take my time with my boy, Blackjack, giving him apples and brushing him well before I settle a blanket on his back and kiss his cheek.

"You did great today, boy." He nudges my shoulder, and I grin, ignoring the twinge that's always there in that joint. "Yeah, we both did, huh? Good boy. I'll see you in the mornin'. You get some rest."

I kiss him once more and then close the door of his stable behind me as I walk out with the others.

"Want to come in for dinner?" Remington asks me, then narrows his eyes on me when I roll that same shoulder.

"You could join us, too, if you want," Bruiser adds. We have a house here for the hands to live in, and those cowboys make some damn good food.

I usually eat at either my brother's or with the hands, but I shake my head.

"Thanks, guys, but I have a date tonight."

My brother turns and frowns at me in surprise. I don't usually date at all, and I would never announce it to anyone, so the look on his face makes me laugh.

"I'm taking Daisy to the father/daughter dance at her school."

"Shit, that's right," Rem says, dragging his hand down his face. "I have to take Holly to that. I'd better go get cleaned up."

"Me, too."

"Have fun," Lucky says with a wave. "I'm gonna go put some chili on the stove."

The other two men walk in the direction of the bunkhouse, and I walk with Rem out to his truck.

"I guess I'll see you there," I say with a wink.

"I hate these things," Rem complains with a sigh. "I *love* my girl, but I hate dances."

"Come on, it's only a couple of hours." I laugh again and head over to my 4Runner. "See you later."

"Wait," Rem says, his hands on his hips. "That shoulder giving you trouble?"

I shake my head with a sigh. "You know my long list of injuries over the years, Rem. Something's always giving me trouble. It's the cost of being a cowboy."

"You're an idiot," he reminds me.

With a laugh and a wave, I hop into the vehicle and drive the couple of miles over to the old cabin that I live in here on the Wild River Ranch. It's the oldest dwelling on the property, and it could use some updating, but it suits me fine. I've lived in the tiny two-bedroom, one-bathroom cabin for almost a decade, and I haven't needed anything more.

Besides, I really only sleep here. I'm always working the ranch or riding a bull. At the very least, I train on the drop barrel daily so I don't get rusty. There's no time for anything else.

But when Daisy asked me to take her to her little dance, the night that my brother Ryan proposed to Polly, I couldn't say no. She reminds me of Snow White, with her dark hair and deep brown eyes. She's the cutest little thing, and she was so...earnest when she asked.

Only an asshole would have turned her down.

Besides, I *like* the kid. She hangs out with Holly all the time, and Daisy's mom, Abbi, is always with my sisters, since they started up their women in business group. And that part, the part where Abbi's always around? That's harder to swallow.

Because she's fucking beautiful. I want to have my way with her, and nothing good can come of that, so I have to keep my distance.

"Good job doing that," I mutter as I finish in the shower and towel off. "Taking her kid somewhere is definitely not the way to stay away from the mom."

I shake my head in disgust as I get dressed. I'm wearing a goddamn *suit* tonight. I usually only do that for weddings and funerals.

And yet, here I am, the consummate bachelor, taking a little girl to her dance.

My phone pings with a text, and I see that it's Abbi.

Abbi: Hey! The snow is really coming down here. We understand if you don't want to brave the roads to come all the way into town from the ranch tonight. It might not be safe.

I smirk. I've been driving into town from this ranch

for half my life. Sure, I'll take it easy, but it's nothing I can't handle.

Me: I'll be there in an hour.

The bubble bounces, then stops for several seconds before it comes back, as if she doesn't know what to say.

Abbi: Okay, we will see you soon. Please be careful.

After I tie my purple tie—Daisy was sure to let me know that she'd be wearing her favorite color, *purple*, to the dance—I grab my black Stetson and head out. Of course, I have a stop to make before I get to Abbi's place.

Abbi was right; the roads into town are a bitch. I have to slow way down because it's hard to see through the blowing snow, but I reach Bitterroot Valley without a mishap.

And just before my sister-in-law, Summer, closes her flower shop for the day.

"I just caught you." I grin at Summer as I walk into her store. "Sorry, would have been here sooner, but the roads were shit. Hey, Chase."

My brother, Chase, is standing by the counter, obviously waiting for his wife to finish working for the day.

"It's bad enough out there that I'm taking Summer home with me, and we'll get her car tomorrow," Chase says.

"Good idea. That bend at Half Moon is icy. Be careful."

"Will do," Chase says with a nod.

"I have your flowers ready," Summer says with a big grin and hurries into the big walk-in refrigerator where she keeps the flowers. She returns with a clear plastic box holding a corsage of purple roses and a bouquet of pink and orange flowers whose name is completely lost on me.

"Nice," Chase says with a grin. "All of that for Daisy?"

"Fuck off," I warn him, but my brother's smile only grows. "I can't take flowers to one and not the other."

"Right, 'cause that would be rude," Chase says, and Summer rolls her eyes.

"Be nice to your brother," she tells her husband. "He's doing a really fun, cute thing for that little girl."

"Yeah," I agree, making Chase laugh.

"It *is* nice of you," he concedes. "And you look... spiffy."

"I don't want to have to punch you and get blood all over my outfit."

"I'm in uniform," he points out. "I don't want to have to arrest you for assaulting an officer."

I smirk and pay Summer for the flowers.

"Be careful out there," I call out to them as I walk to the door.

"Have fun," Summer calls back.

Abbi lives in a little neighborhood of townhomes on the edge of town. It's a newer area, with a park for Daisy and sidewalks and trees. It's a nice part of town, which makes me feel good because I know that they're safe.

And I don't even want to *think* about why that's something I worry about.

I pull into the driveway of Abbi's end unit and cut the engine, and with the flowers in hand, I make my way to the door, which is immediately opened by Daisy, who is currently jumping up and down in her ruffly purple dress.

"You're here! You're here!"

"Well, hello there, Princess." I wink at her and step inside when Abbi gestures, keeping most of the cold outside. When the door is closed, I offer Abbi her bouquet of flowers, and her gorgeous blue eyes soften. "For you."

"You didn't have to do that." But she buries her nose in a bloom and fusses over them in that way that women do that makes a man feel like he gave them the world. "Thank you."

"And for my *gorgeous* date, we have this." I present the box, and Daisy frowns down at it.

"What is it?"

"A corsage," Abbi says with a laugh. "Come on, let me set these in the kitchen, and we'll get the corsage on you, baby."

"Okay." Daisy takes my hand and leads me into the kitchen. I like this townhome, with its open floor plan. This floor is just the kitchen and living room, with a door out to the garage, and another that I assume is a half bath.

The bedrooms are upstairs.

"You look handsome," Daisy says with a bright smile. "And your tie matches my dress!"

"I heard a rumor that you'd be wearing purple."

Daisy giggles. "I told you, silly."

"Oh, yeah, that's right. Well, your dress is super pretty, and your hair is all curly."

"Mommy did it," she says shyly, gently touching the curls that fall around her shoulders.

"Here, I know how to do this, thanks to prom about a million years ago," Abbi says as she takes the corsage out of the box and slips the wristband around Daisy's wrist, tightening it to fit.

"This way," Daisy says, "it's easier for me to sniff them."

She does and then closes her eyes, as if it's the best thing she's ever smelled.

"Good?" Abbi asks.

"I'm gonna smell them all night. Can we go now?"

"Pictures first," Abbi says, grabbing her phone. "Here, stand by the fireplace."

We pose for photos. In some, I'm holding Daisy's hand. In others, I'm squatting next to her, and she has her arms around my neck.

It all makes me wonder where her father is. Who would willingly miss out on something this great?

Before long, we're on our way to the school where the dance is being held. Daisy's in the back seat of my 4Runner, chatting away.

The kid never shuts up, but it's kind of cute.

"Robert is nice," she says, "but he has red hair."

"You don't like red hair?"

I glance in the rearview and see her frown, thinking it over. "I do. Polly has red hair, and I like her."

"Okay, so what's wrong with his red hair?"

"It's just...I can't say because Mom says it's mean."

I frown back at her. "You're not a mean girl."

"*I know.* Okay, if I tell you, you can't tell Mom I said it."

"Cross my heart."

"What does that mean?"

I grin as I pull into the parking lot.

"It means that I promise not to tell."

"Okay. So, I don't like Robert's hair because it looks like spaghetti sauce."

I wait, positive that there's more to this story, but she doesn't say anything else. So, I pull into a parking spot and cut the engine, unbuckle my seatbelt, and turn to look at the little girl who's staring back at me with sober brown eyes.

"*That's* why you don't like him?"

"I don't like spaghetti." She leans her head back in despair. "We had to play duck, duck, goose the other day in the gym, and I didn't want to touch his hair."

"Because it looks like spaghetti."

She nods solemnly.

"And what don't you like about spaghetti?" Now I'm starting to wonder if *I'll* ever eat it again.

"It looks like Robert's hair," she says, and I can't help but laugh.

"Well, sweetie, I think of all the things in the world, this isn't so bad. You don't have to touch his hair *or* eat spaghetti."

"Okay, good. Let's go in!"

I learned a few things during the dance.

One, little girls will dance forever if given the chance, and they give zero shits about silly things like keeping their shoes on or if anyone cares what they look like.

Two, my brother may have moaned and groaned about going to this thing, but he indulged the hell out of Holly all evening and never once frowned or complained.

Three, Robert's hair does, indeed, look like spaghetti sauce.

And four, I am completely smitten with a little girl.

Of course, I already knew number four. I've had a soft spot for Daisy since the first time I met her, so I'm glad that I came tonight and that she didn't have to sit this one out because her dad isn't around.

"I'll see you tomorrow," I say to Remington, keeping my voice down. We're each holding a little girl, and both of them are passed out cold. "They danced until they dropped."

Rem grins and waves before we go our separate ways to our vehicles. I ease Daisy into her booster seat and then drive the five minutes to her house.

The snow hasn't stopped falling. If anything, it's only started falling harder, which means the drive home will be an adventure.

Daisy doesn't even stir when I lift her out of the 4Runner and walk up to the door, where Abbi must be watching because she opens it when I approach.

"I saw your lights," she says and smiles at her daughter, her eyes softening. "She must have had fun."

"I've only seen more dancing on *Footloose*," I confirm, making her chuckle. "I'll carry her up."

"Thanks." Abbi gestures up the stairs. I know which

bedroom is Daisy's because I helped them home a couple of weeks ago after Ryan and Polly's engagement party.

It doesn't take us long to have Daisy in her pajamas, her corsage off and safely in its box, and tucked into bed, and I follow Abbi back downstairs.

"Are you hungry?" Abbi asks.

Truthfully, I'm *starving*. And it must show on my face because Abbi grins and crooks her finger for me to follow her into the kitchen.

"I have some leftover meatloaf from dinner. I can make you a sandwich, if you want?"

"That sounds damn good." I take off my jacket and set it on a chair at her small kitchen table, loosen my tie, and sit at the kitchen island as I roll up my sleeves. I love the way her home feels warm from the fire and from the glow of Christmas lights from the tree in the corner.

When Abbi turns back around, her eyes go wide.

"Problem?" I ask.

"No. No, of course not. You should get comfortable. Was Daisy good for you?"

"Daisy's always good," I reply with a grin. "She's smart, and she listens. She had a blast dancing with her friends, and I even cut a rug with her a couple of times. That seemed to make her happy."

"I'm sure it did," Abbi says with a chuckle as she slices the meatloaf and sets it on the buttered bread. "My daughter is quite taken with you, in case you hadn't noticed."

"It goes both ways." She slides the plate my way and then opens her fridge.

"Would you like some lemonade? Water? I don't keep soda because Daisy likes it too much, so we save it for a treat. I do have beer, if you want that."

"Water's perfect, thank you." I'd tell her she doesn't have to go to so much trouble, but the truth is, I *like* being here with her, even though I know I shouldn't. I take a bite and sigh when the flavor hits my tongue. "Jesus, this is good."

So, she's gorgeous, *and* she can cook. I'm fucked.

"If I'd known you hadn't eaten, I would have fed you before you went to the dance." She puts the rest of the leftovers away and wipes down her countertop. Abbi's house is *clean*. Sure, there are a few things out here and there that show that the house is lived in, but it's all clean. Which makes sense, given that she owns a private cleaning company here in town.

"It's okay," I reply. "I just had a busy day. We had to herd cattle from higher ground, down near the barn so we can keep an eye on them in this weather. We don't want to lose any of them."

"Of course not." Once she's finished tidying up, she leans on the counter, and I get a front-row view of her impressive cleavage.

What am I doing here? I should go home. I should get the hell out of here, where I'm not tempted to make moves on a woman that I absolutely can't fuck around with.

"This was delicious," I say after finishing the last bite. "Thanks for it."

I take my plate to the sink, rinse it, and then set it in her dishwasher.

"Are you sure it's safe for you to drive home?" Abbi asks with a frown as she nibbles on her bottom lip. "It's snowed another foot since you picked up Daisy."

I sigh, looking toward the windows where the snow is coming down hard, and shoot my brother, Chase, a text. "Let me check with Chase."

Me: How nasty are *the roads?*

Almost immediately, he replies.

Chase: Rem just texted. He barely made it home without going off the road. Had to crawl. It's a shitshow out there.

I show her the response, and she cringes.

"Stay here," she says, and my whole body reacts at her suggestion. "I have a guest room upstairs, and I'd feel better if I knew that you were safe. The storm should pass by morning."

"Abbi, you don't have to—"

"Am I that repulsive?" she demands, her hands on her hips now, and we're caught here, between the island and the sink, and I want to kiss her more than I want my next breath. "I know I'm not a skinny woman, and I'm a mom, but I'm only suggesting you stay here, where it's safe. You don't have to worry about me getting naked and trying to have my wicked way with you when my daughter is twelve feet away."

Her eyes go wide, and she covers her mouth with her hand, clearly horrified that she said the words out loud.

"Oh, God," she whispers.

"Number one," I begin, and immediately move in,

sliding my hand over her round hip, my fingertips pressing into her, as I cage her in against the countertop. "You're every fucking fantasy I've ever had, so don't *ever* say that shit about yourself again. Got it?"

She's watching me intently as she nods, and her hand falls from her face.

"Number two." I lick my lips as my gaze slips down to her mouth. "I want to kiss you. I won't take it further. I know Daisy's right upstairs, but fuck me, I want to kiss you, Abbi."

She doesn't pull away. She doesn't say no, and by the way her breathing has just gone ragged, I take that as consent.

My hold tightens on her hip, and I cup her jaw with my free hand as my mouth descends to hers, and I nibble. I take my time tasting her before I sink in and *take*. She moans deep in her throat as she shifts closer to me, presses those fan-fucking-tastic tits against me, and her hand dives into the hair at the nape of my neck, and I am completely lost to her.

Fuck me, I've wanted this for *months*. I have no business doing it. None whatsoever, but I'll be damned if I can stop.

Finally, though, I loosen my hold on her, and she pulls away, just out of my reach. She's breathing hard. Her blue eyes are on fire as she watches me, and her blonde hair is the perfect halo of light around her, illuminated by the firelight and Christmas lights in the living room.

"Every goddamn fantasy," I repeat before swallowing

hard. “And your curves? Jesus Christ, Abbi, your curves are enough to kill a man.”

She giggles, pushes her hands through her hair, and turns away from me, pacing.

“You’ll sleep here,” she insists after swallowing hard and clearing her throat. “Because I don’t want to worry about you getting home safely.”

“Yes, ma’am.” I shove my hands into my pockets so I don’t reach for her again. “I have a bag in my SUV with necessities.”

She lifts an eyebrow, and I grin.

“I get pretty messy at the rodeo and at the ranch. It pays to have extra things on hand.”

“Ah. Makes sense. Go ahead and grab it.”

With a nod, I hurry outside, through the falling snow and wind that’s just flat-out obnoxious, and retrieve the bag from the back seat. When I return inside, the lights are off, and Abbi’s waiting to escort me upstairs.

Her ass sways back and forth as she climbs the steps ahead of me, and I have to swallow hard and think about something other than burying my face between her legs. Baseball. Branding season. Getting bucked off of a pissed-off bull and dislocating my shoulder.

Again.

Nope, even that didn’t do it.

“You’re in here,” she says, gesturing to the fourth door on this floor. “You’ll have to share a bathroom with Daisy.”

“No problem.” I grin and walk inside, setting my bag on the queen-sized bed. “I appreciate it.”

"You're welcome. I'm making pancakes for breakfast, in case you want to stay in the morning."

"Just for me?"

She laughs softly and shakes her head. "No. We have pancakes every Sunday. Good night, Brady."

"'Night, Abs."

She bites her lip and flushes, as if she wants to say something else, but she decides against it and closes the door behind her.

When I'm alone, I blow out a breath and shake my head. I shouldn't have kissed her, no matter how badly I wanted to. But damn it, hearing her say that I might not find her attractive was fucking ridiculous. Does the woman not know how damn hot she is?

I guess not.

I was happy to remind her.

But this can't become a habit because I can never commit to her, and she's a *mother.* You don't fuck around with that. She deserves so much more than I can give her.

CHAPTER TWO

ABBI

The man who has starred in all of my sexy fantasies for the past year and a half is still sleeping just down the hall from me.

How in the hell was I supposed to sleep through the night with Brady Wild so damn close? Especially after that kiss in my kitchen. I almost stripped out of my clothes and begged him to fuck me right there on the island. Has anyone ever made me feel so sexy? So *wanted*?

Nope.

No one. Not even Nate, and he was always attentive, but I knew that I wasn't really his *type*. In my experience, the curvier girls are typically overlooked for someone more...athletic.

Which is funny because I'm in excellent shape. I clean for a living, which means I carry heavy vacuums and buckets full of water up and down stairs and in and out of my SUV. I push and pull furniture, and I bust my ass to do a good job in a timely manner so I can move on to the next job.

I'm *athletic.*

But I'm also naturally curvy, and sometimes, men are assholes about that. At least, the men in my past have been.

But not Brady. Not only did he assure me that he found me hot, but he kissed me like I was the sexiest thing he'd ever seen in his life. And that kiss alone is going to fuel all my spicy dreams for months.

As if he didn't already.

With a sigh and resigned to dragging ass today, I pull on some wide-legged yoga pants and a cropped sweatshirt, twist my hair up into a bun, and wash my face. It's too early for makeup, and it's Sunday, so Brady's going to get my lazy look today.

When I step out of my room, I notice the guest room door is open and, with a frown, walk down to peek inside. The bed is made, and his bag is gone.

Daisy's door is closed, so she's still asleep. Otherwise, she'd come looking for me.

I pad downstairs and find it empty, and my stomach drops.

He left.

He didn't even say goodbye. He just left. And for some reason, that hurts my feelings.

I blow out a breath and scrub my hands over my face.

"Get over it," I mutter. "He doesn't owe you anything."

Walking to the windows, I glance out at the snow.

It's still falling, but it's a normal, light snowfall now, and the wind is gone. There are piles of snow where Brady shoveled it out of my driveway, clearing it for not only his vehicle, but mine, too.

Yep, he's gone.

And he shoveled my driveway. A chore I *hate*. I would kiss him again, just for that alone.

Not that I would need a reason to want to kiss him again. The man is a grade A kisser.

I check the time and see that it's still quite early. Daisy will probably sleep for another hour or so, but I can get everything ready for breakfast.

I take my time, enjoying the quiet, pulling out the griddle and setting it on the counter, and then I start to mix the batter for the pancakes. Just as I set the oven to preheat for bacon, my front door opens and in walks Brady, a tray of to-go cups in his hand, looking fresh and sexy as hell in blue jeans and that black Carhart jacket.

His eyes find me and warm, and my mood is instantly a million times better.

"I thought you'd left," I admit as I step around the island, watching as he sets his tray down so he can take off his jacket, hang it by the door, and step out of his snowy boots. He's in a green Henley that hugs his shoulders perfectly, making me salivate.

Okay, fine, *everything* Brady does makes me salivate.

"Thanks for shoveling the driveway. It's my least favorite chore, and now I don't have to."

"You're welcome. And I wouldn't have just left without a word. I wanted to get you some coffee. Millie knows your order." He offers me a cup, and I take a sip and let my eyes close with that first jolt of caffeine.

"Your sister brews the *best* coffee," I say with a sigh, and when I open my eyes, Brady's watching me, his jaw tight. "What's wrong?"

"Nothing." He shakes his head and pulls his own cup out of the tray, leaving a little one still nestled inside. "I like the way you look in the morning. All sleepy-eyed and soft."

In all of the months I've known Brady Wild, he's never looked at me like *this*. Of course, we've never been alone before for this long. His family, my *friends*, are always with us, and the way he's watching me now isn't exactly appropriate for mixed company.

It makes my insides tingle with glee.

"Are you flirting with me?" I ask with a grin.

"I shouldn't be," he says with a frown. "But yeah, I guess I am. I got Daisy some hot chocolate. Is she still asleep?"

I hear her feet hit the floor above us, and I smile at him. "Not anymore. Thanks for the coffee. I hadn't made any yet."

"That was the goal." He sips, eyeing me, as my daughter comes bounding down the stairs.

She's always been like this. Wakes up fully alert and ready to take on the day. Her curly hair is messy, and there's a crease in her cheek from her pillow. When she sees Brady, she stops cold as pure joy fills her precious face.

"Brady!"

"Hi there, Princess," he says with that easy grin. "I brought you some hot chocolate."

"Can I have it, Mom?"

"Of course. Come sit at the island and drink it. You guys keep me company while I make breakfast."

"We have pancakes on Sunday," Daisy informs Brady as she climbs into her favorite stool and sits as Brady sets her cup in front of her. "Did I get whipped cream?"

"You did," Brady confirms with a wink and sits next to her.

"So, tell me about your dance," I say as I take the bacon out of the fridge and peel it apart, placing it onto a tray for the oven. "Who did you boogie with?"

"Holly, of course," Daisy says. "And the other girls, too."

"What about boys?" I ask her.

"Ew. No, they danced together. Sometimes we were all in a big group, and that was fun. They had cookies there. Brady danced, too, and he was goofy."

"Hey." Brady frowns down at her. "I was *not* goofy. That's just how I dance."

Daisy giggles, and I slide the pan of bacon into the oven and then get started on the pancakes.

"Did you stay here last night?" Daisy asks him, and my heart stutters.

Shit.

I twirl, ready to jump in, but Brady's already nodding his head.

"Your mom was nice enough to offer me the guest

room because the blizzard got pretty bad last night, and it probably wasn't safe to drive to the ranch."

"Oh," Daisy says and sips her drink. "You didn't sleep with Mommy?"

"No, he didn't." I frown at my daughter as I pour pancake mix onto the griddle. "Why would you think he would?"

"I don't know, sometimes people sleep in the same bed. Like Holly's mom and dad do. And sometimes my mommy has nightmares, and I go to her room and snuggle her for a while."

My eyes go wide, and I wish the floor would just open up and swallow me.

"She does, huh?" Brady asks, and I can just *feel* his eyes on me.

"Yeah, so I thought maybe you had to snuggle with her to make her feel better."

"No, he didn't," I say softly and smile at my baby. "But thank you for thinking of me. You're very sweet."

Daisy smiles and drinks her hot chocolate, and I glance over to Brady. Sure enough, those hot hazel eyes are on me, full of questions, but I just shake my head and get back to work.

Brady asks Daisy about school and what she wants for Christmas as I finish breakfast, and I'm happy for the reprieve from any more uncomfortable topics that my precious daughter wants to bring up.

One thing about my girl is, she's not afraid to speak up. And I *love* that about her. I envy it sometimes. But I'm also learning that it might be a little uncomfortable around a man that makes my insides quiver.

"Let's sit at the table," I suggest as I make a plate for Daisy and get her settled and then join Brady in the kitchen to make my own breakfast. He puts three pieces of bacon on my plate, and I shake my head. "I don't usually do the bacon."

"You don't like *bacon*?" He scowls down at me like I just told him that I hate kittens.

"Of course, I *like* it; I just don't eat it." I bite my lip when his eyes narrow.

"She worries about her hips," Daisy pipes up, and I close my eyes in embarrassment as Brady scoffs.

"Thanks, baby."

"Eat the bacon, Abs." His voice is low so only I can hear, and it sends tremors right through me. Actual *tremors*. "This smells damn good."

"You said a swear," Daisy informs him. "A dollar goes into the jar."

"What jar?" Brady demands, looking around the room.

"It's on the mantle," Daisy says, pointing to the living room. "We're saving up."

"For what?" he wants to know.

"I don't know," she admits with a giggle. "What are we saving up for, Mommy?"

"A rainy day," I murmur as I take a bite of the bacon and savor the salty taste of it on my tongue. I don't remember the last time I had a piece. I sit next to Daisy, across from Brady, and watch him inhale the pancakes. "Good?"

"Da-dang good," he says, catching himself. "You said you do this *every* Sunday?"

"Yep." Daisy takes a bite and hums with happiness. "They're my favorite."

"Mine, too," he says and high-fives my daughter. "You have good taste, Princess."

"I know."

When we're finished eating, Brady helps me clear the table, and then Daisy announces, "You should just live here and be my daddy."

I blink, and my gaze whips up to him. He's staring down at a plate, frowning, and if I'm not mistaken, he's gone pale.

"You know, I should probably head out," he says quietly and sets the plate back in the sink. He doesn't meet my gaze as he turns away and gathers his coat and slides his feet into his boots. "Thanks for breakfast, ladies."

"Daisy, why don't you go upstairs and get dressed."

"But—"

"No arguing," I snap back at her and hurry after Brady, who's already outside and striding to his SUV. "Brady, hold on."

He's shaking his head as he opens the door, and I rush over, in my *socks*, through the snow and worm my way between the door and the 4Runner so he can't shut it on me.

"She didn't mean to upset you," I say, breathing hard

and feeling awful that Daisy's words are making him run away. "I apologize."

"No, don't." He shakes his head and sighs. "She didn't do anything wrong. It was just a reminder that I need to watch myself. I can't let her get too attached to me."

"She *really* likes you, that's all."

"I'll keep my distance." He still won't look me in the eyes. "You're going to get frostbite on your feet, Abbi."

"Brady—"

"Go inside." The words aren't harsh, but they leave no room for argument, so I back away and let him shut the door and return inside, where Daisy's sitting on the stairs, holding the bunny she's had since she was a baby, looking at me with wide brown eyes.

"Did he get mad?"

I don't know what in the hell he is. He looked...*lost.* "No, baby. I think he had to get home. There's a lot to do at the ranch, you know."

"He doesn't want to be my daddy."

"Come here." I take her hand and lead her to the couch where we snuggle in like we do when we're watching movies. "Sweetheart, it's not that easy."

"He likes us."

"Sure, he does. And he's nice to us, but that doesn't mean he wants to live with us and be married to me. That's what it means, Dais, and that's a big deal. It's not something that's decided over breakfast after a dance."

"Okay."

My heart breaks at the defeat in her little voice, and I kiss her head, breathing in her shampoo.

"I love you, pumpkin."

"I love you, too."

"What do you want to do today?"

"Can we make cookies?"

That's my girl, forever with the sweet tooth. "Sure. Why not? Snowy days are for cookies."

I HAD to take matters into my own hands.

So to speak.

I've been living with perpetual sexual frustration for the past two weeks since Brady spent the night during the snowstorm. I haven't heard *one word* from him, and I can take a hint when a man just isn't interested.

Although, I'll admit, there were some mixed messages there, what with the hottest kiss of the goddamn century, but if he was interested in more, he'd contact me.

He has my number.

But there has been nothing. Nada. Zilch. And I need relief from this constant ache for the stubborn son of a bitch.

Not that Joy's a bitch. Brady's mom is the best.

Anyway, I broke down and bought a toy. An *adult* toy. Online.

And it just arrived. I've unboxed it and am frowning

at it, wondering where the batteries go, when Daisy gets home.

Of course, she sees the packing box.

"I want to see what we got," she says as she lets her bookbag drop and starts to shed out of her coat.

"No, ma'am," I reply, shaking my head, shoving the toy in the back of my jeans and covering it with my sweatshirt. "It's too close to Christmas for you to be looking in delivery boxes."

Thank God for that excuse.

"Come on, we have to get you ready for your overnight slumber party at Holly's house. I packed most of your stuff, but I need to know what pillow you want to take."

The toy is digging into my back, so I take it out of my pants and shove it into my pocket as I follow Daisy up the stairs. Once I'm in her room, I stash it under her pillows.

"The pink one," she says, as if I should just automatically know that.

"You always change which one is your favorite," I remind her. "Erin will be here soon to get you."

Once a month, Holly and Daisy get a slumber party, and we switch back and forth on which house they stay at. This month, it's at the Wild River Ranch. The girls look forward to it every month.

"Are you excited to be out of school for the holiday break?"

"No," she says with a frown.

"Why not?"

"Because I'll miss my friends," she says.

Daisy is the most social person I know. She *thrives* around other people. She's never met a stranger, and sometimes that makes me nervous.

Beep-beep.

"Well, you'll get to see everyone in a couple of weeks. Come on, that was Erin's horn in the driveway."

"Yay!" Daisy runs out of her bedroom, leaving me to carry her backpack and pillow and Mr. Bunny.

"Hi, guys," I call out with a smile as I walk outside, carrying all of Daisy's gear. My daughter is hugging Holly like she hasn't seen her in a month. "Didn't you guys just see each other at school?"

They laugh and hop into Erin's big SUV, and Erin offers me a hug.

"So, what are you going to do with a whole night to yourself?" she asks.

I can't exactly say, *"I'm going to use the new toy I got to get my rocks off."* So, I smile and shrug a shoulder. "I'll catch up on some stuff."

"Let me know if you get bored. You're always welcome to come out to our place, have some wine, and chat."

"I'll keep that in mind. Thanks, friend."

Erin grins and then climbs into her SUV.

I return inside and unpack Daisy's backpack, clean her lunch box, and get everything put away before I take an hour to clean the house a bit. I got home from work just twenty minutes before Daisy arrived, and I've felt like I've been ignoring the things that need to get done around here.

Finally, with one last glance around the living room, I head upstairs to Daisy's room and check under the pillows for my toy, but it's not there.

I toss all the pillows onto the floor. Nothing.

With my heart hammering in my chest, I yank the covers back on the bed and still come up empty.

"You've got to be shitting me," I mutter as I pull my phone out of my back pocket and call Erin.

"Hey, are you coming out here after all?"

"No, listen, I need to ask you to do something for me, and I don't want you to judge me."

Erin clears her throat on the other end of the line. "Are we going to bury someone, Abbi?"

I can't help but laugh at that. "It's not *that* dramatic, but it's embarrassing." I tell her about the toy and my attempt to hide it from my daughter.

She's laughing on the other end of the line when I say, "I need you to check Daisy's overnight bag and her pillow and see if I managed to put it in there."

"This is *hilarious*," Erin says with glee. I can hear her walking through her house, and I bite my fingernail as I wait.

"You can't tell anyone."

"My lips are sealed...until we meet with the other girls and have a couple of margaritas. And then the secret will be between the five of us."

I cringe and then can't help but laugh with her. "Tell me you found it."

"Nope, not here. Let me check the pillow."

She's quiet for a second, and then I hear something land on the floor. *Hard.*

"Found it," she announces. "Hey, this is a nice one. Send me the link."

I giggle now and blow out a breath. "Thank *God* you found it and not Daisy. I'll come out and get it."

"Don't worry, he's safe with me until you get here. You might as well plan on staying for dinner. I'm making sloppy joes."

"I never could turn down a sloppy joe. Thanks, friend. See you soon."

CHAPTER THREE

BRADY

"You coming up to the house for dinner?" Remington passes me the tack from his horse, and I hang it up for him. "Erin's making sloppy joes."

"Sure." I'm fucking *starving*. It's been another long day of work on the ranch. If the damn weather would just let up, even a little bit, it wouldn't be so bad. Instead, we're getting more snow every day, and it's colder than shit outside. "I just have to go home and shower, and then I'll be there."

"See you in a bit," Rem says with a nod as he heads for his truck, and I climb into the 4Runner.

Thirty minutes later, after a quick shower and a change of clothes, I'm headed over to the farmhouse, the one that all of us grew up in, for dinner.

Several years ago, when our parents decided to build themselves a smaller, more manageable house for the two of them, Rem moved himself and his kids into the big house. We all supported that idea because

Remington is now running the show at Wild River Ranch, and he had the kiddos, too. It felt like a tradition, a passing of a torch.

And it just made sense.

I park near the back door and enter through the kitchen, like I usually do. I can hear Holly telling a story in the dining room, and it makes me grin.

Holly and Johnny own me, and they know it.

"Uncle Brady," Johnny exclaims when he sees me. "I'm glad you're here. We're outnumbered."

"By who?"

I walk all the way into the room and come up short.

"By the girls," he finishes, just as Daisy shoots me the biggest smile and comes running to me, wraps her arms around my waist, and gives me a hug.

"I haven't seen you in *forever*."

I pat her back and look across the room at Abbi, who's watching me with serious blue eyes.

Yeah, I'm an asshole. I've done nothing but think of these two for the past couple of weeks, but I didn't call or stop by. Because that's pointless and does nothing but send mixed signals.

"We're having sloppy joes," Daisy informs me, pulling me out of my reverie.

"I heard," I say with a grin and boop her little nose. "Did you save some for me?"

"We haven't had any yet," she replies and then hurries back over to her bestie.

"Now that you're here," Erin says as she crosses to the kitchen, "we can all dish up."

"You didn't have to wait for me."

"It wasn't a big deal," Erin assures me as she walks by. Remington joins her to help, and I'm stuck here in the dining room with Abbi and three kids.

"How have you been?" I ask her, shoving my hands into my pockets.

"Doing well," she replies with a nod. "And you?"

"Fine, just fine. Been busy out here, what with the sh—crappy weather."

Her lips tip up in a grin. "Same, actually. When there's snow, there's mud, and I've been getting a lot of calls for cleanings lately, so my team has been busy."

I nod and rock back on my heels. "Makes sense, I suppose."

"Boy, grown-ups are boring," Johnny mutters and rolls his eyes, making me smirk.

"It's ready, everyone," Erin announces, and we get to work making plates for the kids, and then ourselves, and settling at the long dining room table. As luck would have it, I end up right next to Abbi, and throughout the entire meal, I'm hyperaware of her scent, her warmth, how she moves, and the sound of her voice.

Fuck me, I'm so damn attracted to her, it's as if I'm a magnet and she's the north pole.

Finally, dinner's done, and the dishes are cleared, so I can say my goodbyes.

"When will I see you again?" Daisy wants to know as I hug her goodbye.

"Oh, I'm sure I'll see you during the holidays," I assure her. "We always have parties and stuff, right?"

"Yeah, okay." She kisses me on the cheek and then runs off to play with Holly. I guess the two girls are having a slumber party here tonight.

And that means that Abbi will be home alone. All freaking night.

Erin and Abbi are huddled together by the front door, and I decide that I'll walk Abbi to her car. It's already been a full evening of torture, so we might as well just carry on the vibe.

"I'll walk you out," I offer, and Abbi smiles and waves at the family.

"Be good, Dais. I'll see you tomorrow."

"Bye, Mom!" Daisy hardly spares her mother a glance.

"I'm glad that she loves being here so much," Abbi says when we're walking down the steps to the driveway. "At first, I was afraid that she'd want to come home in the middle of the night, but she's totally comfortable here."

"She knows she's welcome," I reply as I press my hand to the small of her back.

As we get closer to her car, Abbi almost slips, and as she rights herself, something falls out of her bag onto the snow below.

"Shit," she mutters as I bend down and retrieve...a *dildo*?

I hold it up, staring at it and then at her.

"Don't tell me you're *borrowing* this from Erin."

"Oh, my God, no!" She reaches for it, but I hold it out of her grasp. "Give that to me, Brady."

"I'm intrigued." I eye it again. It's big. And teal. "Why is it so colorful?"

"I don't know. Don't be a child and give that to me."

I shake my head and press the button, but nothing happens. "It's broken."

"I haven't put batteries in it yet." Her face is flaming red, and now she won't meet my eyes, and I feel like an asshole. "It ended up here by...accident."

She tells me a quick tale about trying to hide it from Daisy, and it ended up in the kid's pillow case, but luckily Erin found it, and Abbi came out to retrieve it.

"So, you haven't used it."

"Not that it's any of your business, but no." She frowns and reaches for it, and this time, I let her have it.

I fucking *hate* that she thinks she needs that thing. And the idea of playing with her, of using that on her myself to make her lose her pretty mind, and then fucking her the way she should be fucked makes my jeans too tight.

"Why are *you* scowling?" she asks as she stows the toy in her bag.

"Why do *you* need that thing?"

"For fuck's sake," she mutters, shaking her head. "Just drop it, okay? It doesn't matter. It's just a silly toy."

But *I* think it matters. I think it matters a lot, actually, and I tip her face up so I can look her in the eyes.

"Tell me, Abs."

"You're impossible. Don't you ever hear the word *no*?"

"Sure. It's fine, you don't have to tell me." I brush my

thumb over her lower lip and then back away, and her tongue darts out to touch where I just was, and it's almost my undoing.

"You kissed me," she whispers and bites that lip, frowning as if she's mad at herself. I want to smooth the frown lines between her eyebrows with my thumb, but I don't. "And then you were just *gone*. So, yeah, I bought a toy. I'm a grown woman who can do...those things."

She bought a sex toy because I got her hot and bothered and didn't follow through.

I'm the lowest piece of shit there is.

"Abbi."

"It's cold," she says and opens her door, climbing inside. "Have a good night, Brady."

Without a backward glance at me, she pulls out of the driveway, headed toward town, and I stand in the goddamn snow, cursing myself as a fool.

Finally, I run around back to my own vehicle, start it, and drive into Bitterroot Valley, but instead of following Abbi to her house, I end up at The Wolf Den. The bar is trendy and serves good food, and on Friday nights, it's usually packed.

Tonight is no exception, especially since we're in the heart of winter tourist season.

Since I'm not in the mood for company, I find a single empty stool at the very end of the bar and order a beer.

I'm halfway into the pint when someone taps on my shoulder.

"I thought that was you," Jen's voice purrs from just behind me, and I turn on my stool to look at her. She's a barrel racer, and she's been a fuck buddy for years. Her golden eyes sweep over me from head to toe, and she licks her lips. "Let's go back to my place."

"Yeah." I chug the last of my beer, toss some bills on the bar, and stand. "Let's do that."

Jen takes my hand and leads me through the crowd and outside into the crisp evening air.

"I'll meet you there," I tell her. "I don't want to leave my car here."

"I walked, so I'll ride with you."

"Hop in." I hold the door open for her, then walk around to the driver's side and start the engine. Jen's place is less than two minutes away, in a little apartment above a garage. I've been here dozens of times over the years. Less in the last year or so, but I'm familiar with the place and with the woman.

Maybe I just need to fuck Abbi out of my system once and for all.

"I haven't seen you in *forever,*" Jen says as she wraps her arms and legs around me, kissing my neck as I climb the stairs to her place, carrying her with me. "God, I've missed this."

I get her inside and then pin her against the door and kiss her, fisting my hand in her hair. But it's not blonde. It's dark.

And when my eyes meet hers, they're not blue.

They're gold.

Her body is too long and willowy. Not lush and curvy.

Every damn thing about this is *wrong.*

"Come on, Wild," she says, grinding herself against me. "Fuck me."

I carefully lower her to the ground and back away from her, breathing hard. She's panting, too, and her eyes narrow on me.

"What the fuck, Brady?"

"This isn't going to happen." I wipe the back of my hand across my mouth, disgusted that I can still taste her there.

"Jesus Christ, you're not a tease. Come on." She whips her shirt over her head and reveals tits that aren't covered by a bra. "You *love* fucking me. Let's do this. Let me ride that cock."

"Stop." I shake my head and hold my hand up. "This isn't going to happen *ever* again, Jen."

She tilts her head to the side, her eyes narrowing. "You met someone."

"I'm just over this. It's nothing personal."

"No." She crosses her arms over her chest, not shy at all about her lack of clothing. "You met someone."

"It doesn't matter. Good luck to you, Jen. I'll see you around."

She moves out of my way, and I open the door and let the cold air wash over me as I descend the stairs.

Jesus, what was I thinking?

I wasn't.

"When it doesn't work out, you can come back," Jen calls down after me, but I don't reply.

I'm not fit for company. I should go home and sleep

off this shitty mood. I absolutely should *not* go to Abbi's house.

And yet, that's where I find myself driving. And when I pull into her driveway and cut the engine, I can't get up the nerve to go inside.

No, I'll never see Jen again because she isn't who I want. She's who I *should* want. No strings, no expectations, no adorable daughter, nothing that I can fuck up or leave behind someday.

Instead, I seem to want the exact opposite of Jen, and she's inside that townhouse right now, probably fucking a piece of plastic.

And that just pisses me off.

Suddenly, a text comes through my phone.

Abbi: Are you coming inside, or are you going to sit out there all night?

Pushing out of the car, I stride to the door and open it, then step in and see that Abbi's sitting on the couch, her feet up and crossed on the cushions, with a throw blanket on her lap. Her hair is up, and the light from the tree dances on her face.

She's the most beautiful woman I've ever seen.

"Why were you camped out in my driveway?"

"Because I didn't know if I wanted to come inside."

She tilts her head to the side. "Why?"

I have to pace, so I do. "You're under my skin. I can't fucking shake you. You're always just *there.* At events with my family, hanging out with my sisters—"

"If it makes you uncomfortable that I come to family

events when invited, I'll stay away from them, Brady. It's *your* family."

"It wouldn't matter," I explode, shaking my head. "Because you're still here."

I point to my head.

"I've stayed away for weeks, as you pointed out. I've buried myself in work, freezing my balls off out there in the goddamn snow. And you're still there."

I shake my head and pace some more.

"Hell, after you left tonight, I came into town and went to The Wolf Den. Thought I'd get a beer, and low and behold, there's Jen."

"Who's Jen?"

"My fuck buddy." I turn to look at her, and she flinches as if I've just hit her. "*Former* fuck buddy. She invited me to her place, and I went."

"How nice for you. I'm going to ask you to leave now."

"No." I shake my head, frustrated all over again.

"Yeah, you're going to want to go. I don't want to hear about how you fucked Jen tonight, Brady. We're not friends like that."

"I didn't fuck her!" I throw my hands up in the air. "I *couldn't*. I didn't have any desire to. I don't want Jen, and I made it perfectly clear that I will never be doing that with her again."

Abbi's eyes narrow as she watches me.

"So, you want me to console you after a breakup?"

"Jesus," I mutter and pinch the bridge of my nose. "I'm messing this up."

"I don't even know what *this* is, Brady."

"I want *you*." The fight has gone out of me now, and I drop into the chair directly across from her. "I want you so fucking bad that everything aches, but I can't have you, Abs."

"Why not?" She tosses the throw aside and sits forward on the couch. "I haven't said no."

"I'm not a good bet." I shake my head and push my hand through my hair, suddenly feeling really fucking nervous. "I can't make a commitment to you, and you're a *mom*. Daisy's already way too attached to me, and I would *never* want to hurt her. I don't want to hurt either of you."

"Okay, then don't."

I can't help but laugh at that, and Abbi scowls.

"I don't think this is funny."

"It's ridiculous." I sober again and watch her. "I can't do promises because my job is dangerous, and...I just can't. And you of all people deserve promises, Abbi, and I don't even know you all that well."

"Nobody has proposed anything," she reminds me, irritation filling her voice. "So just slow down a minute. We're attracted to each other, and we're friends. We have the same circle of people. My daughter likes you. Why does it have to be anything more than that for right now?"

I shake my head again, but she continues.

"I'm not asking you for anything, Brady. Not a damn thing. Well, that's not true. I would ask that you don't break my daughter's heart. That if we decide to sleep together, and if sex with you sucks, and we don't want to do it anymore, you'll still be kind to Daisy."

"Why would the sex be bad?"

"Promise me."

"I want to know why you assume that the sex will be *bad*, Abbi."

Her lips twitch. "It was just an example. I don't think it'll be bad. But if you and I don't work out, I don't want Daisy to suffer for it."

This is a bad idea. A bad, bad idea. I know better than to get involved, but fucking hell, I can't walk out of here tonight without knowing what she tastes like.

"I will *never* make Daisy feel unwanted or suffer for any feelings that I might have for you."

She watches me closely and then finally nods.

"I believe you."

"I wouldn't do that, Abbi."

"I know. Now, what are you still doing way over there?"

CHAPTER FOUR

ABBI

His eyes, those glorious hazel eyes with flecks of gold in them, narrow on me, and his jaw clenches. I've managed to keep my cool since he walked through that door, but my heart is pounding, and the mixture of emotions tonight has been exhausting.

Everything from embarrassment when he found the toy, to anger, to frustration, back to anger and jealousy, and now I simply want him.

The wanting him never goes away.

I want to know *why* he thinks he's a bad bet. Why does he think that he can't make a commitment to someone? There are so many questions, so much I'd like to talk with him about, but first, I'd like to have his hands on me.

And I haven't felt this way about a man in a long, *long* time.

There's a war going on in his eyes as he watches me, and finally, he stands and crosses to me, takes my hand,

and pulls me up, then simply scoops me into his arms and sits with me in his lap.

"I might crush you." I smile and drag my fingers down his cheek, but he doesn't smile back. "Brady, if you don't want to be here, it's okay. You don't owe me anything, and I'm sorry if you think you do because of what I said in the driveway earlier."

"It's not that," he whispers, his voice ragged as he hovers, mere inches from my lips.

"What is it?"

He growls, and then his lips are on mine, and just like last time, I'm immediately full of electricity and yearning for him. His hand dives into my hair and fists at the nape, holding me where he wants me so he can plunder my mouth, his tongue bold and firm, taking exactly what he wants from me.

"You feel damn good," he murmurs against my lips before he loops one arm around my back and easily shifts me to lie flat on the couch, hovering over me. He nudges my legs apart and settles between them, and I can feel the full, hard length of him nestled in my cleft. "So fucking beautiful."

My hands fist in his shirt, and I've just managed to get it up and off of him, revealing rock-hard abs, sculpted so *perfectly* they'd make the gods weep, when my phone starts to ring with Erin's ringtone.

"Ignore it," he urges, but I shake my head.

"Can't. It's Erin. Could be Daisy." I reach for the device on the coffee table and swallow hard before I accept the call. "Hello?"

"Hi, I hope I'm not interrupting time with your new boyfriend." My heart stills, and then I remember that she's talking about the toy, and I can't help but bark out a laugh. "I have bad news. Both girls started getting sick about thirty minutes ago. I figure they caught something at school."

"Oh, no. I'll come get Daisy."

"No, Rem's already on his way in with her. She really wanted to go home."

"Of course." Brady backs away so I can sit up, but he doesn't leave. "What's wrong with the girls?"

"Upset stomach, nausea. They said their tummies hurt. I'm hoping Daisy makes it home before she starts to throw up. Holly's already lost her dinner twice."

"Ugh, thanks for the heads-up. I'm sorry."

"No, *I'm* sorry. Keep me posted."

"Same goes. Thanks, Erin. Bye." I hang up and sigh, tossing my arm over my face. "Damn it."

"What do we need to do?"

I move my arm and stare up at him. "Huh?"

"What do we need to do to get ready for her? Puke bucket? Cold compress?" He stands and heads for the kitchen as if he's on a mission.

I slowly rise from the couch and simply say, "Brady."

He turns to me, those eyes no less hot, but his body less intense.

"Your girl's sick, Abs."

"I know, and I'm sorry."

"Don't be. Now, what do we need to do?"

We spend ten minutes getting things ready. The big

bowl, a cold compress, and fresh pajamas on hand. When everything is as ready as it can be, Brady pulls me against him and kisses me, long and slow.

"You'll never apologize to me again for being a mom."

"It's just such bad timing." I drag my fingers down his cheek, enjoying the way the stubble feels on my skin, imagining the way it would have felt in other areas. "Rain check?"

"Rain, snow, sleet, hail...you name it."

I laugh, and he kisses me again, and then I see the headlights through the window, and Brady pulls back from me.

"Let's go get her," he says.

The back passenger door flies open, and Daisy leans her head out and upchucks all over the snow, then immediately begins to cry.

"Oh, baby," I hurry to her and scoop her up. She's not a baby anymore, and she's gotten heavier, so I'm grateful when Brady hurries over to take her from me. "Did she get the inside of your truck?"

"No," Rem says, shaking his head. "She held it in until I pulled in here. I'd better head back. I'm pretty sure I have a mess waiting for me to help clean up."

"Thanks for giving her a ride," I say and notice the way Rem eyes Brady's truck. Brady's already inside with my daughter. "You'll have to talk to him about this."

"Plan to." He grins at me and gets back into his truck. "Good luck."

When I get inside, I hear Brady cooing to Daisy in the

bathroom, where I hear her throwing up again, so I grab the cold compress and join them, placing it on the back of her neck.

"Mama," she manages to get out as I kneel next to her.

"I know, baby. I'm so sorry. Do you need to throw up some more?"

Brady appears with a wet cloth and wipes her little face and lips, and Daisy shakes her head no.

"I don't think so."

"Okay. Let's go snuggle on the couch."

Brady lifts Daisy and gives her a ride to the living room, but Daisy shakes her head.

"I want to rock," she says, her little voice weak.

"She's always been a rocker," I say with a small smile. "You can give her to me, and I'll—"

But he's already sitting in the chair, Daisy curled up against his chest, and they're rocking back and forth.

"What else can I do?" he asks me, his voice hushed as Daisy starts to fall asleep.

"Will you just...*stay*?" I bite my lip, hating how vulnerable I sound, but he smiles at me over Daisy's head.

"Looks like you're stuck with me for a while," he replies as he brushes his hand down her long hair.

"I'll get some things, just in case."

I bustle about, gathering the puke bowl, wet cloth, and cold compress and then pour a sports drink from the pantry—on hand for just these occasions—into a bottle with some ice so it's cold, and set everything on the table next to Brady and Daisy, and then I lower myself onto the couch and rest my elbows on my knees, watching them.

Brady kisses the top of her head, rocking gently back and forth, back and forth.

"She's already asleep," he says in surprise.

"Throwing up's hard work." I offer him a half smile and then rub my hands down my face. "Hopefully, she'll stay that way, but she'll probably be in and out. Oh, I need to check for fever. I'll be right back."

I rush upstairs to Daisy's bathroom and grab the thermometer, then return to them and point it at her forehead.

"One-oh-one," I mutter. "Damn. We'll keep an eye on that, and when she wakes up, I'll give her some Tylenol."

"Does she get sick very often?"

"Thankfully, no, but schools are cesspools of germs, so it happens a couple of times a year. I just hope that *you* don't get sick."

"I'm fine," he says as I return to the couch and sit, then relax against the cushions, watching this handsome, sexy, sweet man rock my daughter. "Can I ask you a personal question?"

"Sure." I bite my lip, hoping that he doesn't ask something that I'll have to lie about.

"Where's her father?"

Nope. Don't have to lie. "He passed away." I pull my legs up under me and sit crisscross. "She wasn't quite two yet, and her dad contracted pneumonia, and it got really bad. The infection spread through his body, and they couldn't help him."

Brady scowls and shakes his head. “That’s not what I was expecting. I thought you’d say that he took off at some point and hasn’t paid child support in years.”

I smile and shake my head. “No, Nate wouldn’t have done that. He was a good guy. Loved her to pieces. He was...comfortable.”

Brady raises an eyebrow at that, and I feel myself squirm.

“I don’t usually talk about him. In fact, I haven’t talked to Erin, Millie, and the others about him. They know he passed away, but that’s all.” I frown at the coffee table and then decide to just let the words come out. “Nate and I were best friends in school. I always wondered why he liked me so much. We were from opposite sides of the tracks, you know? His family was wealthy, and I didn’t have a family at all. I was in foster care. Maybe he thought he could help me or save me. Either way, we were really close, like I said. But never romantically. I was absolutely *not* Nate’s type of girl.”

“What was his type?” Brady asks.

“Tall, thin, brunette. I’m not even one of those things.” I smile at the memory. “Which was fine, because I didn’t think about him that way either. Our relationship was platonic.”

Brady raises an eyebrow and then looks down at Daisy and back at me.

“Yeah, well, we were at a college party—his college because I didn’t go—and there was alcohol involved.”

“Ah.” He nods slowly. “I get it.”

“Young and drunk and stupid.” I blow out a breath.

"And Nate, being the responsible, kind, good guy that he was, insisted that we get married. And this might sound really bad, but at the time, I thought, I could do far worse. I knew him, I *liked* him, we got along well, he had a stable family, and we'd never have to worry about money. I talked myself into it. I was selfish."

"You were young," he reminds me.

"And scared," I agree. "And pregnant. But, we were excited for her, and we continued being friends. We even had sex sometimes, even though it wasn't exactly... passionate, I guess is the word. But it was fine. Everything was just *fine.*"

"Until it wasn't."

"Yeah." I blow out another breath. "He got sick. The truth is, I can't imagine that we would have stayed married forever. *Fine* doesn't cut it for the long term, but we always would have co-parented together, and he was my best friend. He protected us, and he loved us, and I was grateful. I *am* grateful. Because of him, I was able to start my business and buy this house, and Daisy will be able to go to college without worrying about how to pay for it. So, yes, I'm grateful to him, and I wish he was still here to be with her because he would have been a great dad."

"I'm sorry he's not."

I nod, watching them rock. "Me, too. Now, tell me something about yourself that makes you tick because I'm pretty sure you didn't watch your best friend die a horrible death."

Brady brushes Daisy's hair off of her forehead, kisses her there, and then clears his throat.

"Actually, I did."

My heart sinks into my stomach. "Oh, shit, Brady."

"I ride bulls for a living, and have for a long time. I think this will be my last season because I'm getting older, and it's hard on the body. Anyway, Dirks Johnson was my best friend in the circuit. We'd compete against each other, and every year, our prize money was neck and neck. Some years he'd beat me, and some years I'd come out on top."

I nod, listening, and wish I could be the one curled in his lap so I could wrap my arms around him and comfort him.

"About six years ago, we were in Colorado. His wife, Amy, and their daughter, Sierra, would come to every ride. They were in the stands that night."

"Oh, no." I cover my mouth, listening.

"I'd just finished riding and made it the whole eight seconds. I was on top, and if Dirks didn't beat me, I'd win about a hundred thousand dollars that night."

"Wow. Good money."

"Yeah, and you risk your life for it," he reminds me. "Anyway, I kept hoping he'd fall off. I wanted him to do well, but not *too* well. Because I'm a competitive bastard. Six seconds into his ride, everything went very wrong. He was bucked off and couldn't get out of the way in time before the bull trampled his chest. Sent him into cardiac arrest and was dead before the eight seconds were up."

"Jesus, Brady." I do cross to him now and take Daisy

out his arms, lay her on the couch, and then return to him, curl into him, and hold him tightly. "Jesus, I'm sorry."

His arms come around me, and he holds on, buries his face in my neck, and breathes deeply.

"He left a wife and daughter, and they watched him die."

I press a kiss to his cheek. "That's horrible."

"I don't let my family watch me," he says softly. "They want to, but I won't let them because if anything happened to me, I refuse to have them see it."

At just the mere thought of something like that happening to Brady, my blood runs cold, and tears spring to my eyes.

"How often does that happen?"

"Not often," he says and rubs his hand up and down my back. "But it *could*."

"And that's why you won't let yourself get involved in a relationship."

"Bull riders aren't—"

"A good bet," I finish for him.

"It's what I do, Abbi. Riding that bull is the highest high in the world. It's worth it to me, the sacrifices and the what-ifs. I'm pissed as hell that I'm starting to age out. And you've already been the one left behind with a baby to take care of by yourself. I won't ever put you or anyone else through that. It's selfish and irresponsible, and I won't do it."

Before I can reply, Daisy whimpers behind me, and

I'm off his lap in a flash to take care of her, grabbing the puke bowl on the way.

And it's a good thing because round two is underway, and Daisy gets sick again.

Brady walks into the kitchen and wets the cloth, then returns to wipe it over Daisy's face.

"Can you sip on some juice?" I ask her. Daisy frowns, but when I put the straw against her lips, she takes a few tiny sips for me. "Good girl. I'm sorry, baby. Should we put you to bed for a while?"

"Rock," she says, already closing her eyes again. "I just want to rock."

"I can do it," Brady offers, but I shake my head and lift her, muscle my way to the chair, and sit with her.

"I'll take this shift," I reply, settling her against me the way I've done since she was a baby.

Brady takes the bowl to the kitchen and cleans it out, not seeming to be bothered by it at all, and then returns with it and sets it next to me, in case there's a round three.

"What else do you need?" he asks softly.

"I think we're good here. You can head out if you want. I have a feeling that it's going to be a long night."

"I'm not going anywhere." Brady sits on the couch and kicks his sock-clad feet onto the coffee table, crosses his arms over his chest, and watches me for a while. "Why do you have nightmares, Abbi?"

My throat closes, and images too horrible to talk about run through my mind. I kiss Daisy's head and level Brady with a stare.

"I'm not going to tell you that."

He raises an eyebrow.

"I can't," I add softly. "It'll put me in a bad place if I do, and I need to keep it together for Daisy."

"Are you okay?"

I nod slowly. "Yes. I'm okay."

"Are you safe?"

My eyes narrow at that. *I am now.* "As safe as I've ever been."

"And if you're not okay or safe, you'll tell me?"

No. No, I wouldn't tell him. I would simply disappear again. And this is the first time I lie to Brady Wild.

"Yes. I'd tell you."

CHAPTER FIVE
BRADY

My phone is vibrating in my pocket, waking me. I open my eyes and frown, then check the time.

It's not even seven.

Which means that Abbi and I got about two hours of sleep.

My phone stops vibrating, and I sit here in the chair, watching the woman I can't seem to get enough of and Daisy curled up together on the couch where they landed after the last round of violent vomiting from the poor little girl. How she had that much in her to throw up, I'll never know. They're sleeping peacefully, and after last night, I have a whole new respect for Abbi. How she manages to do this on her own, day after day, is beyond me. The two of us pitched in throughout the night, and it was still exhausting.

My phone vibrates again, so I pull it out and check it.

I've missed two calls from my agent, and Rem just texted.

Rem: Let's meet for coffee at Millie's. I'm headed there now.

I sigh and run my hand down my face. I *do* need coffee, and it looks like the girls are going to sleep for a while anyway. So, I stand and push my feet into my boots, grab my jacket, and then return to the couch, where I gently kiss them each on the head.

Abbi's eyes crack open, and I shake my head at her.

"Sleep," I whisper before kissing her again. I can't keep my lips off of this woman. "I have to go, but I'll call you later. Just get some rest."

"Thank you," she whispers in return and then falls back to sleep, and I turn to the door. I push the button on the keypad that locks it behind me and then head for the 4Runner, but before I start it and leave, I return Sandy, my agent's, call.

"Wild," she says with a happy smile in her voice.

"Sandy, why are you calling me before the sun is up on a Saturday?"

"The sun is up in New York," she counters, "and you know that I don't take days off. Honey, I've got some *big* news. Huge."

"Okay, what's going on?"

"Sponsorships are starting to pour in for the coming season. You have *three* offers, and none of them want a non-compete, so we can sign with all three if you want to."

She outlines the terms for a popular cowboy boot company, a hat manufacturer, *and* a denim company. I wear all of them on a regular basis. And *all* of them want to pay me well into the seven figures. Jesus.

"They *all* want me?"

"That's right. You're hot stuff, you know. All the cowboys want to be you. Of course, you'll need to travel to LA for photo shoots—"

"No."

"What was that? I know for a fact you didn't just tell me no."

"I can't travel, Sandy. I'm a *real* cowboy, and we're in the middle of a bitch of a winter. If they want photo shoots and video, they'll have to come to me."

"Hmm." I can practically hear her tapping her long fingernail on her chin. "You know what, that's good. Can they shoot at the ranch?"

"I'll double-check with my brother, but I don't see why not. They'll have to pay for it."

"Of course, honey. You know I have your back there. Okay, let me make some calls, and I'll take care of it. Talk soon."

She hangs up before I can even reply, and I sit for another moment, not a little shocked.

This will be the highest-grossing year of my career. It's a good thing I have my brother, Ryan, helping me with investments.

Pulling out of Abbi's driveway, I head into downtown and park in front of Bitterroot Valley Coffee Co. My little sister, Millie, bought this place last year. She's changed a few things in the past year, bought new tables, updated the signs, and added some things to the menu. We're all damn proud of our baby sister.

I'm the only one in the place when I walk inside, and I grin when Millie smiles over at me.

"Good morning," she says. "You want your usual?"

"How do you remember everyone's *usual*?" I ask her, leaning on the counter.

"Steel trap," she replies, tapping her head. "You want?"

"Yes, please."

"I hear you spent the night with Abbi." She turns and grins at me, and I narrow my eyes.

"How the hell did you hear that?"

"Well, Rem told Erin that you were there when he took Daisy home, and Erin called me this morning. Not to gossip, we had to talk about the New Year's Eve party for the collective, but she happened to mention it to me. So. Spill it."

"Fuck that."

"Come on." She finishes my coffee and adds a lid. "She's my friend, and you're my brother. Don't give me details, because gross, but what's going on? Are you a thing? Are you sleeping together?"

"We're..." I shrug and sip my coffee. "Friends. I helped with Daisy. She was really sick."

"Poor baby," Millie says, frowning. "Was she better this morning?"

"They were sleeping when I left. Hopefully, she's through the worst of it. I'm meeting Rem here."

"I know. Erin called." Millie winks at me. "And you're not going to tell me any more, are you?"

"No." I sip again. "I'm not."

The bell over the door chimes when Remington walks in, takes his hat off, and nods at us. "Mornin'."

"Good morning," we reply in unison.

"How's Holly this morning?" I ask him.

"Sleeping. Puked her guts out last night. Daisy?"

"Same."

"He won't tell me anything," Millie says as she passes Rem his coffee. "It's damn annoying."

"Nothing to tell," I reply, ignoring them when they both narrow their eyes at me. "Let's sit."

I gesture to a table, and Rem and I have a seat. A few seconds later, Millie walks over with two slices of huckleberry-lemon pound cake.

"On the house," she says with a wink. "'Cause I love you."

She bustles away, and I take a bite.

"Damn, this is good. So, what's up? Do you want to drill me about Abbi, too?"

"Not drill," Remington replies slowly, watching me. He's always been the most serious, the broodiest out of all of us. And although I'm close to all of my siblings, Rem is the one I'm closest to. "But I *am* curious."

"I like her." I shrug. "It's really that simple."

"Yeah, except you don't date."

I nod, thinking it over. He's not wrong. "Not usually. We talked about it last night, and we're just taking it one day at a time for now, and we're both okay with that. I'm not dicking with her or lying to her. I'm not an asshole."

"Not usually," he echoes.

"She's a good mom," I say quietly, fidgeting with my coffee cup. "And Daisy's the sweetest. I tried to stay away, but damn it, I'm attracted to her. She's so fucking beautiful. Who wouldn't be attracted to her? Hell, I was pissed last night. Mad at myself, irritated with her. So, I went downtown, and Jen ended up being there."

His eyes narrow, and now I can't stop talking. It's like the faucet's been turned on, and it's all just rolling out of my mouth.

"And I went back to her place."

"Whoa." Rem holds up a hand. "Are you telling me that you fucked around with the barrel racer and *then* went to Abbi's?"

"I didn't have sex with Jen," I reply, scowling. "Jesus, I *couldn't*. I kept thinking about Abbi, so I told Jen the fuck buddy thing was over, and then I couldn't help myself. I drove over to Abbi's place."

"And then the girls got sick and ruined your plans." He laughs now, and that's unusual for my oldest brother. I don't love it when he laughs at my expense. "Oh, man, you're fucked."

"But that's just it, it didn't ruin anything. Sure, it... interrupted. But I didn't mind helping with Daisy. I don't know how Abbi does it by herself. It's hard fucking work."

"Yeah," my brother says, eyeing me. He was a single

dad for more than five years after his first wife passed away while giving birth to Holly. "It *is* hard damn work."

"I don't know what the fuck is up except that I can't stay away from her," I admit, running my hand down my face. "I guess we'll take it one day at a time."

"Fair enough." He takes a bite of the cake. "What else is going on with you?"

"I got a call this morning." I fill him in on everything that Sandy said, and Rem's eyes widen when I tell him how much they want to pay me for the sponsorships.

"Holy shit, Brady."

"I know."

"Good for you. I'm proud of you."

"We're going to try to get them all to come here for photos and to film so I don't have to be away from the ranch. I don't want to go to fucking LA. Today or any other day."

"Can't say that I blame you."

"If they want to film at the ranch, they'll pay a fee for it. Would you allow it?"

"Of course. Tell them to include the event space and mention it in the ads."

I grin at him. "I like the way you think, big brother."

"Hey, this New Year's Eve party that the girls are throwing for their collective is a big deal for them. You should escort Abbi."

"She didn't invite me."

He shakes his head at me. "You're not stupid. Ask *her*. And shit, Christmas is in a few days. I still have to shop."

"Damn it, so do I, now that you mention it. I haven't

got the kids anything yet. I guess I can do that while I'm downtown. I'll be out at the ranch later today to help with the livestock."

"Take the day off," he says, shaking his head and waving me off. "Lucky and Bruiser have it handled. There's not much going on, anyway."

"Yeah, okay. Thanks. Is this all you wanted to meet for? To shoot the shit and get the scoop on my sex life?"

"What can I say?" he asks before finishing his coffee. "I missed my little brother."

"Right."

I SHOPPED until I just couldn't do it anymore, and I managed to get everything that I needed. As a bonus, there's a store at the end of the street that offers gift wrapping for a good price, so I left all of my bags there. and I'll pick everything up tomorrow.

You can't beat it.

Just as I'm about to call Abbi to ask her how Daisy's doing, my phone rings, and it's my nephew, Jake.

"Hey, bud," I say into the phone.

"Hey, Uncle Brady. Are you busy this afternoon? I have a horse that I'd like you to look at. I think something's wrong with her."

"Yeah, I can come by now. I'm about fifteen minutes away. Want me to meet you at the stables?"

"That would be awesome. Thanks. See you soon."

I hang up and start the vehicle, then call Abbi so I can talk to her while I drive.

She answers on the third ring. "Hello?"

"Hey, beautiful. I'm sorry I didn't call earlier. How are things there?"

"Oh, we're doing okay. Daisy hasn't thrown up any more, and I've been able to keep some food and fluids in her. She's been sleeping off and on, poor thing."

"And how are *you*?"

She sighs, making me frown. "Just tired. I think I'll nap with her here in a few. I just wanted to clean up a bit. I might have Merilee from next door come stay with her while I run to the grocery store in a bit."

"No, just send me your list, and I'll pick up what you need. I'm headed out to Ryan's place now because Jake wants me to have a look at a horse, and then I'll come back into town."

"Brady, you don't have to do that. You should just go on to the ranch."

"Are we going to argue about this when you could be napping? Seriously, send me the list. You'll have what you need before dinner time. No arguments."

"You seriously rock," she says, relief heavy in her voice. "I didn't want to leave her yet, even though Merilee is like a surrogate grandmother. Okay, I'll text you the list, if you're sure."

"I'm sure. Get some rest, and I'll see you a little later."

"Thank you, Brady. Seriously."

"You're welcome."

With a grin, I disconnect the call and then turn off of

the highway, into Ryan's driveway, and stop at the gate. Within seconds, the gate slides open, and I drive through.

My brother's enormous house comes into view, but I drive past it to the barn and stable area about a quarter of a mile away and park next to Jake's truck.

It's too fucking cold outside to walk back and forth from the house to the barn.

When I push inside, I find both Jake and Ryan standing just outside of a stall, looking grim.

"What's up, guys?"

"We need a third opinion," Jake says, shoving his hands into his pockets. "Thanks for coming out."

"Of course. I figured I'd come out and visit anyway." I hug each of them and then turn my attention over the gate to the pretty white mare, Lullaby, just inside. "Hey, beautiful girl. What's going on in there?"

"She's more lethargic than normal," Jake says, his voice full of worry. "I mean, Lullaby is usually the laziest of the bunch, but she doesn't seem to have any energy at all."

I push inside the stall and walk around the horse, running my hands over her, cooing to her gently.

"She's dry," I say, taking stock. "Has she been drinking enough water?"

"Her water trough hasn't been getting lower," Jake says thoughtfully as Ryan listens. "I did notice that."

"It's winter, and horses naturally slow down a bit," I tell him. "And if she's a lazy girl by nature, you have to make sure she's getting the nutrients she needs, especially water. She might need an IV, and I can't help you there, but let's encourage her to get some fluids into her."

The three of us work together to urge Lullaby to drink, and finally, she does. And once she starts, she doesn't want to stop. Finally, she comes up for air and nods her big head.

"Good girl," Jake croons as he runs his hand down her neck. "Don't worry me like that, baby. You scared me."

Ryan and I smile at each other and walk toward the doors.

"Are you coming inside?" Ryan calls out to Jake.

"Nah, I'm gonna hang here for a while longer," he replies. "Thanks, Uncle Brady."

"You're welcome. Anytime."

I was here with him a few months ago when we lost one of the horses. Ryan and his fiancée, Polly, were in Paris, and it was a heartbreaking mess.

I'm glad that this won't have the same outcome.

"We're headed up to the house," Ryan calls back with a wave. "I'm riding with you. I walked down, and that was a big mistake."

"It's fucking cold," I agree, and we hurry to the 4Runner, and once inside, I set off for the house. "You should have known she was dehydrated."

"I suspected, but I kind of wanted to see how Jake handled it. I *like* that he thought to call you for help. That if I'm gone, and he's here alone, he knows to call you."

"He can always reach out to me."

"And that means a lot to me. Now, what were you going to come out here for?"

"What, I can't just hang out with my brother?"

Ryan smirks as I park in front of the house. "Sure. Wanna play pinball or something?"

"No. We need to go to your office."

His eyes sober as he watches me, and then he nods and pushes out of the 4Runner.

I follow him up the stairs of the porch and inside, where we shed our coats and boots. Polly comes around a corner and smiles when she sees me.

"I thought you'd be working today," I say as I catch her up in a hug. "What with it being almost Christmas."

"I wasn't feeling well this morning." She shrugs. "My girls are covering for me."

"Are you okay?" I frown down at her. Polly is a tiny little woman with fiery red hair, and she's currently pregnant, which has all of us brothers on edge.

"Oh, I'm fine. It was just a horrible bout of morning sickness."

"You might have caught a bug." I tell them about Holly and Daisy getting sick. "Could have been a stomach thing."

"Oh, I hadn't thought of that," Polly admits with a shrug. "Could have been, I suppose."

"You need to be in bed," Ryan reminds her, kissing her on the head.

"I was just grabbing some water when I heard the door. Don't worry, I'm taking it easy." She smiles up at me. "He hovers."

"I'm allowed to worry," he replies before Polly leaves to go sit on the couch, cuddled up with a blanket and the remote. "We'll be in the office."

Ryan's office is *big*. And it should be. As the owner of Wild Industries, he has a lot of responsibility and a lot of work to do, most of which he does out of this home office.

"Have a seat," he offers, and I lower myself into the chair on the other side of the desk from him. "What's up?"

"Well, it looks like I'm about to come into a lot of money, and we'll need to invest."

That piques his interest, as always, and I fill him in on the sponsorship opportunities that Sandy called about just this morning.

"You're pretty fucking badass, Brady."

"Yeah, I know. Now, let's make this money grow because this is my last year on the circuit."

That has his head whipping up. "What? Why?"

"I'm old," I reply.

"You're thirty-three."

"In the rodeo world, that's old as fuck. You know my list of injuries, and I'll only injure easier as I get older. I don't want to be forced out, I want to leave on my own terms. I'm sore, and I'm tired. Hell, sometimes I have the walk of a sixty-year-old man, and I knew that I was signing up for that, but it's time to step down. And given that I'm retiring at the age of thirty-three, half the age of normal retirement, I have to make the money stretch."

"Rem would pay you for the work you do at the ranch."

"Fuck that." I shake my head in disgust. "That's my family. I don't get paid for taking care of my family. Besides, I live there for free. That's all I need."

"You're really going to live in that tiny cabin for the rest of your life?" The look he sends me says, *get real.*

"Probably not. Maybe I'll build something out there."

"Well, you're a wealthy man, Brady." He taps the keys on his computer, logging into my portfolio, which I let him dick with. Having a billionaire brother has its benefits. "Even before being paid for these new sponsorships, you're well into the eight figures. Rodeo has done well for you."

"Yeah. It has."

"You can build whatever you want. Pretty much any*where* you want. I don't see any reason why you can't comfortably retire from riding after this season and then do whatever pleases you."

"Good." I nod, satisfied that Ryan has my financial stuff under control. "I figured that was the case, but I wanted to talk it through."

"I'm proud of you," he says, his eyes earnest. "Looks like I'll be buying a bunch of new hats and boots soon."

"Don't forget the jeans."

He grins. "Trust me. I won't forget."

Abbi: Please don't feel pressured to stop at the store for me. But if you're willing, here's my list: OJ (no pulp), ...

I read through her list and feel myself grinning as I pull a cart from the carousel and head for the produce. Her list isn't short, and I don't mind a bit. I know she'd rather stay home while her daughter recovers, so I'll gladly take this chore off her plate.

Noticing that the strawberries actually look good for this time of year, I check Abbi's list and see that she didn't have any on it, but I add them to the cart anyway. For the next hour, this is how it goes. I am sure to get everything that Abbi's noted and toss in a few extra things that I think they might enjoy. I know that Abbi loves chips and salsa from the cookouts we've had together, so I grab those. Daisy has a sweet tooth, like me, but I know that Abbi tries to keep the sweets for treats, so I just add some whipped cream for the strawberries. And, maybe, I snag a little bag of sour candies, too.

By the time I check out, I've far surpassed the twenty or so items on Abbi's list, and I don't really give a shit. I'm discovering that I enjoy doing things for Abbi and Daisy. I like *being* with them. We've said we're going to take it one day at a time in this—whatever it is—and I'm still nervous as hell to start something when I'm still going to be riding a bull in just a couple of months. But by fall, I'll be retired.

Maybe I can hang in there for that long. Maybe I won't try to date her or touch her or hell, anything, until then. It sucks, and it won't be easy, but I can do it.

And then, I won't have any of the what-ifs hanging over my head when I finally do allow myself to feel something for a woman.

I can finally make promises. It's the right thing to do, for both of them.

With that decided, I load the groceries into the back of the 4Runner and drive over to Abbi's townhouse. I back into the driveway so there's not as far to go with the bags and open the tailgate to retrieve them.

The front door opens, and Abbi comes jogging out, grinning. "Hey there, Cowboy." When she sees the pile of white plastic bags, her eyes go wide. "I know I didn't have that much on my list."

"I might have found a few extra things," I reply with a shrug as she loads up, and we walk inside. "You stay in, I'll get the rest."

"I can help—"

"It's too damn cold," I reply, shaking my head as I set the bags near the front door so I don't track snow through the house. "I'll be right back."

I'm able to get the rest of the groceries in one trip, drop them off inside, and then hurry back out to close the tailgate. When I close the front door behind me, intending to just talk to her for a minute before I head home, Abbi's frowning at me from the kitchen where she's unloading the groceries.

"What's wrong? Is that the wrong kind of salsa?"

"No, it's actually my favorite salsa, but I didn't have it on my list."

"I know, but you like chips and salsa, so I grabbed it." I shrug and shift on my feet. "How's Daisy?"

"She's napping, but she's much better. I think she'll be as good as new tomorrow."

"Good." I nod, relief flooding through me. "That's good.

"Thank you," she says, leaning on the counter that separates us. "For last night and for this. I'll get you some cash."

"No." Her gaze whips over to mine, pausing on her way to her purse. "I don't want your money, Abs."

"You don't have to buy my groceries."

I don't respond to that. I'll be damned if Abbi will give me a dime for anything, ever. "I should probably head home—"

"Before you do," she interrupts, taking a small, hesitant step toward me. Jesus, if she gets any closer, I won't be able to make it one hour into my new plan of holding off with her until the fall. One. Fucking. Hour. She stops and bites her lip, then squares her shoulders. "Our collective is hosting a New Year's Eve party, and I'd like to take you. As my date. Jesus, my daughter had no problem at all asking you to be *her* date, and I'm nervous as hell."

I soften at that, and there's no way I can stop my feet from crossing to her and cupping her face. I brush my lips over hers, careful not to take it too deep.

"I'd love that," I whisper. "What time should I pick you up?"

"I'll be at the ranch," she says and swallows hard. "You can pick me up at your brother's at eight."

"Done. Is it fancy?"

She grins, clearly excited. "Hell yes, it's fancy."

"I figured." I nod, and it takes every fiber of strength to back away from her. "It's a date. But I'll see you at Ryan's in a couple of days for Christmas. Right?"

"Yes. Daisy's excited to spend the day with your family. If it's okay with you, that is."

"Of course, it's okay. I'll see you there. Call me if you need anything."

She nods. "Thank you."

I hate this sudden awkwardness between us. It wasn't there last night when we were taking care of Daisy and talking the night away.

But today, my insecurities are back. I feel like an ass.

And suddenly, Abbi moves quickly, closing the gap between us, and wraps her arms around me in a hug, pressing that gorgeous, curvy body against me. It's not a desperate hug.

It's...sweet.

"Aside from Daisy," she murmurs softly, "I don't hug very much. But this is nice."

"Yeah." I kiss the top of her head and wish with all my might that I could retire today. "This is nice."

CHAPTER SIX

ABBI

"Oh, my gosh!" Daisy bounces with excitement, hugging Holly as they both celebrate their shiny new Christmas presents with hugs and dancing. "We *both* got new bikes!"

Erin and I had the bikes delivered here, to Ryan's house, and Jake offered to put them together for the girls so they'd be by the tree, waiting for them when we arrived.

The Wilds decided to gather at Ryan and Polly's for Christmas, rather than at the family farmhouse, because they've added so many members to the clan over the past couple of years, and this house is *big*. The tree in the main living room has to be thirty feet tall.

And it's decorated, from the tippy top to the bottom with shiny, glittery balls and lights.

Polly said that a company came in to do most of it and that she, Ryan, and Jake decorated the bottom few limbs with special ornaments.

I thought that was sweet.

"I got a scooter," Johnny adds, doing his own happy dance.

"We want to ride," Holly announces.

"It's a little too snowy for that," Erin reminds her. "Sorry, baby."

"We have a shop that's pretty much empty," Jake says with a wink. "Come on, you guys, I'll take you out so you can ride."

"Yay!" Daisy yells as the three kids follow Jake out the back door. The young man has a red bike under one arm and a purple one under the other, carrying them as if they weigh nothing at all, and Johnny follows behind with his scooter.

The shop is only a few yards away, and knowing Ryan, I'm sure it's heated, so they're fine running over with just boots and jackets.

"I got you something," Brady says quietly as he sits on the couch next to me, passing me a box wrapped in red with a gold bow.

"You didn't have to get me anything," I reply softly as my heart thuds. "You made Daisy's year with the pink Stetson. She'll never take it off."

He laughs and continues to hold the small box out to me, so I accept it and rip the paper off.

Inside is a pair of teal fuzzy socks. And these are way better than the ones I usually get. They're thick and lined with what looks like sherpa fuzziness, and I know without a doubt that they won't get holes in the heels like the ones I usually buy myself.

"I notice that you wear these a lot," he says after clearing his throat. "And I thought you might like them."

"I can't wait to get home and wear them," I admit and lean in to kiss his bicep. "Thank you. I have a little something for you, too."

"Wait," he says with a smile. "There's something else. Do you think that I'd just get you *socks*?"

Brady scoffs and lifts another box from under the tree, and I feel my eyes widen. This is a *small* box. Also red with a gold bow.

"Brady."

"Take the gift, Abbi." I look up and see him watching me with humor-filled hazel eyes, and I know that I can't resist him.

Taking the box, I tear the paper and flip open the lid, and I'm pretty sure I just swallowed my tongue.

Twinkling up at me are a pair of *gorgeous* diamond earrings. Not simple studs. No, this cowboy bought me diamond studs with huge teardrops hanging from them.

My jaw drops, and then I close it again. I don't know what the fuck to say.

"Brady." It's a whisper now. My lungs are having a hard time taking in air, and finally, Brady reaches over and takes my hand in his.

"I couldn't pass them up," he says, drawing my eyes back to his face. "Nothing could ever be as beautiful as you are, but these earrings are trying, and they'll look fucking amazing on you."

I bite my lip and brush a fingertip over the diamonds. "I can't accept these."

"Oh, you don't want them?" Brady shrugs and tugs the box out of my hand, then starts to unfasten one from the black velvet. "Too fucking bad, Blue Eyes. They're yours."

He fastens them to my ears and then pulls back to admire them.

"Just as I thought."

"What?"

He leans in and brushes his lips over my cheek, then presses his lips to my ear. "You're the most beautiful woman I've ever seen."

Heat floods through me, and I have to clear my throat before taking a deep breath.

"Thank you." I lick my lips. "And I got you something, too."

Leaning over, I snatch up a box from under the tree and pass it to Brady, who's frowning at me.

"What's wrong?"

"You didn't have to get me a Christmas present."

"That was *my* line. And after freaking *diamond earrings*, I'm glad I did get you something. Here, it's small."

He narrows his eyes at me and then rips the paper, opens the box, and *smiles.*

God, that smile melts me every time. It's an arrow right to the heart.

"What is it?" Erin wants to know as she saunters in from the kitchen, where the others have been picking away at Christmas morning cinnamon rolls. "I want to know. She wouldn't tell us."

"It's a leather bracelet," he says. "With a silver bull head."

Erin's gaze meets mine, and I can see in her eyes that she *knows.* Hell, they all know that I've had a crush on Brady for a while. I don't make a big deal out of it, but it is what it is.

And when I saw this, with the rugged leather strap, I knew that I had to get it for him.

"You could really put it on anything," I reply. "Doesn't have to be your wrist."

He takes it out of the box and loops it around his wrist, admiring it.

"Thanks, Abs."

"You're welcome."

"Whoa," Erin says, rushing to me. "You weren't wearing *those* earlier."

I finger one of the earrings. "They're from Brady."

"Damn. Good job." She high-fives Brady and then smiles softly at me. "You can wear those to the party next week."

Oh, I already planned on it.

"I'll be right back."

Needing a minute, I stand, walk into the kitchen, and pour myself some juice. Millie, champagne bottle in hand, raises an eyebrow, and I nod, giving her the go-ahead to add it to my glass.

The kids run in through the back door, their cheeks flushed with happiness.

"It was *awesome*," Holly says, and Daisy nods.

"I can go faster than both of them," Johnny says.

"I didn't fall down," Daisy adds. "Not even once. I remembered how to ride, even though it's not summer anymore."

"Because you're *amazing*," I remind her and bend down to kiss her cheek. "I'm proud of you, baby."

"Would you like a cinnamon roll?" Brady's mom, Joy, asks the girls.

"Yes, please," they say in unison.

"Grandma, can I please have some juice?" Daisy asks, and my eyes go wide.

"Daisy, her name—"

"No, ma'am," Joy says, interrupting me. "I love being called Grandma. Nothing brings me more happiness than these kiddos, and Daisy is absolutely one of mine. Now, of course, you can have some juice. Come on, you can help me pour it."

I have to take a long, slow breath as tears threaten.

I don't know what I did to deserve being welcomed into this big, amazing family, and as I watch Joy with all three of the little kids, helping them get their breakfasts, I'm suddenly overwhelmed with gratitude.

Blinking, I excuse myself from the kitchen and walk down the hall, looking for the half bath.

But before I can get there, Brady takes my elbow and pulls me into a theater.

"Hey." He frowns as I wipe away a tear. "What's wrong? Who the fuck made you cry? I'll kill them."

"No one," I reply with a half laugh. "It's happy tears. And maybe I'm a little overwhelmed, too. I'm not used to this."

"What? Christmas?"

"Not like *this.* With all the people and the food and the presents. Feeling included and loved. And I'm so grateful that Daisy has it. That your family makes her feel like she belongs here. She called your mom Grandma, and when I tried to correct her, Joy wouldn't allow it."

"Of course not," he says with a half smile. "Being a grandma is her favorite thing. Hell, she'd let *you* call her grandma."

I laugh at that, already feeling much better.

"I'm just...grateful," I say again. "I don't have another word to describe it. And you got me this incredible, outrageous gift, and I really shouldn't accept them, but I'm going to because they're so beautiful, and I couldn't stand it if someone else wore them."

"No one else is going to wear them, Abs. I bought them for you."

"What was Christmas like for you, as a kid?" he asks as we sit in two of the wide, deep theater seats, turning to face each other.

"Before I was twelve, it was pretty normal. Or, my mom tried to make it as normal as possible. She was a single mom, and she was *so* poor. Always poor. She cleaned houses for a living, and sometimes I helped her. I enjoyed it."

"I guess so. You followed in her footsteps."

I grin, nodding. "Yeah. We always had a tree. I had at least one thing to open, and we had a good meal. Every year. She made sure of it."

"What happened when you were twelve, Abs?" He takes my hand in his, links our fingers, and I hold on tight, not wanting to tell him this part.

"Mom died," I whisper. "She had been sick. Cancer. And I went into foster care, and that piece is not a conversation for Christmas Day."

"Fair enough," he replies, not pressing the subject. He reaches over and tucks a stray piece of hair behind my ear. "I'm glad that you and Daisy are here. I know we're big and loud and kind of obnoxious most of the time. Okay, that's mostly just Chase."

I bark out a laugh, and he smiles, as if that's exactly what he was going for.

"But," he continues, "we're mostly harmless."

"You have a wonderful family."

"Yeah. I do. I have to say, Daisy's been a kick today. So happy and excited, like she usually is, but on steroids."

"My kid *loves* presents. Giving and receiving, as she proved today by giving every single person a piece of art that she made herself."

"My picture of a horse actually *looks* like a horse," he says, obviously impressed. "I should have bought her art supplies."

"She didn't want to go to bed last night," I confess. "She wanted to stay up for Santa. So, I had to wait her out before I could do the Santa thing."

"Wait." He holds up a hand, scowling. "You mean, Santa's not *real*?"

I grin at him. "Of course, he is."

"And what did Santa bring her?"

"He filled her stocking, and mine, actually. I always fill my own stocking because otherwise, Daisy would think that Santa doesn't love me." I shrug a shoulder. "It's kind of nice to get some new shower gel and chocolate of my own that I don't have to share. Anyway, she got some clothes, a couple of Barbies with clothes for them, and a couple of small toys. The bike was the biggest thing, and Erin and I decided we wanted to give them to the kids at the same time."

"It was a hit," he replies with that sexy grin. "What else did Santa bring *you*?"

"Uh, a healthy kid and a thriving business. I don't need anything else, Brady. Besides, you got me socks and these glorious diamonds."

"Hold up. Are you telling me that the only Christmas presents that you opened today were from me?"

"No. Erin, Polly, Summer, Millie, and I exchanged gifts. Daisy made me an ornament for the tree in school... Don't look at me like that." He's scowling at me, and it makes me shift in my seat. "What did *you* get this morning? Did you even have a stocking?"

"That's different."

"Why?"

"Because it just is." He's still scowling, so I reach over and smooth the lines between his brows with the pad of my thumb.

"Merry Christmas, Brady."

He sighs, then lifts my hand and kisses my knuckles, sending shivers up my arm. "Merry Christmas, Abs."

"What are you *doing*?" Daisy demands as she opens the door. "Oh, are we watching a movie?"

"No, baby, we were just talking." Daisy climbs into my lap and wraps her arm around my neck. "What are you up to? Are you having fun?"

"I had a ciminim roll." She grins happily, and I can't resist kissing her smooth cheek. She smells so good.

"Was it delicious?"

"Yes." She smiles shyly at Brady. "Did you have one?"

"Not yet. We'd better go get our share before my brothers eat them all."

"Come on!" she exclaims, jumping off of my lap and running out the door, and Brady smiles at me.

"Come on, then," he says, offering me a hand and pulling me up to my feet. "Let's go find a sugar coma."

THE WEEK between Christmas and New Year's is always chaos for me. I want my employees to have time off, too, so they rotate the holidays between them, and I cover. Typically, I only clean a couple of houses each week for clients that I especially enjoy and spend the majority of the week in my office and doing all the laundry that comes in from the rentals.

It's paid off big time to buy sheets and towels and offer them to the short-term rentals that we clean, so we can just haul them back to the office to launder and put them back into the rotation. I have two industrial washers and dryers that are running pretty much all day.

But, this week, I'm short by two cleaning teams, so I'm picking up the slack, spending my days cleaning rather than in the office.

And that's okay. I *enjoy* cleaning. If I were to see a therapist, they'd probably tell me that my love for keeping things clean and tidy stems from a need for control, and that's something that I actually have control over. When I was in foster care, my rooms were always sparkling. And even now, if I'm stressed, I clean.

It's just who I am, and it's likely something I inherited from my mother.

I have two clients today, both short-term rentals in the condos at the ski resort. One asked for a late checkout, so I have them on deck for later this afternoon. I'll take the bigger of the two units first.

I *love* Bitterroot Ski Resort. I've never been on a pair of skis in my life, but being at the resort is just *nice.* It's new, with so much recently remodeled or added, and the mountains are beautiful. The restaurants are great, too. Our Iconic Women's Collective meets up here often for our monthly meetings, and the lunch provided by the on-site restaurant, Snow Ghost, is always delicious.

I might just have to take something to go on my way home.

Daisy's spending the day with Merilee, our next-door neighbor. She's a retired school teacher, and she loves spending time with my girl, so if I ever need a sitter, Merilee is my go-to.

Having her just steps away is convenient.

Since Daisy will eat with Merilee, I might as well grab

a burger and onion rings from Snow Ghost to eat at my office as I process the day's laundry. God knows I'll be working off those calories today.

Merilee isn't expecting me home until well into the evening. It's rare that I have a day that I don't have to worry about what to fix for Daisy, so I'll indulge a bit.

With that decided, I park my SUV in the visitor parking and cut the engine. These two units both have a locked closet with most of our supplies inside, so I have minimal things to carry in with me, which is nice, as they're both on the second floor.

I ease around the car gingerly, since there is a lot of ice on the ground, and I don't want to fall. I pull out a bucket with rags, a tote full of clean sheets, and my favorite mop, then close the SUV and turn for the building.

Once the elevator doors open, I muscle my gear down the hallway to the first condo and knock on the door before unlocking it and stepping inside.

"Housekeeping," I call out, just in case the guests haven't left yet, but the condo is still and quiet, so I shut the door, set my stuff down, and slip out of my coat and boots before hauling the bucket and rags into the kitchen to get started there first.

There are pots and pans in the sink, which is an irritation. We always ask that guests at least load the dishwasher on their way out, so this will take me longer, but it is what it is. I've just finished loading the dishwasher and started the cycle when I turn to scrub the glass top stove that has dried spaghetti sauce stuck to the surface.

What a mess. I'll let the owner know that they shouldn't refund any of the cleaning deposit.

Suddenly, the hair on the back of my neck stands up, and I feel the air in the room shift.

"I don't think we've met."

I yelp and spin, my heart climbing into my throat at the sound of a man's voice, and I grip the countertop behind me as I swallow hard.

"I called out when I got here," I reply, my voice sounding calmer than I feel. Jesus, he can probably hear my heart hammering against my breastbone. "I can come back later or tomorrow."

"No need for that." He's a tall man with blond hair and a sneer as he looks me up and down. He's shirtless, covered only in a pair of jeans that ride low on his hips. Under any other circumstances, I might think he's handsome. "I must have fallen asleep."

"Like I said, I can come back." I start to move toward the door, but he blocks my path. I move to the right, and he moves with me, as if we're kids playing a game, and it irritates the hell out of me. "You're going to want to get out of my way."

"Or what?" He lifts an eyebrow. "Why don't you just calm down and come back to bed with me? It's warm, and I'd like to have a little fun with you."

"Absolutely not." *This* is why I make sure everyone on my staff works in teams. "I'm leaving."

He moves way faster than I give him credit for, and suddenly, he strikes out and hits me, right on the cheekbone, and I fall against the counter, seeing stars.

"I'm going to fuck you either way," he drawls, and I hear the sound of his zipper, and every cell in my body goes ice cold.

Never again. I'll never be used like this ever again. His hands are on me, my shoulder, my hip, and he reaches around to grope my breast, trying to pull me around, and my hand closes around the handle of a frying pan on the stove, and I spin, moving with the force of him pulling on me, and smack him right on the side of the head with a loud *bang.*

"Ah!" He falls to the floor, moaning, and I *run,* my sock-clad feet sliding on the hardwood floors. I can hear him still moaning behind me, but I don't look back to see if he's chasing me.

I just need to get the hell out of here.

I don't stop running, bypassing the elevator to take the stairs down two at a time, and then out to my car, running on the ice in my socks.

Thanking all the gods above that I forgot to lock it because my purse is still upstairs, I climb inside, lock the doors, and pull my phone out of my pants, calling 9-1-1.

"Nine-one-one, what is your emergency?"

"I was just physically assaulted." I have to swallow hard against the hysterical tears that want to come. My face is *killing* me. "I'm at the resort. Cleaning rooms."

"Take a breath," the operator says calmly. "I'm sending someone up there now. What unit?"

I give her all the information that she asks for, but I feel the panic attack coming. It's *right* on the edge of taking over, and I have to hang up this phone so I can try to breathe.

Usually, when this happens, and if Daisy is with me, she holds her fingers up and tells me to blow, like I'm blowing out the candles, and she puts the fingers down as I blow them out.

But she's not with me. Thank fuck.

"Do you hear the sirens?" the operator asks.

"Yes, ma'am." My accent kicks in when I'm upset. "I hear them."

"Okay, they'll be there soon. You can hang up and flag the officer down. It's Officer Wild."

Thank God.

"Thanks. Thank you."

I hang up and open my car door as the cruiser pulls to a stop in front of the building, and I stand, waving my arm.

"Abbi?" Chase scowls and hurries over to me, bracing my shoulders in his hands. "Shit, Abbi, what happened?"

I can't breathe. I just can't catch my breath, and it pisses me off.

"Whoa," Chase croons, as if I'm an upset horse that needs calming. "Deep breaths, honey. Are you hurt?"

I look up at him, and his eyes immediately narrow.

"Black eye," he says with a hard voice. All crooning is gone, and now he's good and pissed. The fierce cop has taken over the kind friend. "Who the fuck did this?"

"C-condo 210," I reply. "Guest who didn't leave. Was going to r-r-rape me. Oh, Jesus, Chase."

"Hey. You got away, you hear me? I'm going to take

care of this. I want you to sit in your car and wait for me." He looks down and scowls. "Where are your shoes?"

"Inside."

With his jaw set grimly, he urges me into my seat and speaks into the radio at his shoulder, calling for more help.

"He didn't leave?" he asks me.

"Not that I saw."

"You hang tight here." He hurries away, pulling out his phone, and I give into the tears. The fear.

The memories.

CHAPTER SEVEN

BRADY

"You need a new suit for the party," Millie says, leaning against the counter at her coffee shop, her arms crossed over her chest as she looks me up and down, as if she's examining me. "You've worn the hell out of the one you have. It's time for something new and fashionable."

"It's a black fucking suit." I scowl at her. "I can buy a new tie. Maybe a new hat."

"No." She shakes her head, reminding me why my baby sister drives me bananas. "New *suit.* I'm serious, this party is important, and you have a date. Abbi deserves to have her date look extra hot."

"Who are *you* going with?" I counter, and she scowls.

"I don't need a date," she replies, lifting her chin. "I complete myself."

"You should write a book about that." I shake my head when she scowls at me. "Do *not* throw something at me. Anyway, this party is in four days. I can't buy a custom suit in four fucking days."

"It doesn't have to be custom, fancy pants. Go across the street and buy something off the rack."

"You know, this would have been good to know a couple of days ago."

"You know," she counters, "you're a complainer."

"I am *not.*" My phone rings, and I answer when I see Chase's name. "Yo."

"Get up to the resort," he says, his voice hard and brisk. "Abbi needs you *now.* Condos, near the restaurant."

"Is she hurt?"

"Get here," he says and hangs up, and I stare at Millie for two seconds before running out of the coffee shop and to my 4Runner, my heart pounding, as I drive a couple of miles up a winding road to the resort near the chairlifts.

I can't get there fast enough. Did she get hurt on the job? I know she's working more in the field this week. God, did she fall?

I come around a corner and spot Abbi's SUV, so I park next to it and see that she's in the driver's seat, crying.

"Fuck." Within seconds, I open her door and am squatting next to her, brushing her hair off of her cheek. "Hey, sweetheart. Deep breath."

She's not just crying. She's having a panic attack. Her eyes are round and bright, her hands clenched on the steering wheel so hard that her knuckles are stark white. She hasn't even acknowledged that I'm here. I don't think she realizes that I'm right next to her.

"Come on, beautiful. Breathe with me."

She finally glances my way, and her face crumples.

And I see the huge bruise across her cheekbone and her eye. Rage fills me, spreading through me like fucking wildfire, but my hand is gentle as I brush my thumb over her chin.

"Hold...your..."—she gulps—"fingers...up."

I frown, but I do as she asks, spreading my fingers and holding my hand up, like a child telling someone their age.

And she systematically blows on each finger, then reaches up and tucks it down to my palm.

She's shaking but concentrating on blowing on my fingers, and after the third time of going through each one, she starts to settle.

"Oh, God," she sobs and brushes at the tears on her cheeks.

"Okay." Shaken to the core, I cup her face and lean in to kiss her cheek, sure to be gentle so I don't hurt her. "It's okay now, Abs. Where's Chase?"

"Upstairs," she says, gesturing with her chin toward the building. "I was cleaning. I thought the condo was empty, but—" She shakes her head, and the tears start again, fueling the bright red anger pulsing through me. I'm going to kill whoever did this to my girl.

"Brady."

I stand and turn at Chase's voice, and see that he, along with two other cops, is leading a shirtless man out of the building, his hands cuffed behind his back.

"You motherfucker." I charge him, fist cocked, but

Chase catches me, holding me back. “I’m going to rip your goddamn heart out. I’m going to be your worst fucking nightmare, you hear me, you piece of shit?”

“Stop.” Chase’s voice is hard in my ear.

“Let me kill him.”

“I can’t let you touch him,” he says, jerking me. The asshole smirks at me, but I see blood running down the side of his face.

“Tell me she did that to him.”

“Oh, she clocked him good with a frying pan,” my brother replies, pride in his voice. “And *she* needs you. Abbi is who you’re here for. This asshole will get what’s coming to him. He confessed to everything, gleefully. Fucker.”

“I’m going to hurt him,” I promise my brother.

“I didn’t hear that.” When the asshole is in the back of the squad car, headed to jail, Chase turns to Abbi, who’s just staring straight ahead now, the look in her eyes breaking my fucking heart, and squats next to her. “Abbi, I need to ask you some questions, but first, we should take you to the hospital.”

“No.” She focuses on him and licks her lips. “Absolutely *no* hospital. I’m fine. It’s nothing I haven’t had before.”

Jesus fucking Christ.

“I have to clean that condo,” she continues.

“Definitely not.” I shake my head and take her hand in mine, lacing my fingers through hers. “You’re going home. Or to my house. And we’ll call someone else to take care of this.”

"I'm the only one who can."

"Then we'll call the owner and tell them they have to find someone else. You're not working today," I stress when she tries to argue, and then she deflates, blows out a breath, and nods.

"I can't go home," she says softly. "Daisy is just next door, and she'd see me come home and would want to be with me, and I need some time."

"Polly's house," Chase says, sparing me a glance before he calls our soon-to-be sister-in-law. When she picks up, he says, "Tell me your house in town is empty right now. Good. I need to take Abbi there. She's okay. Yeah. Yeah. Thanks, Polly."

"I'll drive you. Shit, where are your shoes?"

"Inside," she says, looking down. All I want is to pull her against me and soothe her. "I need my purse."

"I'll go get your things," Chase says before jogging back inside.

"Come on." I tug her out of her car and get her settled in my 4Runner. "Everything's going to be okay, baby."

"Would you really kill him?" Her voice is low, but she's watching me shrewdly.

"In a motherfucking heartbeat." I let the anger show in my eyes and in my voice. "He fucking *touched* you. He marked you. If Chase hadn't stopped me, he'd be a dead man."

She swallows hard and turns to look out the windshield, and I worry that I said too much. Chase returns with all of Abbi's things, including a bucket of supplies, and we stow them in the back of the 4Runner.

"I have to come with you," he says grimly. "I need to get her statement."

"Let's do this, then," I reply with a nod, and we follow Chase down the road into town.

Polly decided to keep her little house near the high school and use it as a short-term rental property. I'm surprised that it's empty right now, given that it's the holidays and rentals are hard to come by.

But I won't complain about it.

Abbi's quiet as we make the short drive, and when I park in the driveway, she wiggles into her shoes, pushes the door open, and steps out. I take her hand to lead her inside, where Chase is already waiting.

"How are you doing?" Chase asks Abbi as I close the door behind us. Abbi sits on the comfy sofa, then drops her head in her hands. "Is that a stupid question?"

"No," she says as I cross to the kitchen and open the freezer, pulling out ice to make a pack for her face. "I'm okay. A little shell-shocked. Sore. Dealing with some PTSD."

Her eyes slide over to me, and she licks her lips.

"You don't need to tell me about your past," Chase says as he sits across from her. "I just need to know what happened today."

"Okay." She accepts the ice pack from me and gently presses it against her cheek and eye, sighing when the cold hits her skin. "Oh, that helps. Thanks, Brady."

I sit next to her, not sure if she wants me to, but I'm relieved when she takes my hand and squeezes, holding on tight as if I'm a lifeline.

“I’m short-staffed,” she begins. “Some of my people are on vacation for the holiday. So, I’m cleaning places this week that I normally wouldn’t. I also don’t have a partner, and I *demand* my people team up for just this reason.”

She blows out a breath.

“Anyway, I had two short-term rentals to clean up there today. I knocked and called out that I was there, and the place felt empty. There was no response when I called out, so I started on the kitchen. It was a fucking *mess*. I got the dishwasher packed up and had just turned to start on the stove when I heard him.”

She swallows hard, and her hand on mine tightens.

“He was a slimy piece of shit. Suggested I get in bed with him. I said absolutely not, that I’d just go and come back later, and he b-blocked my way.”

Her voice wavers, but she clears her throat.

“He said he’d fuck me whether I was into it or not, so I should just calm down and go with it. Grabbed me. Smacked me.”

Seeing red, I have to stand and pace the room. Christ, I want to hurt him. I want to tear his heart out through his fucking asshole.

“I reached for the frying pan on the stove and hit him, hard, and then I just ran. I didn’t stop to see if he was chasing me. I knew I had to get out of there because he was going to rape me, and I had to run.”

“Okay,” Chase says calmly when her voice rises, and it sounds like she might spiral into another panic attack. “You’re absolutely right, Abbi. You did the right thing. I can tell you that I did a run on his name, and it turns out this is not his first sexual assault. The fucker is a rich brat whose daddy paid for attorneys to get him a plea bargain on the last case, but part of his parole stipulation was that he not offend again. He's going back to prison."

"For how long?" My voice is a growl.

"Twenty more years," Chase replies.

"You found all of that out?" Abbi asks. "That was fast."

"My office does good work," he says with a smile. "He can't hurt you, or anyone else, again. I'm so sorry this happened, Abbi. Are you *sure* I can't take you to the hospital?"

"No hospitals," she repeats, shaking her head. "But thank you. Thanks for coming so quickly."

Before he leaves, Chase takes his time, assuring Abbi that she can call him anytime and that everything will be okay. Then we're alone in the quiet house.

Abbi stands, blows out a breath, and calmly walks into the kitchen to freshen up her ice pack, before turning to me with big, sad blue eyes.

Those eyes are going to be the death of me.

"So, I guess this means that anything you and I might have started is over."

I blink at her and then scowl. "What? Why would you even think that? None of this is your fault."

She sighs and, if I'm not mistaken, chuckles.

Chuckles.

"This isn't funny, Abbi."

"No." She presses the pack to her face and cringes.

"It's not funny. But it's typical. I'm a fucking mess and a half, Brady. You don't need to bring my bullshit into your life."

"I don't see any bullshit."

"No, you've seen what I want you to see, and I don't mean that as deceitful as it sounds."

She walks back into the living room and sits on the couch, pulls her feet up under her, and looks so...*sad.*

"Maybe you should talk to me."

I take Chase's seat across from her so I can look her in the eyes.

"I don't ever talk about this," she replies quietly and shivers, and I pull the throw blanket off of the back of the chair I'm in and take it to her and wrap her up in it, before returning to the chair. "I'm not going to go into the nitty gritty because I *can't.* I have to go home later to be with Daisy, and if I go there, I might not come out of the darkness that it puts me in. But I was in foster care. You know what Jake went through."

My brother's son was in foster care for over a year after his biological parents died in a car accident. He was brutalized in that house, over and over again, until Chase and Ryan saved him.

I narrow my eyes on her and nod. Christ, I want to hold her.

"I was abused in every way there is to hurt someone. In. Every. Way."

Unable to stand it, I cross to her and lift her into my arms, settling with her in my lap, and press my face to her neck.

How could *anyone* want to hurt this beautiful, smart, sweet woman?

"Never again," I say, my voice rough with emotion as we cling to each other. "No one will *ever* hurt you again, Abbi."

"I didn't think so. Until today. And I was unprepared, unarmed, and so damn *stupid*."

I pull back and frown down at her. "What are you talking about? Are you supposed to carry a gun every time you leave the house?"

"I should have been more aware of my surroundings," she says. "I should have checked every room before I started cleaning, and I should have had a partner with me."

"I won't argue about the partner," I agree. "That's just common sense, but it's the holidays and you were short-staffed. Jesus, Abbi, it's not your fault."

Her lower lip quivers, and I cup her cheek, pressing my lips to hers.

"I wish..." She stops talking and closes her eyes.

"What, baby? What do you wish?"

She takes a long, deep breath. "I wish you hadn't seen me like that. The panic attacks don't happen very often anymore, and it's bad enough that poor Daisy has to help me through them. I didn't want you to see it."

I don't like that Daisy is the one she has to lean on.

"Well, to answer your previous question, *no*. This doesn't change anything between you and me. We all have a past, Abs. We all have stuff. If you need to fall apart, then *fall the fuck apart*. I can handle it."

She leans in and buries her face in my neck.

"I have secrets, Brady. You don't deserve that."

"Will any of your secrets hurt my family?"

She jerks back as if I've just hit her, her big, blue eyes full of fire. "Of course not. Jesus, of course not."

"Then I don't give a shit. When you want to tell me, you will."

"As simple as that?"

"It doesn't have to be hard. Now, what do we need to do? Who do we need to call?"

She chews her lip, and it looks like she might cry again, but she squares her shoulders and pulls her phone out of her pocket.

"I need to call my people and find out if anyone can cover those two condos. Then, I have to call the owner of the one I was cleaning. And I really, really need to eat something."

I grin at her. "You make those calls, and I'll handle the food."

"Deal. And, Brady?" She smiles up at me. "Thank you. No one has ever had my back like that. Not since my mom died."

God, I want to tell her that I'll have her back every goddamn day for the rest of her life, but I can't promise that.

Instead, I gently kiss her sweet lips and brush her hair over her shoulder.

"I'm right here," I whisper before I set her on the couch and stand to cross the room to place my own call for food.

An hour later, once we've polished off a pizza and Abbi seems to be much calmer, she sighs and smiles over at me.

"As much as I'd like to stay here with you all night, I should go home to Daisy. I have some arnica there for this bruise, and I need to do some rearranging on the schedule for the rest of the week."

"I understand. I'll take you home, and my brothers and I will get your car for you later."

"You can just take me up there now, and I'll drive it home. It's no big deal."

"No. I'll take you home." I soften the statement with a kiss and then help Abbi clean up from our surprise visit to the rental before I drive her the short distance to her townhouse. "Do you need anything?"

"No, I'm honestly fine. Do you want to come in?"

Surprisingly, no. I don't want to come in. I want to work off some pent-up aggression.

"Actually, I think I'm going to go to the gym for a while, unless you need me."

"By all means, go to the gym," she replies with a smile and leans in to kiss my cheek. I grip her chin, turn her lips to mine, and kiss her long and slow, until she whimpers against me. "Maybe we should have stayed at Polly's place, after all."

I grin at her. "Soon, I'd like to have uninterrupted, kid-free time with you. But for today, I'll say goodbye."

"Soon," she says and turns away to get out of the car. "Now, go lift some weights. Your arms are my favorite."

I quirk up a brow. "Is that so?"

“Super hot,” she confirms and steps out of the 4Runner. “I’ll see you at the gala, if not before.”

“It’ll probably be before,” I assure her with a wink, and once she’s inside, I pull out of her driveway and let the fear, the absolute *rage* pulse through me. I’ve held it back over the past couple of hours because that’s not what she needed from me.

But now, I need to beat the shit out of something, so I dial Ryan’s number.

“Chase told us,” my brother says by answering. “What do you need?”

“Your gym,” I reply grimly. “More specifically, the bag.”

“It’s yours, help yourself. Need someone to spar with?”

“Maybe. I don’t know. I’m pretty shitty company right now, Ry. I want to kill that motherfucker.”

“I get it. I’d want the same in your shoes. Hit the bag for a while.”

“Thanks.”

I park just outside of Ry’s shop, where the gym is also housed. It has its own entrance in the back, and because my brother is who he is, this gym is likely outfitted with better and more state-of-the-art equipment than the *actual* gym just outside of town.

When I walk in, I find Jake on the treadmill, earbuds in his ears, sweating as he jogs. I wave at him and head straight to the corner, where a punching bag hangs.

After slipping on gloves so I don’t tear my knuckles apart, I start in. First, I see that asshole’s face from today, and I pound it as hard as I can. Then I make my way through the fuckers that were supposed to protect Abbi when she was a teenager. The ones who not only hit her, but raped her, and tore apart her mental health, as well. She didn't spell it out for me, but it was clear.

And I wish I could make them all pay.

So, I hit and hit and hit until my arms and shoulders sing in protest. Until I'm fighting for breath and every inhale is pure fire. Until all the injuries I've ever had—and there are more than I can list—scream in protest.

And then I hit some more.

The bag falls from the ceiling, catching me by such surprise that I step back, and then applause breaks out around me.

When I turn, I find Ryan, Jake, Remington, and Chase all standing nearby, hands on hips or in pockets, watching me.

"You're going to hurt tomorrow," Rem says.

"I hurt now. Give me just five minutes alone in a cell with him," I say to Chase as I wipe my arm over my forehead.

"I can't do that, no matter how much I want to," Chase says quietly. "He threatened to sue her for assault."

"You're fucking kidding me." I turn and kick the bag now.

"He dropped that idea when we reminded him that what she did was in self-defense." Chase crosses his arms over his chest. "How is she?"

"Better. She's a lot better. Bruised and sore, but she

ate and wanted to go home with Daisy. And I needed—" I point to the bag. "I'm just so fucking *pissed*."

"Did this help?" Jake asks quietly, watching me with sober eyes.

"A little. I pictured his face." I blow out a breath as I tug my sweat-drenched shirt over my head and then accept the bottle of water that Ryan offers. "I hate that there's nothing I can do."

"You did it," Ryan replies. "You stayed with her. You took care of her. That's all you can do."

"It's not enough." I chug some of the water. "Hey, you're fancy."

Ryan's lips twitch. "Are you insulting me?"

"No, Millie says I need a new suit for this big party. But I only have a couple of days until the gala."

"Oh, I can take care of that," Ryan says, pulling out his phone. "What color do you want?"

"It's a fucking suit, I don't know." I eye Jake. "Sorry, buddy."

"I figure you have the right to swear a lot today," Jake replies. His face is still sober. "Did he hurt her really bad?"

"He got one hit in," I reply and walk to him, patting him on the shoulder. "And she smashed a frying pan over his head. Made him bleed."

Jake nods, relief obviously moving through him. "Good. That's good. Maybe I'll go see her tomorrow and see if she needs anything. I'm gonna go kill some zombies."

He waves at us and then walks out of the gym, closing the door behind him.

"Fuck," I mutter, shaking my head. "I should have thought of how he was feeling before I went on my rampage."

"He's okay," Ryan says. "He'll go kill some zombies and feel better. The way you killed my bag over there."

"Sorry." I grin at him. "Not sorry. Hey, this asshole is the son of a rich fucker. I can't hurt him physically, but—"

"I'll take care of it," Ryan says with a lethal grin. "That family might just have to lose all of their money."

"Jesus, you guys are scary," Rem mutters. "How can I help?"

CHAPTER EIGHT

ABBI

"Look at those *earrings*," Summer breathes, her voice full of awe and admiration, from her seat next to mine.

"I can't," I reply. "I'm getting lashes, and I'm not allowed to open my eyes. Whose earrings are we admiring?"

"Polly's," Summer replies.

"Describe them."

"Rubies," she said. "Big, fat, red rubies the size of my baby toe. With diamonds. Did you get those for Christmas?"

"Yes," I hear Polly reply. "Ryan spoils the shit out of me."

"As he should." That's Erin's voice. "And oh, my God, your baby bump is *so cute* in that red dress."

"Okay, hurry up with the lashes already," I say with a laugh.

"There, all set," my makeup gal, Stacy, says with a chuckle of her own. "Go ahead and admire everyone."

"*Finally*." I turn in my chair and sigh in happiness. Polly looks incredible in a fitted, red velvet dress that *does* make her bump look adorable, and those earrings are just stellar. "You're *so* beautiful, friend."

"You're all really good for my ego," she replies happily and passes me a glass of champagne. She's holding a glass of sparkling cider. "Also, your makeup is amazing. And you have some pretty incredible earrings of your own. Brady did *good*."

"Oh!" I turn back to the mirror to have a look and am immediately relieved to see that there's no sign of a bruise on my cheek or my eye. "You did a great job on that coverup."

"It was my pleasure, and the makeup should stay in place for a few days, even if you wash, as long as you don't scrub too hard."

I stand and hug Stacy before hurrying over to the dress hanging in the doorway of Erin's bathroom.

Since all five of us were already going to be at the ranch all day, getting the Wild River Ranch event space ready for tonight, we decided to just bring all of our stuff out here to get ready together. We even hired hair and makeup artists to make us feel extra fancy.

We also decided that we would all wear gold and/or red. Polly has the red more than covered in her amazing ensemble. After pulling my dress down, I turn and take in my best friends.

Millie's in a strapless gold dress that hugs her in all

the right places. Her dark hair is down, falling in waves around her shoulders.

Erin's dress is red with ruffles that flow down the slim skirt and a high neckline, but no sleeves.

And Summer's dress is a gorgeous ballgown, with a red skirt and gold bodice that is going to make her husband break out into a sweat.

"You need to get dressed," Erin says with a grin. "Your date will be here soon."

"Maybe I should have gone with something more... modest." I bite my lip, having second thoughts, but all four of my besties immediately shake their heads.

"Fuck that," Millie says.

"What she said," Erin agrees.

"This dress was *made* for you," Summer adds, and Polly simply walks over to me and takes my hand in hers, grinning.

"You *wear* this dress, Abbi. It doesn't wear you. It hugs your curves, yes, and shows off your perfect breasts."

"I'd *kill* for your tits," Millie says with a grin. "Seriously. Smoke show right here."

I can't help but laugh at that. "Okay, you guys *are* good for the ego. Help me into this thing."

I step into the dress, a long column of gold sequins that's heavy and not at all comfortable, but once I'm zipped up, I turn to the mirror, and my jaw drops.

My blonde hair is teased into a smooth roll at the nape of my neck. My boobs are pushed up, and even I have to admit, the cleavage is impressive. The bodice is a tank style, and the skirt falls straight down, almost touching the floor.

My heels are also gold and match perfectly.

"Photo," Stacy calls out, and the five of us hurry to stand side-by-side, hands on hips, chins up, chests out, posing for the photo.

"We'll take more when we get there," Erin says.

"The red and gold is *so pretty*," Stacy says, admiring us. "Good call on the color choices."

"A toast," Millie says, holding up her glass. We all grab our own glasses and join her. "To five badass women who had a good idea and ran with it. Next year is going to be even better than the last, and that's saying a lot. And to my best friends. I admire you, and I love the shit out of you."

"Don't make us cry," I say with a laugh. "We just finished our makeup."

"To us," Erin agrees, and we all clink our glasses together before taking a sip.

The doorbell rings, and Erin grins. "I think our hot-as-hell men are arriving."

"Let's get this party started!"

Downstairs, Remington and Ryan are already here, and when their girls walk down the staircase, they both have to swallow hard. It's actually really adorable.

The bell rings again, and this time it's Chase on the other side. When he sees Summer, he dips her back and kisses the hell out of her.

Without knocking or ringing the bell, Brady pushes through the door, and I feel my heart rate speed up. I've never seen this suit before. It's a dark hunter green that fits his lean body perfectly, with a gold tie and a gold handkerchief in his pocket. Jesus, he's handsome. And when he glances around, looking for me and finding me, his gaze darkens, and he blows out a long breath as he stalks toward me.

"You look—" I begin, but he cuts me off, sweeping me up in his arms and kissing the breath out of me, right here in front of his family. When he finally sets me back on my feet, I realize that we're surrounded by applause, and I can't help but laugh. "You know how to make an entrance."

"You're so fucking beautiful I can hardly breathe."

"Aww," Millie says. "That's sweet. Come on, let's party."

Thankfully, the weather has been working in our favor, so we're able to have sleigh rides from the bigger parking area over to the event center. As the others climb into the sleigh and bundle up in the white blankets we've provided, Brady and I hang back, and he wraps me in a hug, then tips my chin up so he can look into my eyes.

"You're beautiful, Blue Eyes."

"You know, before I was interrupted back there, I was going to say the same to you. This suit is amazing."

"Ryan came through," he says with a chuckle.

"Are you getting in this sleigh or what?" Ryan calls out. "Let's go."

Brady offers me his hand and helps me into the sleigh with the others, and then we bundle up together under the blanket as the driver gets the horses moving toward the event center.

It's a gorgeous, clear night, with a billion stars and a big full moon casting a glow on the snow around us. Aside from the horse's hooves and the skids in the snow, it's perfectly still and quiet.

"It's so beautiful out here," I say with a sigh and lean against Brady. "Maybe the most beautiful place in the world."

"We tend to agree," Remington says with a wink. He doesn't *quite* crack a smile, but Remington rarely does.

He's so stoic.

Some might call him grumpy. At least, that's what Erin calls him, and it never fails to make me laugh.

It doesn't take long before we pull up to a stop, and the guys help us out of the sleigh and onto the red carpet. There aren't any photographers out here—we don't want anyone to freeze— but we laid the carpet so it wouldn't be slick.

"Wow," Brady says when we step inside. "This is really pretty."

From the thousands of twinkle lights hanging all around us to the gorgeous white flowers on the tables, the space is absolutely gorgeous. There are already some members of our Iconic Women's Collective here, having their photos taken, mingling, and drinking champagne.

I love that for four events a year, we include spouses or significant others. A fancy party for everyone to enjoy. We're never disappointed in the turnout, and I'd say that this event won't be any different.

"Oh, this is just *gorg*!"

We turn and smile at Katie, the young woman who works for Polly and has been dating Jake for a few months. She's in a pretty silver dress, and Jake is in a tux, and I think my heart just melted into a puddle at the look he sends his date.

Our Jake is very smitten with Miss Katie.

"Well, aren't you two just absolutely beautiful?" Erin asks as we make a little semi-circle around the couple. Jake's face flushes all the way to the tips of his ears.

"Thank you," Katie says, executing a perfect curtsy. "This is *so* fun. I'm going to make Jake dance all night."

"Great," Jake says with a smile. "Just what I love to do most. Dance."

The guys all laugh, and Chase claps him on the shoulder, and then we start to disperse so we can mingle with our guests.

The night flies by. Everything goes smoothly, and finally, it's almost midnight.

The DJ counts down from ten seconds, and when he reaches one, he yells, "HAPPY NEW YEAR!"

I'm a bit tipsy from all the champagne, but when Brady pulls me to him and lowers his magical mouth to mine, I fall the rest of the way into happy bliss.

I hear the buzzing around us, the commotion, the song. But all I feel is this man. He's been so attentive to me all night, not afraid at all to show me affection, as if it's a simple, foregone conclusion that we're a couple, and he doesn't care who sees.

It's just moments after midnight when people start

to filter out, ready to go home. The music continues, but the crowd thins significantly, and finally, around twelve-thirty, I turn to Brady and grin.

"What now?" I ask him.

"Depends," he replies, looping his arms around my back. "Where is Daisy tonight?"

I smile slowly. "She's having a sleepover at your parents' house with Holly and Johnny."

His hazel eyes narrow. "And you're just telling me that *now*? Shit, I would have left hours ago."

"I know, and as a co-host, I had to stay." I laugh as I run my hands up and down the lapels of his suit. "This color is really great on you."

"Your place or mine?" He's laser-focused on me and it makes my core tighten in anticipation.

"Yours is closer."

"Mine it is." He nods and takes my hand, leading me toward the door. We're stopped several times to say our goodbyes, and finally, we're in his 4Runner, driving away from the venue.

"How did your car get there?" I ask him. "We rode a sleigh to the event."

"The guys and I knew we'd want our own cars when it was all said and done, so we parked them out here earlier."

"Smart." I shift in the seat, suddenly nervous. Sure, we've kissed and *kissed,* and I feel like I've grown to know Brady so well over the last month or so, but it's clear that we both intend to have sex tonight.

And I haven't had sex with anyone in a really, *really* long time.

"Whoa, you're thinking pretty hard over there."

I smile softly and look over at him. "Are you nervous?"

"No. Absolutely not. Wait, are *you* nervous?"

I shrug a shoulder and bite my lip. "Maybe a little."

He tugs my hand up to his lips and nibbles them. No, he doesn't simply kiss my skin, he bares his teeth and *nibbles.* Now my nipples are hard.

"You'll keep the earrings on," he says, almost casually. "Because I'm going to fuck you while you wear my diamonds."

Well, damn. Now, my panties are completely soaking, and I can't help but squirm in the seat.

"Still nervous?" he asks me.

"No. No, I wouldn't use that word to describe what I am."

"Good."

Brady takes a turn, and less than thirty seconds later, he pulls up in front of a small log cabin. He cuts the engine and hops out of his 4Runner, crossing around to my side. When he opens the door, he simply scoops me into his arms.

"I can walk, silly."

"No way. You're in those fuck-me heels, and there's a foot of snow out here." He's not even breathing hard when he opens the door and steps inside with me, then sets me on the wood floor.

I remember Erin saying that this is the oldest

dwelling on the ranch. That the original owners, more than a hundred years ago, lived here. Obviously, it's been updated through the years with electricity and plumbing. There's a pot belly stove in the corner, with a fire smoldering inside.

The space is clean and neat, and when I turn to Brady, I find him watching me with his hands shoved in his pockets.

"I like it," I say at last.

"It's small." He rocks back on his heels, looking around the room. "But it's just me, and I don't need anything more than this."

"I *like* it," I repeat and walk slowly to him. In my heels, I'm able to tip my head back and kiss his chin, and I grin when those hands slip out of his pockets and around to my ass. "It's warm in here, and I have you all to myself."

His eyes heat as his lips meet mine. Softly at first, gently brushing back and forth, just barely tasting me. Then his tongue licks across my bottom lip, and I open for him. Brady sinks into me, his hands tightening on the globes of my ass, tugging me harder against him, and I can feel his need for me pressed against my stomach.

I push his coat off of him, and he tosses it onto the couch behind me as I get to work on his tie.

"I love dressing up," I murmur against his lips, "but I hate all of the layers."

His lips twitch up into a smile as he helps me unbutton his shirt and pull it out of his pants. It takes longer than I'd like, but eventually, he's standing before me in just his trousers, and I'm quite sure the air has just been sucked out of the room because I can't quite catch my breath. His muscles are hard behind smooth skin, and I can't resist reaching out to touch his chest, letting my fingers drift down those rock-hard abs.

"And I like that you *don't* have as many layers," he says, but he doesn't reach behind me to unzip my dress. Instead, he drags his fingertips gently along the material of my bust, sending goose bumps down my arms. "I'm going to take you to my bedroom."

"Please, by all means, do."

He chuckles and takes my hand, leading me down a short hallway and into a small bedroom where a king-sized bed takes up 90 percent of the space. He flips a switch and a bedside light comes on.

"You said earlier that you're nervous," he whispers as he kisses down my cheek to my ear. "I won't have that, Abs. You're with *me*. I won't hurt you. I won't do anything you don't want to do. And I plan to worship every goddamn inch of your amazing body."

I bite my lip when his teeth nip at my earlobe. "I wasn't nervous because I don't want this. It's just...been a long time."

I feel him grin against me, and then those magical fingers of his find the zipper at my back, and he slowly tugs it down.

"I'm a bastard because I'm damn glad that it's been a long time." He kisses the ball of my shoulder after one strap of my dress falls down. "But if you want to stop, we stop. You're in control here, sweetheart."

I swallow hard and let my fingertips drift up and down his sides. He lets my dress pool at my feet, but he doesn't lean back to look.

Not yet.

No, I don't want to stop. I don't *ever* want this to stop. I've wanted Brady Wild for what seems like eons, and we're finally here. As far as I'm concerned, this could last forever and I'd be perfectly fine with that.

"Holy God."

I blink and then grin when I realize that he's checking out my bra and underwear set. They're gold, like the dress, and all lace.

With a teasing smile, I take two steps back and prop my hands on my hips, not even a little self-conscious about my curves, thanks to the fire in Brady's eyes. "You like?"

He swallows hard, wipes his hand down his face, and then shakes his head. "No."

I pout and try to keep the sudden nervousness out of my voice. "You *don't* like?"

"What I'm feeling right now is way beyond *like*. I'm... fuck, I'm speechless."

Suddenly, I'm on the bed, still in my underwear and heels, and his lips are all over me. His hands are everywhere at once, and everything in me is on fire.

My hands dive into his thick, dark hair as his lips move to my breast. He teases the nub through the lace, and finally, he reaches behind me to unfasten the bra and casts it aside.

"Abbi," he breathes before pulling a nipple into his

mouth, his fingers toying with the other one, and my hips have a mind of their own, twisting and moving beneath him. I've never wanted a man the way I want Brady Wild.

"I want to see *you*," I groan, but I hold him close, loving the way his mouth feels on me, the way his hands make me tingle all over.

And before I can complain anymore, Brady shoulders his way between my thighs, spreads me wide, and loops my panties with his finger to pull them aside, and then his mouth is on me. I'm pretty sure the veil between heaven and earth just lifted. My back bows as I cry out, gripping onto his hair as he feasts on me. He moans, and it sends me over the edge, screaming with the first real orgasm that I think I've ever had in my life.

He tugs my panties off, tosses them over the side of the bed, and shimmies out of his trousers.

Before he can reach for a condom, I sit up and reach for him, palming him, moving up and down.

"Abbi," he moans, his head falling back. "Christ, I want you."

After stroking him three more times, he leans over for the condom, rolls it on, and nestles against me, rubbing up and down my slit as he brushes my hair away from my cheek and smiles down at me.

"You're sure?"

"So sure." I kiss his nose. "I've never been surer of anything."

CHAPTER NINE

BRADY

I don't have to worry about dying in the arena after being thrown off a pissed-off bull because this woman, right here and right now, is going to kill me. She's lying on my bed, that beautiful blonde hair falling out of her fancy twist, my earrings sparkling on her ears, her blue eyes shining in the low light of the lamp, and don't even get me started on her lips.

Those lips, all pink and swollen from my kisses, are parted, and her tongue darts out to lightly lick her lower lip.

"Jesus fucking Christ, Abs."

She's soaked where my dick rests against her, and I want to slide in hard and claim her. I want to ruin her for all other men.

But I also don't want to hurt her.

"Brady," she breathes, her hand running down my torso.

I lean in and kiss her, unable to resist those pretty

pink lips, and move my hips back and forth, slipping through her folds.

But I'm still not where I want to be: buried so deep inside of her that we don't know where I end and she begins.

"Now," she whispers against my jawline. "Please."

I lean up a bit, and her hand slips between us, wrapping around my shaft, and I suck in a breath through my teeth as she guides me to her. *Nothing* can stop me from inching my way in, a little at a time, watching her face as she takes me so well.

"God, baby, you're so damn tight."

She purrs, fucking *purrs*, and digs her nails into my back, and I know without a doubt that I'm right.

She's going to end me. Right here, right now.

But what a damn fine way to go.

I take one of her hands in mine, kiss her fingers, and then press it over her head against the bed, holding her there as we find our rhythm, gazes locked. The room is buzzing with energy as we climb, reaching for a climax that's way closer than I'd intended.

But I can't hold back with her.

"You're incredible," I tell her, dragging my nose against hers.

"No," she breathes, her voice hitching when I grind against her. "*You* are."

I smile and pick up the tempo, and she moans long and low as her walls clench around me, contracting with her climax.

"That's it, Blue Eyes. Let go. Let me feel you come on my cock."

I can't hold back. With a growl of my own, I rock into her while my world shatters around me.

After a moment, when I've managed to take a breath and reassure myself that I haven't actually died by orgasm, I lift my head and smile down at her, releasing her hand. She cups my face and kisses me as we roll to our sides, still linked.

I'm not ready to let go of that incredible connection.

But, finally, Abbi sighs and rolls away, pads into the bathroom, and I also get up to deal with the condom and clean myself up a bit.

When she returns to the bedroom, she's not shy at all about climbing onto the bed and crooks a finger at me.

"I have questions," she says, making my eyebrows climb in surprise.

"I will answer them if I can." I join her and pull her against me, covering us up with the blankets, and she sighs as she settles against my chest. God, it feels good to have her wrapped around me. "What do you want to know?"

I kiss her hair as she drags her fingertips up and down my chest.

"You have a lot of scars, Brady." She leans back so she can look up at me. "Like, a *lot.*"

"Probably more than the average guy, yeah." I smile, but she doesn't lose the concerned look in those beautiful baby blues. "Would you like a rundown on what's what?"

"Kind of," she admits. "I mean, I *know* that bull riding is dangerous, but I've never been to an arena. I've never been to a rodeo. Hell, I've never even ridden a horse. I don't know what the dangers really are, aside from the worst-case scenario you told me about a few weeks ago."

She cups my cheek, and I turn my mouth so I can kiss her palm. I don't ever want her anywhere near an arena.

"This one," I say softly and guide her fingertips to the long scar over my right pectoral muscle. "It was my second year professionally riding. I fell wrong, tore the skin open."

She swallows hard, and I kiss her forehead.

"What else?" she whispers after she leans over to press a kiss to the scar, making butterflies come to life in my belly.

"You want the *whole* list?"

"Yep." She sits up, drawing the covers up over her breasts. "Give it to me, Cowboy."

"Oh, I'll give it to you."

She laughs and shoves my shoulder. "Focus. This first, then you can give me the good stuff."

"Ah, incentive. Now we're talking. Well, the shoulder you just shoved has been dislocated twice."

She gasps, and I shake my head.

"You're fine. You don't have to be gentle with me."

Abbi leans in and kisses my shoulder. "What else?"

"Too many concussions to count."

"Don't you wear a helmet?"

I press my lips together and then shrug. "No. It's not required. Honestly, studies have shown that with this sport, the helmet doesn't prevent the concussion. You have to learn not to land on your head when you fall."

"Can you even control that?"

"Not really." I grin at her, wondering how much I should really tell her because it might freak her out a bit, and I don't want to add to her anxiety.

"Don't get apprehensive on me," she says, as if she can read my mind. "Tell me."

"Okay, I've had six broken ribs, not all at the same time."

She bends over and kisses my torso, and my dick has decided to get in on this action.

"Liver laceration."

"God, Brady," she whispers and kisses under my breastbone. "I don't know where your liver is, so this is close enough."

I grin at her. Jesus, she's beautiful.

"I've broken both hands." She lifts each one, kissing them. "And I ripped my knee apart a few years ago."

She shakes her head as she pulls the covers off of me and leans in to press her lips to the knee sporting the scar.

This turn of her body lifts her ass in the air, and I don't miss the opportunity to cup it, let my fingertips brush over her slit, and she lets out a gasp but doesn't pull away.

"We're not done," she says breathlessly.

"That's close enough," I reply and push onto my knees, moving behind her, keeping her ass in the air. "You have the most perfect ass I've ever seen, Abs."

"Right. It's the size of *two* asses."

And with that, I smack one cheek, hard enough to leave a little pink on the skin, and Abbi sits up and stares back at me.

"You did *not* just hit me."

"I spanked you." I pull her face in for a kiss. "Keep talking shit about your amazing body, and I'll keep spanking you. Ball's in your court, Blue Eyes."

Those eyes narrow on me, and then she shrugs and pats me on the cheek.

"As long as it's just spanking, we're fine."

"I will *never* touch you in anger."

"Good. Now, where were we?" She leans onto her elbows, that ass in the air. "Ah, yes, right here."

I lean over for a condom, but I toss it onto the bed and instead spread her lips with my thumbs and bury my face in her.

"Ah, shit," she moans as I lick and nibble. I sink my tongue inside of her, fucking her, and I can feel her start to quake around me.

But I want to feel her come on my dick, so I roll the condom on and then push inside of her, making us both moan.

"So good." She swallows hard and glances back at me. "It's almost too good."

I fucking love the way she pushes back against me, as if she can't get enough, and I reach around to circle her clit with my finger, making her start to lose it again.

"That's it, baby. Let go."

She buries her face in a pillow and cries out, pushing

against me as I grip her hips and come with her, unable to hold back any longer.

This time, after we clean up and collapse back onto the bed, we fall asleep almost immediately.

Abbi's still asleep as I creep into the kitchen to start a pot of coffee and find my phone in last night's trousers. It's not quite seven, but that means that it's nine on the East Coast, and I need to make a call.

The same call that I make every year, on the morning of New Year's Day.

After pouring a cup of the brew, I sit on the couch and press *dial.* Two rings later, she answers.

"Happy New Year, Brady."

"Hey, Amy. Happy New Year. Were you guys up too late last night like the rest of the world?"

"No," she says with a laugh. "I slept through the ball dropping. Sierra spent the night with some friends. How are things in Montana?"

I glance out the window and see that we got about six new inches of snow last night.

"It's white," I tell her with a grin. "And cold. And how about North Carolina?"

"No snow here, and the ocean looks pretty calm right now." After her husband passed, Amy moved herself and Sierra back to her hometown in North Carolina. "Brady, I have some news that I need to share with you, and I don't want you to be upset."

I narrow my eyes, still watching the snow. "Okay. What's up?"

"I'm getting married. I got engaged on Christmas Day."

Well, that hits like a punch to the gut, but I shouldn't be surprised. Amy is young and beautiful, and she shouldn't be alone forever.

"Congratulations."

She's quiet for a moment.

"Who's the lucky guy?" I ask, trying to lighten the tension that's suddenly between us.

"His name is Hugh. He's a real estate agent here in town, and I met him through friends. He's a good man, Brady. You and Dirks would have liked him. He thinks the world of Sierra, and she loves him, too."

"Good." I clear my throat, nodding even though she can't see me. "That's good, Amy. Dirks would want this for both of you."

She sniffles on the other end. "I know, but that doesn't make me feel like I'm betraying him any less. Even though my therapist has told me over and over again that I'm not doing anything wrong."

"You're not," I agree gently. "Honey, he's been gone for more than six years. We'll always miss him, but you can't stay where you were six years ago. You can't live in that grief for the rest of your life. You deserve so much better than that."

"Shit, I should have paid you instead of a therapist."

I laugh at that and wish that I could give her a hug. "I hope I get an invitation."

"Duh. Actually, you know my daddy passed away a few years ago, and I don't have any brothers. Brady, would you walk me down the aisle?"

Well, hell. I didn't have *getting choked up* on my Bingo card for today, but here we are.

"Of course. You name the time and place, and I'll be there. I'm honored you asked me. Plus, it's time I saw my goddaughter. Two years have gone by fast."

"She'll love it." Now she has a smile in her voice. "And, you know, if you have a date to bring..."

I chuckle and glance down the hall toward the bedroom. "Actually, I just might."

"Brady Wild, you're holding out on me!"

"Hey, you got *engaged* a week ago, and I'm just now finding out about it."

"Okay, that's fair. Tell me about her. Send me pictures."

I spend ten minutes filling Amy in, and when I'm done, she sighs, obviously envisioning a Hallmark romance in her head.

"And now, you're snowed in at your tiny cabin, wasting time with an old friend when she's in your bed, pining for you."

"Uh, I don't think that's quite accurate, but okay. Anyway, I'm having a few bad moments of my own over here. I have no business starting something with her."

"Why the hell not?"

"Because I'm not retired." I blow out a breath. "Although, this will be my last season. But you know how I feel about starting a relationship with someone,

Amy. I won't do to Abbi what happened to you and Sierra."

"Good. Don't do that. Zero out of ten stars, do not recommend. But that doesn't mean you can't start a relationship with her. Weren't you the one just lecturing me on not living in my grief?"

"Number one, it wasn't a *lecture*. Number two, it's not the same thing at all, and you know it."

"Nope, I don't know it. I'm going to tell you right now that you're *wrong*, Brady Wild. You and I know that life can change in the blink of an eye. You're stupid to pass on happiness because of *what-ifs*. Promise me you won't do that. If she's the one for you, and you're crazy about her, you hang on to her. And you bring her here so I can meet her and her amazing daughter. Send me photos. Hell, I might get impatient and have to bring Sierra and Hugh out there to ride some horses."

"You're always welcome to come here," I remind her. "I hope this is the best year of your life, Amy. You deserve it more than anyone I know."

"Right back at you, Brady. We've both earned it. Now, I'm going to go out to breakfast with my *fiancé*, and I'll have Sierra call you later."

"Sounds good. Take care."

"Bye."

I hang up and let out a long breath before sipping my tepid coffee. I sit in the silence for a while before getting up to stoke the fire, and then I pad down the hallway, fresh cup of coffee in hand, and open the bedroom door to check on Abbi.

She turns over in the bed and smiles at me sleepily. "Hey."

"Good morning. I *think* I got your coffee right. I'll do better next time."

She sits up and takes a sip, closing her eyes. "You did great *this* time. Thanks. I thought I heard you talking to someone out there."

"Yeah, I call Amy every year on New Year's morning. We talk sporadically during the year, but this has been a tradition since Dirks died."

"Oh, I like that tradition." She smiles and sips, and I reach out to tuck her hair behind her ear. "How is she?"

"She's great, actually. She got engaged on Christmas."

"Oh, wow, that's awesome." Abbi looks almost as excited as if she got engaged herself, and I can't help but lean over to kiss her lips. "How did *you* take the news?"

"I was a little surprised, but I'm really happy for her. She deserves happiness. She asked me to walk her down the aisle."

"Holy shit. I hope you said yes."

"Of course, I did." I take the coffee from her and take a sip of my own. "Now, what would *you* like to do today?"

"For starters, I need to call and check in with your mom and see how Daisy's doing. I have no idea where my phone is."

I laugh and stand, passing the coffee back to her. "I'll go look for it."

Her purse is on the floor just inside the doorway

where she dropped it last night when I couldn't take my lips off of her, so I pick it up and take it to her.

"Thanks. It also occurs to me that the only clothes I have is that dress, unless I want to wear this sheet like a toga."

"Togas are coming back in."

She smacks my arm and pulls her phone out of her purse.

"No messages or calls, so that's a good sign," she says as she taps the screen and then holds the phone up, and it starts to ring on speakerphone.

"Hello, dear," my mom says in greeting.

"Hi, Joy. Good morning and happy New Year. How's Daisy today?"

"Oh, she's great. She's watching cartoons with Holly and Johnny. Do you want to speak to her?"

"Sure, just for a moment."

There's some rustling around and then Daisy's voice comes out of the phone. "Hi, Mama! I'm having so much fun! We made homemade pizza last night, and today, we had bacon and eggs from eggs that we collected out of the *backyard*, from *chickens!* And Grandma made fresh bread for toast. And now we're watching TV, and Grandma told us that we can stay again tonight. Can I?"

"Uh," Abbi looks a little stunned at the turn of events. "I'm glad you're having so much fun, baby, but I should talk to Joy about another night."

"You can totally talk to her. Okay, bye, Mom! Love you!" The phone is passed, and *my* mom comes back on the line.

"She's such a happy child," Mom says with a chuckle. "I just love her to pieces. Like she said, it's fine with us if the kids stay another night. I think John is going to take them down to the barn to ride around on a pony, and I thought I'd have them help me make some homemade pasta this afternoon."

"Are you *sure*?" Abbi asks before biting her lip. "I'm happy to come get her."

"I'm sure," Mom says. "She's not a bother at all. We love her. You have a fun day, and don't worry about a thing. We'll see you tomorrow."

"Well, okay. Thanks, Joy."

"You're welcome. Tell my son I said hello."

"Hi, Ma." I laugh as Abbi turns bright red. "Have a good day."

"Love you, Bubba," Mom says, calling me the name she's used since I was a toddler, and then ends the call.

"Your *mom* knows that I'm here," Abbi says in a loud whisper.

I glance around the room and then back at her. "Why are we whispering?"

"I don't know, but your mom knows. And that means your *dad* must know. Holy shit."

Now I'm laughing my ass off and fall over on the bed, holding my stomach. "We're adults, Abs. And everyone saw us leave last night. I couldn't keep my hands off you."

"Oh, my God," she groans, throwing her arm over her eyes. "And now, I don't have any clothes, and I'm going to have to do the walk of shame out of here with last night's dress on."

"Whoa." That has me sobering, and I crawl over her, pinning her to the mattress. "No shame here, Blue Eyes. We are two consenting adults with a babysitter. If it makes you feel better, I'll run you into town so you can change your clothes and grab another change for tomorrow."

"My car is still at Erin's house."

"We can work out the details." I can't resist leaning down to nibble those enticing lips. "Later."

CHAPTER TEN

ABBI

After another round of sex this morning, Brady drove me to the farmhouse so I could grab my things from yesterday, along with my car. Of course, before leaving, Erin whispered in my ear that I *had* to call her later to fill her in on everything, and I promised to do that as I walked out with a flaming red face.

Then Brady followed me into town so I could take a quick shower and change my clothes before packing a bag for another night away. And let me just say, I feel *so much better.* My muscles are sore, especially in the areas that have been ignored for way too long, but despite little sleep last night, I feel refreshed and energized. Not to mention excited for the opportunity to spend another full day and night with this incredibly sexy man.

And trust me, Brady is sexy with a capital S.

"I'm ready," I announce as I walk downstairs and find Brady sitting in the chair, thumbing through his phone.

"Sorry for making you wait. Drying my hair takes forever, but it's necessary in the winter."

"I can't have you getting sick on me," he says with a wink as he stands and crosses to me, immediately pulling me into his arms and hugging me close. "You smell good enough to eat."

I grin against him, kiss his chest, and then pull back. "What are we going to do today?"

"Lady's choice."

"I was hoping you'd say that because I *really* want a tour of the ranch."

Brady blinks in surprise. "You've seen most of the ranch, haven't you?"

"I've seen the farmhouse and Summer and Chase's house, along with the event center, yes. And now your cabin. But I haven't seen any animals or heard any stories. I guess I want to see it through *your* eyes."

And right now, those hazel eyes smolder as he stares down at me.

"But if you'd rather not—"

I'm cut off by his mouth as he kisses me hard and long, and I can't help but sway against him, soaking him in.

Brady Wild is an addiction that I may never recover from.

"The ranch it is. Do you have boots that you don't care if they get shit on them?"

I laugh in surprise. "I guess we're going all out. I'm sure I do."

"Grab a good winter coat, too. Layers, babe. You need layers."

"I live in Montana. I have layers." I wink at him and then march back to the small mud room off the garage entrance to gather what I'll need, and then we pile into Brady's SUV and head back out to the ranch. "I'm glad the weather has eased up a bit. Snow is fine, but it's tough when you add arctic temps and wind."

"I couldn't agree more. I work in that shit all day. Temps in the twenties is downright balmy."

When he turns onto the ranch road off the highway, he bypasses the farmhouse and drives us out to the barn first, coming to a stop by a huge rolling door that's currently shut.

"Some of the hands might be out here right now," he says as we get out of the car, and he pulls the door open so we can step inside, then closes it again.

It's warm in here, with the smell of hay heavy in the air. It's cleaner than I expected, and way brighter, with light-colored wood stalls lining one wall where I assume the horses must live.

"Hey, Lucky," Brady calls out, waving to an old man shoveling hay at the other end of the barn. "I'm giving Abbi the tour."

"Hey there, little lady," Lucky says, tipping his hat to me. "Welcome to our little slice of heaven."

"Thank you."

Brady leads me to one of the middle stalls, and a huge black head greets us over the door.

"Hi there, buddy." Brady nuzzles the horse's face and grins, offering him an apple that I didn't realize he had with him. "This is my guy, Blackjack."

"He's gorgeous." Tentatively, I reach out to pet Blackjack's nose, and he leans into my touch, making me smile. "Hi, beautiful boy."

"He likes you," Brady says with a nod. "And he doesn't like just *anyone*. He's picky. Obviously, he has good taste."

"Clearly." I push up on my toes so I can kiss the horse, falling in love with him. "You're a sweetheart."

"Here, feed him an apple, and he'll pledge his undying love for you."

"Oh, it's okay—" I shake my head, moving back, but Brady takes my hand in his and kisses my palm before setting the apple in it.

"I'll help you," he says gently. "It's easy. Hold your fingers out, and he'll take it right out of your hand."

"And my fingers with it."

"Not if you hold them out like this." He shows me how to do it, and I follow suit, and Blackjack takes the apple from my hand, brushing it with his soft lips.

"Oh, his mouth is so soft."

Brady grins down at me, as if he's proud of me. "See? Easy. Want to see some of the others?"

"Will Blackjack get jealous?"

"Maybe, but he'll be okay."

He leads me down the line, introducing me to at least ten horses, and we give them carrots or apples, along with lots of pets and kisses.

"I think I might need a horse," I say, surprising both of us. "Not that I have anywhere to put one. Daisy would *love* this."

"She's been out here with Holly and Johnny," I hear Lucky add behind me. "She's good with them. Never been up on one, but she likes to talk to 'em."

I don't know why that makes me emotional, but I have to swallow the lump that's suddenly in my throat.

"Sounds like my girl," I say with a grin. "She loves animals. Now that she's seen your parents' chickens, she'll be asking for that next. She's convinced she needs a cow."

"A *cow*?" Brady asks. "Why a cow?"

"Have you seen the miniature Highland cows? They're so fuzzy and adorable, and she can't get enough of them. I told her we don't have a place to put a cow, even if it *is* a miniature."

"Hmm," he says, and I narrow my eyes on him.

"You will *not* buy my daughter a cow, Brady Wild."

"Well, *you* might not have a place to put it, but *I* do."

I shake my head and prop my hands on my hips as Lucky cackles like a maniac and leaves the barn.

"Absolutely not."

"Yeah, okay. When's her birthday again? June?"

"I'm not telling."

That only makes Brady grin as if to say *challenge accepted,* and I change the subject.

"Speaking of cows, where are yours?"

"I'll drive you past them," he assures me as he leads me back to Blackjack's stall, where he takes a minute to make sure his horse has everything he needs before we head out again.

Once back in the car, he heads off-road, into a pasture.

"Our herd is over there," he says, pointing, and I see a bunch of black cows, all huddled together in the middle of the pasture. "They're keeping warm. They keep the youngest in the middle, and then they take turns with who's on the outside."

"Smart."

"Cows are *very* smart," he agrees. "And generally gentle."

"What other animals do you have out here?"

"Domestic animals? Chickens, and Rem's making noise about getting some goats for the kids in the spring. We had pigs when we were young, but they're not easy, so we stopped."

"And *non*domesticated animals?"

"Well, we have your typical deer, elk, moose." He steers us toward a spot that just takes my breath away with the view of the mountains. I *love* it out here on this ranch. "Bear, both black bears and grizzlies."

"Wait." I tear my gaze from the mountains and stare at him. "You have *grizzly* bears?"

"Sure, but they're all asleep right now. Or, should be. Grizzlies never truly hibernate. They'll come out and about a little in the winter, but it's not often."

"Grizzly bears. In Montana."

He frowns over at me. "You've been here for a couple of years. Surely, someone has told you about the bears by now. Why do you think people carry bear spray when they hike?"

"In case of *black* bears."

That makes him laugh. "Black bears don't want to hurt you. Hell, grizzlies don't either; they're just more temperamental. Anyway, if it was a nicer day, we'd be sitting on the ground to take in this view. It's our favorite on the ranch."

"I can see why." The mountains are just *incredible*. I can't see all the way to the top because of the cloud cover, but they loom before us, so big and magical, and it makes me wonder how I managed to live all of my life without the mountains.

"What are you thinking?"

I turn to find Brady watching me, and I grin. "Just admiring this view. How about you?"

"Same. This is a spectacular view."

"You're a charming cowboy."

That makes him laugh as he starts the car. "No, ma'am, that's not one of the ways people have described me. Now, what next? You've seen the lake with Chase's house, and you've seen my cabin and my parents' house. I can show you more of the actual ranch when there's not so much snow."

"Then, I guess we can just go back to your place and find...*something* to entertain us."

"I'm sure we can come up with something."

He turns the 4Runner around and heads back the way we came.

"Can I ask more rodeo questions?" I turn in my seat

so I can look at him. Damn, his profile is something to write home about. That jaw is so *chiseled*, and his hands are sexy on the steering wheel. Now that I know how good they feel on *me*, I will never look at them the same way again.

"Abs?"

"Huh?"

He grins over at me. "You said you have more questions."

"Oh, right. I do. So, after Dirks passed, how long did it take you to get back on a bull?"

He blows out a breath, thinking it over. "Geez, about a week, I guess."

"That fast?"

He spares me a look. "A week is a *long* time for a rider to be off of a bull. I was damn rusty by then, and it took a while to get back into shape."

"You're kidding."

"I never kid about riding a bull."

"So, what do you do in the winter? You're not riding bulls out here on the ranch."

"Do you want to see how I train in the offseason?"

"Of course, I do."

With a nod, Brady parks in front of his cabin and then gestures for me to follow him around back to a rustic shed. He opens the door and motions for me to go inside, and he flips on a light before closing the door to keep out the cold.

"It's chilly in here."

"It's heated, but I keep it at fifty. I get sweaty." He

shrugs and walks around the huge...*thing* in the middle of the room. "This is what we call a drop barrel. Mine is electric."

"Is it like a mechanical bull?" I step up to it and run my hand over the carpeted round barrel at the end of a metal stick coming out of a machine.

"No, because the mechanical bull moves differently. This has just one motion, but it's imperative for leg and core strength and for practicing technique and balance."

"Are you going to show me?" I smile boldly before batting my eyelashes at him. "Please?"

His eyes narrow at me, and I shrug.

"Okay, *I'll* do it. Start it up." I move to hop up, but he's suddenly beside me, holding me at the waist.

"Fine, I'll show you."

"Yay. I *really* didn't know what I'd do if you called my bluff on that one."

He chuckles and shakes his head. "I haven't practiced today, so I guess this works."

"When do you have *time*?"

"I usually come out here after early morning chores." He shrugs like it's no big deal and then hops up, as if it's easy and second nature to him. "Put in an hour or so."

The machine starts to move up and down in a rhythmic, rocking motion, and Brady's legs tighten, one arm comes up, and he moves with it, up and down, up and down.

It's...*graceful.* And hotter than I expected. Not that he isn't hot with everything he does, but this is clearly what he knows and what his body is trained for, and he looks damn good doing it.

So good, in fact, that my panties are officially soaked.

After a few minutes, he hops down, shuts off the machine, and turns to me, not even breathing hard.

"And you do that for an *hour*?"

"Usually." His eyes narrow. "Your cheeks are flushed."

Oh, I just bet they are.

I saunter to him, grateful that the floor in here seems pretty clean, and when I reach him, my hands grip onto his button-fly, and I hit my knees.

"Whoa."

"That was—" I shake my head as I ease his pants over his hips. "Sexy. Hot. Wow."

"I guess so. Abs—"

"I'm going to be brutally honest, Brady. I want to suck your cock."

He chokes and then hums as I pull said cock out of his pants. It's already hard and thick, and there's a tiny bead of precum on the tip that has me licking my lips.

"Except, I'm not sure how to do this."

That has his hand tangling in my hair and tipping my head back so I have to look up at him.

"What just came out of that gorgeous mouth?"

"I've never done this before, but I'm sure that what I lack in technique, I make up for in enthusiasm."

"Jesus Christ," he growls, and I didn't think it was possible, but he gets even harder in my hands.

"So, what do I do here?"

"The fact that your hands are wrapped around it is a great start." He swallows hard and covers my hands with one of his. "You move up and down, like this."

He guides my hands up and down his shaft, and more precum beads on the tip, so I lick it off, and Brady growls.

"No?"

"Hell yes," he counters. "You can lick me, suck me, whatever you want, sweetheart."

So, I try it again. I lick him, enjoying the saltiness on my tongue and the way it jerks when I swirl around the ridge of the tip. I take that tip inside my mouth and experiment with brushing my tongue over it, and Brady growls again.

I think that means that I'm doing something right.

"Hell, Abs." He swallows hard. "Look up at me."

I do and find his eyes on fire as he watches me, his jaw clenched.

"I like the way you look with my cock in your mouth."

Oh, that makes me *very* happy. It seems I'm a fan of praise because that fills me with sunshine and makes me want to continue, working for more words of affection from him.

I take him deeper, and when I can feel him at the back of my throat, I swallow, but I don't gag. His hand fists in my hair again, and the tug pulls at my core.

I *want* him.

But first, I want to play with him.

"Fucking hell," he groans when I grip on with my lips and pull up, coming off of him with a loud *pop*.

Suddenly, I'm on my feet, my back against the drop barrel, and Brady is tugging my jeans down my legs, where they get caught on my boots, and we both laugh as I have to work my way out of the boots and *then* the jeans.

"Winter sucks," Brady says with a laugh and then boosts me up, wrapping my legs around his hips. "Ah shit, no condoms out here."

"I have the birth control covered," I whisper in his ear, and before I can say anymore, he's inside of me, and we're both gasping. "Yes. *Yes, yes, yes.*"

"God, you take me so well." He bites the side of my neck, hammering into me as if he's a man possessed. "Seeing your mouth on me almost fucking killed me."

"I plan to do it more later. I need a lot of practice."

He half laughs, half groans, and I wrap my arms around his neck and kiss him, my tongue tangling with his.

I feel the orgasm building in me, moving through me, and suddenly, he's coming with me, rocking into me, and we're clinging to each other as we fall over the edge into insanity.

Being invited over to Chase and Summer's to spend time with all the siblings and have dinner the next day was a welcome surprise.

I'm *desperate* to talk to my friends about recent... developments.

And I just love Summer and Chase's new house on the lake. Now that we're in the heart of winter, that lake is frozen over, and it looks so pretty covered in snow with the mountains in the background.

They definitely chose the most amazing spot to build their home.

"I'm gonna win," Jake calls to the little kids as he leads them outside for a snowman-building contest.

"No way, we will," Holly counters as they run after him as fast as they can in all the layers of clothing, closing the door behind them.

The guys are out in Chase's shop, admiring his latest woodworking project, so it's just the five of us women left, and Summer is pouring chocolate-peppermint martinis into glasses.

Polly's is a virgin drink, but she doesn't mind at all, and Summer is sticking with water.

"Cheers," Millie says, as we all clink glasses and then take a sip. "Oh, that's good stuff."

"I heard a rumor," Summer says, immediately jumping into the gossip, and we all lean in closer. "About our very own Millie Wild."

"What?" Millie blinks and then frowns. "I haven't done anything scandalous."

"I *heard*," Summer continues, "that your vehicle was parked at Bridger Blackwell's house last night."

Millie rolls her eyes at that. "For fuck's sake. I am *not*

screwing around with Bridger, of all people. He's just a friend."

"Uh-huh," Polly replies with a knowing smile. "Only a super-hot firefighter. The *fire chief*. And, in my humble opinion, the sexiest of the Blackwells, but they're all mighty fine, if you ask me."

"I don't know, Brooks is *hot*," Erin says, shaking her head.

"Have you guys seen Beckett?" I fan my face. "What is it about the ranch guys, anyway?"

"I can't go to the doctor if Blake's working," Summer confesses. "He's too hot, and I'll just embarrass myself."

"Okay, so we've established that the Blackwell brothers are sexy," Millie says, laughing. "But I'm not sleeping with any of them."

"Shame," I say with a sigh. "Because as the newest citizen of Pound Town, I can assure you that you're missing out."

There's silence, and then all four of them begin talking at once.

"I need details," Erin says.

"Spill it," Polly agrees.

"Tell us *everything*," Summer adds.

"*Why* must I be punished like this?" Millie demands. "All four of you are now banging my *brothers*, and I do *not* want to hear about it. Yuck. No."

"Listen, it's not our fault that you have brothers that are hung like horses and give the best orgasms west of the Mississippi," Polly points out, making Millie gag.

"Brady is hung like a horse and gives the best

orgasms," I reply, high-fiving my pregnant friend. "Holy shit, does he, and it's only been two days."

"It's about damn time," Erin says emphatically. "It was getting almost *painful* watching you two dance around each other."

"He's so sweet with Daisy," Summer adds, and I nod, tears springing to my eyes.

"He really is, and she just adores him." I sip my drink. "He stayed the night with me when she was so sick. He didn't have to do that, you know?"

"Okay, my brothers *are* sweet," Millie admits with a sigh. "I can talk about this part."

"And the things he can do with his tongue—"

"No!" Millie yells, making us all laugh. "Jesus, have mercy on my poor, battered soul!"

"Oh!" Summer checks her watch and then hurries around the kitchen island, where we're all huddled. "I have to put the chicken in the oven. Keep talking, though. Abbi, I suppose it helped that Daisy was with Joy and John for two nights, so you could go to Pound Town often."

"I need new friends," Millie mutters, shaking her head mournfully.

"It was sweet of them to keep her," I agree, and decide to take pity on Millie. "And the sexy time was fun, but it was honestly really nice to be able to just *be* with him, to ask him questions, and get to know him better when we're not around the rest of the family."

"I hadn't thought of that," Erin admits. "You're always with the rest of us, so it's not like you can have deep, personal conversations between the two of you. I'm glad you had that for a couple of days."

"Me, too, but I missed the hell out of my girl." I lean back so I can see out the window and catch a glimpse of Daisy giggling on her knees in the snow.

I have such a cute kid.

The front door opens, and the guys walk in, and when they see Brady, all four women let out a loud *whooooop!*

Brady's eyes turn to me, narrow, and then he grins in a way that says, *Yeah, I fucked her, and I plan to do it a lot more.*

It makes me shiver with anticipation.

"Now he's fucking her with his eyes," Summer says with a sigh as she leans into Chase when his arms circle around her from behind. "Isn't it the sweetest?"

"Adorable," Rem mutters, grabbing a carrot off of a vegetable platter.

"Oh, baby girl," I mutter, watching as Daisy climbs to the top of a huge snowball that Jake just finished rolling. "Please be careful."

Before I can hurry to the door, Jake's at her side, wraps his arms around her waist, and lifts her off, shaking his head, obviously telling her not to do that.

"He's going to be the *best* big brother," Polly says with a huge grin. And then, to all of our horror, tears fill her eyes. "I just love him so much."

"She's leaking," Brady says, pointing at Ryan. "Fix her. *Fix her.*"

"It's okay," Ryan croons, holding Polly in a hug. "No need to cry, babe."

"It's hormones," she says, sniffling. "Stupid hormones."

"Looks like that's what I have to look forward to," Summer says. "I'll stock up on tissues."

"You'll need lots," I agree, and then my heart leaps into my throat. "Wait, WHAT?"

Chaos ensues as we rush the couple, hugging and laughing, and maybe a few of us are crying, and I love all of this so much. Being a part of these people, this family.

This is my tribe, and God, I love them with my whole heart.

"What's wrong?" Jake demands. "Why is my mom crying?"

"Good tears," Polly assures him as Daisy takes my hand in hers, her brown eyes wide as she takes everything in.

"I'm going to have a baby," Summer says with a sheepish smile. "We just found out yesterday. I'm glad I didn't drink much at the party."

"Cool," Jake decides and crosses over to hug her. "That's awesome."

"He's the cutest," I whisper to Brady, who's smiling like a loon.

"I know," he says.

"More babies," Johnny says, looking up at his dad. "Blech."

"You don't like babies?" I ask him.

"They're loud and smelly, and they don't know any jokes. Plus, they're messy."

"But they're so cute," Holly says, jumping up and down. "And so tiny. I want to hold all the babies. Can we have babies?"

"Not today," Erin says with a laugh, but Remington kisses her on the head, and I can't help but wonder if they're trying.

"It's a good day," Chase says, holding on to his wife. "A damn good day."

"Swear jar!" Daisy yells, making us all laugh.

CHAPTER ELEVEN

BRADY

Despite the spring equinox happening more than two weeks ago, we had a doozy of a snowstorm blow through here yesterday, covering all the spring flowers with three inches of snow. It's not uncommon, and yet every single time it seems to take us by surprise.

Thankfully, that should be the last snow of the year. Although, this was the most satisfying winter I can ever remember having, despite the colder than usual temps and harsh working conditions at the ranch.

I've had Abbi. And Daisy. I can't get enough of the two of them, and over the past few months, we've settled into a routine that seems to be a balm to my battered cowboy soul.

"I'm on my way," I assure Abbi as I drive into town from the ranch. "Do you need me to pick up anything from the store?"

"No, I think I have everything. The bread's toasting in

the oven, so we can eat when you get here. Daisy is *impatient*. You know how she gets."

I grin as I slow down for a deer that's decided to cross the highway.

"Yeah, I know. Friday movie night is her favorite. I'm only a few minutes out. I have to stop by the coffee shop to drop something off to my sister, and then I'm there. Ten minutes, tops."

"I'm not the one you have to answer to, Cowboy," Abbi says with a smile in her voice. "And don't worry. We're fine here. See you in a few."

"'Bye, Blue Eyes."

I hang up and turn onto the main street and park in front of Bitterroot Valley Coffee Co. It's too late in the day for Millie to still be open, but she said she had a book club meeting there this evening, and she left something out at the farmhouse that I'm dropping off to her.

I push through the door and find my sister at the counter, looking at her phone.

"Hey," I say as I approach. "Here's your...whatever this is."

"It's a hair straightener," she informs me with a laugh. "Thank you. I wish Billie Blackwell would pull the trigger and open a bookstore next door so I wouldn't have to stay open for this book club."

"The last time I checked, you're not *required* to do anything. They could have it somewhere else."

"But they're so *cute*," Millie says. "And they buy a lot of coffee and snacks, so at least it pays for itself. Anyway, thanks for this. What are you up to?"

"Movie night with Abbi and Daisy." I grin and tuck my hands into my pockets. "It's a Friday night thing."

"You guys are so sweet, you make my teeth hurt." She smiles and pats my arm. "I'm happy for you. All of you."

The bell over the door dings and Chase walks in. "You're still here."

"Book club," I say, and my brother nods.

"I could use a coffee," he says. "I'm going to work all night, and I can't do that without a shot of caffeine."

"Why are you working the night shift?" I ask him.

"We had someone get sick. It's fine. I just didn't plan for it." Millie whips up what she knows he likes and passes it to him, and then the door dings again.

But this time, it's Holden Lexington who walks in.

No, he doesn't walk. He *stalks*, his blue eyes trained on my sister, and it puts my back up.

Our family has a complicated history with the Lexingtons. We were rival families for more than a hundred years, with property that borders each other and grandfathers who hated each other, so we're not exactly friends.

Holden doesn't spare either Chase or me a glance as he marches right past us and over to our sister.

"Are you fucking Bridger Blackwell?" he asks, leaning into her, his entire body tight with frustration.

"You're going to want to watch yourself," Chase says casually as he takes a sip of his coffee, as if every muscle in his body isn't poised to knock Holden on his ass.

My eyes narrow as Millie's face goes hard, and her

hands fist at her sides, staring up at Holden almost defiantly.

I wonder what in the hell happened between these two?

"That's absolutely *none* of your business," she snaps back.

"Like hell."

"What I do with my life doesn't concern you," she says again, her voice breezier this time. "Now, do you want coffee, or are you going to fuck right off?"

"You've been parked at his house at night all the goddamn time for months now, and I want to know—"

"Get any closer," I say, stepping forward, "and I'm going to put my boot up your ass."

"I'm not doing this with you," Millie says when he doesn't move an inch at my warning. Her voice isn't as hard, and her eyes have softened, but she doesn't back down. "I'm not doing this, Holden."

"Goddamn it." He pushes off of the counter and stomps out of the coffee shop, the door flinging under the force of the shove.

"You ever going to tell me what the fuck happened there?" I ask her as she stares at the doorway that he just stormed out of.

"No." She shakes her head and reaches for a towel, letting out a gusty breath as she wipes it over the countertop. "It doesn't matter. And for the record, I'm *not* fucking Bridger. People have got to stop asking me that."

"Then maybe you shouldn't have your car parked in

front of his house every night," Chase says. "This is a small town, Mill. People talk."

"Obviously. Busybodies." She makes a face, and then the place starts to fill up with the book club girls, so I take my leave and head over to Abbi's.

"Where *were* you?" Daisy demands as I walk through the door. "We've been waiting *forever.*"

"You've only been home from school for two hours," I remind her and kiss the top of her head before I round the island and pull Abbi in for a big hug. God, I missed her today. Her arms tighten around me, and when I pull back, she's grinning up at me. "Got a kiss for me?"

"Maybe one." She boosts up on her toes, kisses my lips, and then turns back to the dinner bubbling on the stovetop.

"I want a kiss!" Daisy races into the kitchen, holding up her arms, and I scoop her up and kiss her cheek, making her laugh. "Your whiskers are scratchy."

"Oh, no, not the scratchy whiskers!" I rub my face against her neck, making her giggle, as I carry her around to the other side of the island so we're out of Abbi's way. "We're having spaghetti for dinner. That surprises me."

"Why?" Daisy asks.

"Because you hate spaghetti, remember? It looks like Robert's hair."

"He got a haircut, so it's okay now," she replies as I set her down, and I share a look with Abbi. "Why were you so late this time?"

"I had to help a calf be born."

That makes Daisy frown. “I thought all the calves were already born.”

I loved telling Daisy all about calving season when the babies started to come in February and then taking her out to see them. It’s our most strenuous time of year, but it was fun to show Daisy the tiny cows at the ranch.

“One decided to come late, and the mama had a hard time delivering him.”

“Oh, no, is she okay?” Abbi asks from the kitchen.

“Yeah, she’s fine now. I think they’ll both recover nicely. They’re tucked in the barn for the night. Now, what movie are we watching?”

“Elsa,” Daisy says with a grin.

“Didn’t we watch that last week? And the week before that? We know all the words.”

“It’s my *favorite*,” she reminds me, patting my arm as if in sympathy.

“Well, I guess the cold never bothered me anyway.” I buss her cheek once more and then turn my attention to my lady. “What can I help with?”

“It’s ready,” she says as she pours the pasta into a strainer. “If you’ll pull the bread out of the oven, we can dish up.”

“I’m *starving*,” Daisy says as she climbs into her chair at the table.

As usual, Abbi and I make our plates, adding one for Daisy, and then we sit at the table to eat together.

“So, what’s happening at the ranch with spring here? Sort of.” Abbi takes a bite of bread and sighs in happiness. God, I love watching this woman eat.

Or do anything at all.

"We have a lot of cleanup," I reply. "Fences need mending. We'll move the herd a little further out so they have fresh grass and more room to spread out. Next week will be interesting, though."

"Why's that?" she asks.

"We have camera crews from Rancher Jeans coming to film me while I work for a commercial and some online ads. I told them I was needed here, so they're coming to me."

"Wow." Abbi blinks in surprise and then smiles at Daisy. "Hear that? Brady's going to be on TV."

I don't bother to tell them that I've been on TV plenty, but it's usually when I'm riding a bull or being interviewed.

Daisy's eyes widen, and then she dances in her seat. "You're gonna be famous, Brady."

"If you say so, Princess." I wink at her and then smile over at Abbi. "You guys are welcome to come out to see what it's all about if you want to."

"I do believe we want to," Abbi confirms. "Just let me know which day, and I'll get it covered at work. I just hired four new people, so it won't be an issue."

"But I have to go to school," Daisy reminds us with a frown. "Will you still be taking pictures when I'm done?"

"I'm sure we will. It sounds like it'll be an all-day thing." I'm already exhausted just thinking about it.

"Then *yes*, I want to go, too," Daisy says, doing another dance.

"Now, tell me about what's happening with *you*," I say to Abbi. "You hired new people?"

"Yes, and I have interviews for three more tomorrow." She smiles at me, her blue eyes lighting up. "The business is growing by leaps and bounds, thanks to tourist season ramping up for the summer and all the lovely people coming to visit our little town. Plus, more locals are hiring us, too, and that *really* makes me happy. Before long, I'll have to move to a bigger office space so I can buy more washers and dryers for linens, but I'm not complaining."

"Your mom is a powerhouse," I inform Daisy.

"I know," she says and swirls her fork in her pasta.

"This also means that I can help out at Daisy's school more often and really cut back to part time for a while, which has been my goal since she was little."

I wish I'd known her then. I would have made sure that she could be a stay-at-home mom, if that's what she wanted to do. I would have made sure that they both were taken care of.

Not that she needed me. Obviously, she didn't. She doesn't need anyone.

"Okay," Abbi says when we've finished dinner. "Let's have some popcorn and watch our movie."

"Can I have M&Ms?" Daisy asks.

"I got you some," Abbi assures her daughter, and as we settle in front of the TV, with the lights low and me in the middle of these two girls, there's nowhere else in the world I'd rather be.

"No," I reply, irritation humming through every pore of me. "I can't do it again. I'm not making a movie here. I'm *working.*"

The guy in the designer suit with the expensive shoes he's already ruined sighs. "Can't you just *try* to lead the horse around again so we can get another shot of it?"

"For fuck's sake," I mutter and grab Blackjack's bridle. "I'll lead him around *one time.* And then I have to ride out to mend a fence."

"Oh, good, we get to catch him riding," he says, turning to his crew.

Why he thought he'd be comfortable in that getup on a working cattle ranch, I'll never know.

"You could walk Blackjack around this ring all day and he wouldn't care," Dad reminds me as he falls into step next to me.

"Yeah, but I have shit to do, and it's not walking my horse in circles."

"Fair enough," Dad says. "Are we going to lead them to the event space? There are some pretty shots over there, and if they use it in the ad, they have to pay more. Which will get me a nice vacation on a cruise ship with your mother. Alone."

"Dad. I don't know if you've heard, but you and Mom live alone already."

"Not the same," he says with a wink and hops onto his own horse, making me laugh.

"I don't even want to think about that." I glance

ahead and see Rem and Ryan riding over on their horses. Ryan wanted to keep an eye on things here, to make sure we're not being taken advantage of, and he always did like riding the fence line with us.

The only brother not here is Chase, but I suspect he'll put in an appearance before the day is through.

For the next few hours, we put the crew through the paces. They're not used to the altitude or the chilly weather, so finally around lunchtime, we take pity on them and head back for the barn to rest for an hour.

When we get there, I'm happy to see that Abbi, Erin, Polly, and Mom are here, too, and Abbi doesn't hesitate to hug me when I get close.

"I'm sweaty," I warn her.

"Don't care," she replies, burying her face in my neck. "Don't care at *all.* Have I ever told you how hot you are when you're doing ranch stuff?"

"I don't think you have."

"Well, you are. It kind of turns me on, Cowboy."

I growl and then kiss her and wish that I could sneak her off to my cabin for a while, but I know that I could never get away with it.

"Break it up," Millie says, rolling her eyes as she walks out of the barn. "We have a bunch of lunch here for everyone. Soups and bread and stuff. You should eat."

"I think I will." I try not to pay attention to the cameras pointed my way as we walk in to get some food. "They won't stop following me."

"That's why they're paying you," Ryan reminds me,

but then his eyes narrow. "However, if they keep taking photos of all of us, they're going to *pay* all of us."

"Today is going *so well*," Designer Suit Man says as he joins me near the food. "We have some great footage already. We'd like you and your brothers to sit on the fence for some shots, since you're all wearing Ranchers today."

"And you plan to pay them for that?" I stare him down until he swallows hard and nods.

"Of course, yes. Now, the magic is *really* going to happen during the golden hour, as the sun begins to set."

"You want a bunch of cowboys to stick around after dinner?" I raise my eyebrows, but then remember the paycheck from all of this and shrug a shoulder. "Fine."

He nods and returns to his team, and I let out a breath.

"It'll go fast," Abbi assures me. "And Daisy will be excited that she didn't miss too much when she gets here. She's coming home from school with Holly and Johnny."

I have to admit, as the rest of the day wears on, I *like* the crew they sent. I don't even mind Designer Suit Guy too much, especially since he took off his jacket and tie and rolled up his sleeves. He's way more likeable this way.

"I have a question," I say as he and I are looking over a few of the shots from earlier. "How is it that a guy who works for *Rancher Jeans*, shows up to a ranch in that suit?"

That seems to stump him for a second, and then he

looks at me and starts to laugh. "You know, that's a good question."

"I'm just saying, man. You gotta loosen up a bit." I clap him on the shoulder, and now that the damn sun is starting to go down, we can shoot the last of the shots they want.

Once again, I take Blackjack into the ring and walk him around, then I get in the saddle and ride, kicking up some dust.

As if we're not already filthy from a long fucking day.

When Designer Suit nods at me, the signal that they got what they wanted, I lead Blackjack into the barn and give him a good wash down and brushing, and they don't stop filming. I'm aware of them around the whole time, and the rest of my family, including Abbi and Daisy, watch from the sidelines.

Finally, I put my horse in his stall and kiss him, lay my forehead against his, and whisper, "Thank you, buddy. You did good today. Get some rest."

"Brady!"

I glance over and grin as Daisy, holding Abbi's hand, hurries to me and then launches herself into my arms and kisses my cheek.

"I'm pretty dirty," I tell the little girl, but she just giggles and kisses me again.

Abbi takes my free hand and offers up her lips, which I greedily take.

"That was *incredible*," Designer Suit says as he joins us to walk out of the barn. "Thank you for today. You have a beautiful home and a welcoming family. Even

Ryan Wild, who's been wheedling more money out of us all day."

"That's just what he does," I say with a laugh as I set Daisy down and then shake the other man's hand. "I hope you got everything you needed."

"I'm sure we have that and more. I actually think we might like to do a short film with what we've collected today. If we do that, we'd need to have you do some voice-over work for us. Would you be willing to do that?"

"Can I do it from Montana?"

"I don't see why not."

"Then I will have my agent ask for more money and be happy to do it."

He laughs, pats me on the shoulder, and then waves as he joins his crew to pack up and go home.

I was right, Chase *did* join us a few hours ago. I was glad that the whole family was here throughout the day. Even though I've done things like this before, this is the first time we've allowed anyone to film at the Wild River Ranch, and I wanted to make sure that it was done respectfully.

So far, I'm happy with how it all went down.

"Good job today," Ryan says, shaking my hand.

"I should say the same to you."

That makes him smile. "I didn't get rich by being dumb, you know. Besides, they can afford it."

"Maybe *you* should be my agent."

"You can't afford me." He winks and then walks away when Abbi and Daisy join me again, but Erin walks over, too.

"I'm going to take the kids to the house," Erin says with a smile to Abbi. "Get them fed and ready for bed. Why doesn't Daisy just stay with us tonight?"

"Oh, but school tomorrow," Abbi begins, but Erin smiles.

"She can wear something of Holly's. Really, it's fine. Come to the house when you're ready to eat," she tells us both and then hurries off with the others.

"Are you going to come with me to the cabin to clean up?" I ask Abbi.

"Duh," she says. "I told you, Cowboy Brady is *hot*. And I have some practicing to do."

CHAPTER TWELVE
ABBI

Brady's taking the longest shower in the history of showers, but that's okay. He's exhausted, filthy, and probably needs a few minutes of quiet after a full day of strangers *and* work. That man works harder than anyone I've ever known in my life, and that's just one of the reasons that I'm falling in love with him. He *loves* the animals on this ranch, and he gives it all 100 percent of his attention and energy.

He deserves a nice, long shower to wash it all away. He was way too dirty for me to even think about joining him in there.

No thanks.

There's a knock at his door, and when I open it, Erin's standing there holding a pan and wearing a knowing smile.

"I brought dinner to you," she says and wrinkles her nose. "I saw the lusty looks you were sending his way at the barn, and I can't blame you. There's just something extra sexy about a dirty cowboy. Trust me, I know."

"In more ways than one," I reply with a wink and earn a laugh from her. "And thanks. I know he has to be starving."

"There's half a pan of lasagna here, some salad and bread, too. Listen, why don't I keep Daisy through the weekend?"

"Erin, I know I'm horny and all, but you don't have to do that."

"I know I don't, but really, she's no trouble. If she wants to go home, I'll let you know. Oh, and I'll swing by after school tomorrow to grab her stuff from you."

"Seriously, if you change your mind, no harm, no foul. And I'll come get her Saturday afternoon. I don't want to lose the whole weekend with her."

"That works for us. We'll just play it by ear. Is he *still* in the shower?"

"I think it's for mental health more than dirt." I shrug, looking toward the bathroom. "It was a lot of peopling today."

"Yeah, I get it. Rem is the same way. I think all the Wilds are just wired that way. Okay, have a fun night, and we'll see you tomorrow."

"Thanks, friend."

As soon as I've closed the door and set the pan in the oven to keep it warm, my phone rings, and when I see who it is that's calling, my blood runs cold.

How could I *forget*? I've settled in so well here, become too comfortable, and it's easy to forget that there's a reason that I ended up in the Middle-of-Nowhere, Montana. And that forgetfulness is *dangerous*. I know better.

"Hello?"

"Hey, Ms. Abbi, it's Jerome. Been a while."

"It has, yes." I swallow hard at the sound of the private investigator's voice, dread sitting heavy in my stomach. "I take it something's happened?"

Please tell me she's dead and I don't have to worry anymore.

"It has." His deep voice is thick with his North Carolina accent, and for about a heartbeat, it makes me just a little homesick. "It seems she's started putting feelers out again, trying to find you. Lots of Google image searches. Now, you and I both know that your appearance has changed somewhat over the past six years, and I don't think she'll come up with a recent hit."

"But?"

"But she could. You know that I keep an eye on you, mostly so I might see something before she does."

"Yes, I know, and I appreciate that."

"And while you don't have social media of your own, you've been in some photos recently. Your friends post photos, and it looks like you're doing some important stuff there in the community."

"I know, but like you said, they can't tag me, and I don't look the same. And I *never* let images of Daisy show up online. My friends know that I don't want that, and they're very respectful of it."

"That's smart. Keep doing that. As of right now, I

don't see anything to be worried about, but I wanted to give you the heads-up, just in case something slips by me. How long do you plan to stay in Montana?"

Forever.

The thought of leaving this town, where Daisy and I finally fit in and feel at home, is devastating.

But we've never stayed anywhere longer than a year.

Of course, that was before she was in school and made friends and we both became entrenched in a community that we love, and that loves us back.

"I don't plan to leave any time soon. We're very happy here, Jerome."

He sighs on the other end of the line. "I'm happy for you, Abbi. I really am. You're far enough away, and in a small enough town, that I think you're fine. Like I said, I'll keep my eyes and ears open."

"Thank you. I really appreciate you. You're doing well?"

"Yes, ma'am." I hear the smile in his voice now. "I'm doing just fine. You go enjoy your evening."

"Thanks. You, too. Bye."

I hang up and lean heavily on the kitchen counter, feeling sick to my stomach and just so...*tired.*

So fucking tired.

I wish she'd just forget about us, but as long as she's alive, that's not going to happen.

The shower has stopped, so I scrub my hands over my face and redirect my energy to the man down the hall. Because if I let myself dwell, I'll have nightmares tonight, and I don't want that.

I don't want to put either of us through that.

I hear him pad down the hallway towards me, and I smile as my breath catches when I see him, shirtless, in a pair of gray sweatpants that hang low on his sexy hips and do what gray sweatpants do: show off his impressive package. He's lean with muscles that seem to have muscles, and his dark hair is wet from the shower. And the look in his hazel eyes as he stares at me tells me that he's a man ready to *consume* me. It's exhilarating and a little unsettling, all at once.

Holy shit, what did I ever do to get Brady Wild?

"Did I hear you talking out here?" he asks, leaning against the doorjamb and crossing his arms, which makes his biceps flex, and that alone almost sends me into overdrive. Is it legal to look like that? Probably not.

"Erin popped by," I reply and lick my lips. "Brought dinner to us. She's keeping Daisy until Saturday afternoon."

He lifts an eyebrow, but he doesn't push off of the wall.

"Are you hungry?" I ask him.

"Fucking starving." His hazel eyes narrow at me. "Did you wear that today to drive me crazy on purpose?"

I frown and look down at my green dress. It's not particularly sexy. I guess it's showing a little cleavage, but with these knockers, that's not hard to do.

"It's just a sundress. It was actually on the warm side today, and—"

Brady pushes off of the wall, and my mouth goes dry, making it difficult to speak.

"I guess you like it," I whisper, and he grins as he strides slowly across the room.

"Oh, I fucking like it," he confirms. "But I like the woman *in* it more."

"I thought you were hungry?"

"I am. Dinner can wait." He grips my hip and tugs me against him, and then that hand slides around to my back and down over my ass as he presses his hard erection against my belly. "Been wanting you all damn day, Blue Eyes."

"Back at you, Cowboy."

Brady smirks, and then his lips are on mine as he walks me out of the kitchen and around to the couch where I'm suddenly flat on my back, and he's braced over me, muscles flexing.

"You shouldn't be doing all the work." I cup his cheek and smile up at him. "You worked hard today."

"You know what? You're right."

He easily pulls me up and switches our positions, making me giggle, and I can't resist biting his chin.

"Hey, you little land shark." His arms wrap around me, and he buries his face in my neck, breathing deeply. "I'm going to want you to sit on my face now, sweetheart."

"Not a chance in hell. I will smother you, and I may be smitten with you, but I'm not going to jail for you or your kinky ways, Brady Wild."

"Smitten?" His smile is wide as he grins down at me. "Is that what we're calling it? Okay, then, smitten girl. I want you to pull that skirt up around your waist and sit on my face so I can make you come once or thrice on my tongue."

I shake my head. Jesus, I don't want *anyone* to see me from that angle. I have a belly and cellulite and thighs and...no. It's better if I'm on my back and gravity is doing its job.

"Hey." With his finger under my chin, he lifts my gaze to his. "You're way overthinking this, babe. I don't know if you've noticed, but you're sexy. From *every* angle. Feel this?"

He moves his hips, nudging me with his hard cock, and I instinctively bite my lower lip in anticipation as my core tightens.

"I want you. I want every glorious, amazing, sexy-as-fuck inch of your body, and right now, I want you to ride my face until I make you scream my name."

Well, when he puts it like that, who am I to argue?

"If you can't breathe, you tell me."

"Uh, there's a hole in your logic, but sure." He laughs as I lift myself off of him, tug my skirt up so I can take my underwear off, and then straddle his face.

Brady's hands find my ass, and he says, "Oh, yeah. Bring it."

And I can't help but laugh at that. I always laugh when I'm nervous as hell. But then he guides me down and licks me, and all thoughts of laughter evaporate from my mind.

Holy. Shit.

I'm still self-conscious, but what he's doing to me is incredible. Licking and lapping, his hands cradling my ass just so, and when he hums in delight, I can't stop the moan that tears its way out of my chest or the sudden climax that rocks through me.

When I would move off of him, he holds firm, keeping me over him as he fucks me with his tongue.

Okay, I'm a little less self-conscious now.

I can't help but move my hips back and forth, loving the way his mouth and tongue feel as they move through my slit. Little jolts of electricity zip through me until I'm shaking and coming all over again.

"I can't hold myself up," I cry, as I reach for the back of the couch, but Brady scoots out from under me and kisses me, the taste of me on his lips. His fingers make a dive for my pussy, and he shakes his hand, pressing his palm against me so hard that it sends me right over into another mind-numbing orgasm.

"That's right," he growls against my lips. "Come for me, Blue Eyes. Ah, God, yeah. Keep those eyes on me. Good girl."

"Shit." I'm coming again because that praise shit is *hot*, and when I come to, he's guiding me onto my back and nudging himself between my legs.

"So fucking gorgeous," he says through gritted teeth as he pushes inside of me. God, I'm so wet that he eases right in, despite his size. "You like it when I call you a good girl."

My muscles contract, making him grin.

"Maybe a little. I guess that's my thing."

Brady rests his forehead against mine, so serious now as he starts to move, pushing and pulling in long, steady strokes. He links our fingers and holds them to our chests as he moves, faster and faster, until we're cresting another peak that sends us both into euphoria.

"That's right, good girl. Come on my cock. Fuck, yes."

I'm gripping onto him *so tightly*, and his jaw is clenched as he rocks against me, pushing every last drop of himself inside of me.

"Wow," he says, his breath still coming fast. "Every time I think I'm used to how you make me feel, I'm hit with it all over again, as if I'm struck by lightning."

I push my hair off my face and lift an eyebrow. "And how, exactly, do you feel?"

"Like nothing and no one else in the world exists. Like I was made just for this. Just for you."

Tears prick the back of my eyes, and I bite my lip as I gaze at him, memorizing every detail.

"Maybe I was." His voice is a whisper.

"Maybe you were," I agree.

He kisses me as he eases out of me. "Let's clean up and eat. Now I'm starving for another reason."

"You get started, and I'll be right back. The food's in the oven, salad in the fridge." I hurry to the bathroom, not just to clean up this epic, wet, dirty mess, but also to catch my breath. It's not just the sex with Brady that turns me inside out. He can be so intense, so filthy when it comes to the physical aspect of our relationship, and then turn around and say the kind of words that make my heart melt. It's...amazing. But I need to catch my breath.

When I return from the bathroom, Brady has already

plated the meal for both of us and has dug into his with gusto.

"So good," is what I *think* he says around the bite in his mouth.

"You worked off a lot of calories today." I take a bite of lasagna and sigh. "But yeah, this is great. Erin's a good cook."

"How was your morning?"

"Productive," I reply and dab at my mouth with a napkin. "I'm officially fully staffed, and I think this crew is going to be awesome. Now, let's talk about you. How did you really feel about today?"

"How did I *look*?" he asks, reaching for bread.

"Hmm." I lick my fork and narrow my eyes, thinking it over. "You looked sexier than any one man has any business looking, and I kept undressing you with my eyes. I mean, I know it was a denim ad, but you're way hotter naked."

"I'm going to make you come just by sucking on your nipples later."

My eyes widen, and said nipples come to full attention.

"But how did I *seem* today, sassy pants?"

"Oh, that." I laugh and steal his bread, taking a bite. "There were moments that you looked annoyed, but those were minimal, and maybe I just noticed because I know you. Otherwise, you looked like a busy cowboy who had shit to do."

"That about sums it up accurately." He watches me

from across the sofa for a minute as we eat our dinner. "I'm taking you to bed after this."

"Is that a threat or a promise?"

"Both."

"I can't wait."

"You're going to pay for that." I don't like his smile. It's scary and mean, and when he smiles like this, I know it's going to hurt.

It always hurts.

"I didn't mean to."

"You like being a bad girl," he says with that slimy voice, and he starts to take off his pants, and I just want to crawl into a hole.

I want to die.

"Please. Please don't hurt me again. I didn't mean to knock the ashtray over."

"Shut up!" He backhands me, and even in this fucked-up dream, I see stars and feel the force of the blow as I fall to the ground. "You're nothing, do you hear me? No one cares about you. No one fucking cares what I do to you. I can do whatever I want. Maybe I'll put a pretty little scar on you right here."

He drags his finger down my cheek, and I jerk my face away. As I do, I know that it's the wrong move because it only makes him angrier.

"Don't you jerk away from me, you little slut."

He grips onto my hair and pulls me to my feet, dragging me down a hallway with doorways that are open, and I can see other foster parents laughing at me. Always laughing at me.

"You deserve it!" one yells out.

"I want my mommy," I cry as I'm tossed into a room, and the door closes behind me. He's not with me, and I breathe a sigh of relief, but then I hear the slithering, and that scares me more.

I hate snakes.

"They won't hurt you."

It's Nate, and he's holding one of the snakes, watching it.

"You hate snakes, too."

"Nah, they won't hurt you as long as you're a good girl."

It doesn't sound nice when he says it.

"I want my mom."

"I'm right here."

I spin, but it's not my mom standing behind me. It's Nate's, and she's holding Daisy, but it's Daisy from when she was a baby.

"Give me my daughter."

"No," she says and kisses Daisy's head, leaving black marks where her lips were. "I don't think I will. She's mine. She's my *daughter."*

"No, she's not." I spin back to where Nate was, but now he's hanging from a rope, his eyes unseeing as he stares my way, and I shriek before turning back to his mother. "I just want my baby."

"You don't deserve her," she says, still kissing her and leaving black stains on Daisy's skin. "You never did. I'll raise her better than you can. I can give her everything. *And what do you have? Huh? Poor little thing, you don't have anything.*

No family. No money. You clean houses and probably fuck the men who pay you, don't you? Whores don't deserve babies."

"I'm not," I cry, reaching for my daughter, but she's suddenly farther away, and I can't reach her. I can't run fast enough to catch them, like my feet are stuck in the sand. "Give her back to me."

I'm trying to run down the hallway, and sometimes, she'll stick her head around one of the doorways and laugh, then disappear again. I can hear Daisy crying for me. Wailing and sobbing, as if she's being hurt, and it tears me apart.

"Daisy! Mama's coming."

"You'll never see her again, you whore."

"Not a whore," I mutter as I continue to fight against my heavy feet, trying to walk, fighting to find my daughter. "Need my baby. Daisy! Daisy!"

There's so much sinister laughter that I can't hear Daisy anymore. It's so loud, echoing off the walls of the long hallway, and now it's all starting to fill with water.

Daisy can't swim! She's just a baby.

Oh, God.

The water rises and rises until I have to swim to keep going because it's over my head. Something grips onto my leg and tugs me under the water, still laughing at me. I tug free and pull myself into one of the rooms, and I can see Daisy, just floating in the water, blinking as she watches me.

"Baby! I'm here. I'll get you."

But then she's snatched away, and I can't stay above the water.

"Daisy!"

CHAPTER THIRTEEN

BRADY

"DAISY!" Abbi is screaming and thrashing out in bed, and no matter what I do, I can't get her to calm down. It's the most terrifying, helpless feeling I've ever had in my goddamn life.

With my heart in my throat, I run my hand down her back.

"Baby," I croon, trying to sound calm, but I feel like I'm going to come out of my skin. "Abbi, wake up. Daisy is safe. Wake up, honey. Abs, I need you to wake up."

She jolts and whips around to stare at me with wide, horror-filled eyes.

"I want my baby."

"Hey." I reach for her, but she jerks out of my grasp and tears my heart out with her. I don't *ever* want her to be afraid of me. "Daisy is safe at Erin and Rem's house. Remember? She's just a mile away."

"I want to see her right now. *Right now.*"

She's hugging her arms around her middle, shaking her head, and stands from the bed stark-ass naked.

"It's the middle of the night, Abbi." I hold my hand out like I might to a scared, wild animal, not sure what in the hell I should do. I want to scoop her up and hold onto her, but she doesn't even want me to touch her, and it's tearing me apart. "Daisy is asleep. She's *asleep*, baby."

She shakes her head again, and the tears start to fall, her face crumpling.

"Ah, baby, let me hold you."

"Outside." She turns and heads for the door, practically running out of the room and down the hall.

It's still cold as fuck at night, so I grab a flannel shirt and rush after her, running as she throws open the door and practically launches herself out into the night.

She's gasping for breath as I wrap her in the flannel and hold her against me, my front pressed to her back.

"Breathe," I croon, not giving two shits that I'm also standing outside completely naked in freezing temps. "Take a breath, my love. Come on, baby, I need you to breathe."

"I know she's safe," she says through her sobs, gasping, "but Jesus, I want her."

"We'll get her first thing," I assure her before kissing her head. "As soon as she's awake, okay? I promise."

She leans against me, crying and wailing so loudly that a coyote calls back from somewhere on the ranch. I rock her back and forth, letting her cry, kissing her hair and her temple, holding her tight.

Finally, she takes a long, deep shuddering breath and

seems to quiet, listening to the night sounds around us as she trembles in my arms.

"Let's go in," she whispers.

I don't let her walk. I bend down and scoop her up, and she wraps her arms around my neck and buries her face against me, still sniffling and softly crying as I walk inside and shut the door behind us, pushing it with my bare foot.

"No bed," she says.

So, with a nod, I carry her to the couch and get her wrapped up in blankets.

"I'll be right back." I kiss her forehead before I return to the bedroom, pull on the gray sweatpants from earlier, and then walk back out to her and sit with her.

"I'm sorry I made you cold."

"I don't give a rat's ass about the cold. All I care about is *you*, Abs."

She leans into me, and I hug her close again.

"Baby, are you ever going to talk to me about this?"

"Yeah." Her voice is so soft that I can hardly hear her. "I am. But I need a few minutes. What time is it?"

I glance at the microwave. "Just past three."

"You should go back to bed. I won't be able to sleep, but you should get some rest." She kisses my chest. "You had a killer day yesterday."

"If you think I'm going to leave you here on my couch and go get some shut-eye, you don't know me at all, Blue Eyes."

I feel her smile against me, and I start to settle for the first time since I first heard her scream out in her sleep.

Jesus, Daisy has to help her through this on a regular basis? The fact that either of them has to deal with this kind of terror is absolutely *not* okay with me.

"I *hate* that it happened with you," she admits and lifts her head to turn those tear-filled eyes up to me. "Because it's not my finest moment, and I know it can be scary. I didn't want you to *ever* see it."

I frown down at her and finally drag my knuckle over the apple of her cheek.

"Abs, it was going to happen eventually. I must have to spell this out for you, and that's okay. I should have done it a while ago. I'm not going anywhere. I love you and Daisy, and at some point, we'll figure out the living arrangements so we're together *all* the time. It would be hard for me to live in town because I work so much out here, and I know you have a business in town, so we'll have to put our heads together and figure it out, but I want *more* of you, not less. The nights that I spend without you are fucking torture. So, yeah, I was going to be there for the nightmares eventually, and frankly, I think it's better if I'm the one to help you through it rather than Daisy."

Her eyes have filled as she stares at me, listening.

"Say it again."

I frown. "Which part? I kind of had diarrhea of the mouth there for a minute."

"The *love* part."

I swallow hard and lean in to kiss her forehead before pulling back to look at her again, gently dragging my fingertips down her cheek.

"I love you. I tried not to. I *really* tried because I'm still not feeling great about being in a relationship when I still have to get on a bull in a few weeks and ride until October, but it seems that I just can't control the way I feel when it comes to you. And I don't *want* to hold back because being with the two of you has changed my life in all of the good ways."

She's crying again, but she's smiling, too. "Same."

"That's all I get?"

She chuckles and brushes a tear off of her cheek. "I love you, too, Brady. And I know that Daisy loves you. For the first time in a *really* long time, I feel like a woman again. Not just a mom or a business owner. A *woman.* You make me laugh, and I know without a doubt that I'm safe with you."

"You are."

She threads her fingers through mine as she seems to gather her thoughts, and I'm reminded that I've never seen anyone more beautiful than this woman. Even when she's vulnerable and a bit of a mess, she's absolutely gorgeous.

"I told you before, I was a foster kid all through my teenage years."

Here we go. The hard stuff. Maybe she needed to hear that I loved her before she felt brave enough to confide in me with the hardest pieces of her life.

"Yes, you did."

"I would say that my experience was very similar to Jake's. Abusive. Mean. Pretty fucked-up."

I clench my jaw, and she reaches up to cup my face in her soft hand.

"I know it's hard for you to hear this, so if you'd rather not—"

"I'm fine, baby. You can tell me. Doesn't mean I don't want to commit homicide, but you can tell me."

Her lips twitch at that. "I was first raped when I was fourteen."

"Jesus." I want to stand and pace. I want to punch the goddamn wall. But I don't because she needs me with her, and from here on out, Abbi will get anything and everything she needs or wants in this life.

I'll make sure of it.

"I never told anyone because it was drilled into me that no one cared. I didn't matter. No one missed me, and no one would check on me. And, for the most part, they were right. I was where I was because there was no one else in the world that wanted me. So, I was used and hurt and beaten. Often. I did get pulled out of one house because a teacher noticed that I had a bruise around my neck, and I really think that if I'd stayed there, I would have died."

"Christ." I can't help it. I lean forward and rest my face in my hands.

"I learned to be small. To not get noticed. To keep things clean, eat what was on my plate, and stay in my room. Don't make a fuss. Don't get sick. I tried *so hard* not to get sick because I didn't want to inconvenience anyone by having to go to the doctor."

I want to kill them. All of them.

"It got a little easier in high school because I could join clubs and volunteer for things, so I wasn't home as much. I had two different homes in high school, and both were close to the school, so I could walk back and forth, kind of come and go. So, by the time I was seventeen, the worst of it was over. By then it was just neglect. They let me live there in exchange for the money the state paid them. But the damage was done.

"When I turned eighteen, I left. On my birthday."

My head snaps up. "Where the hell did you go?"

"Nate snuck me enough money to pay for a tiny studio apartment and food and utilities, and I started to work. I'd already had a job at a fast-food place in the summers, but my foster parents always took my paychecks. Claimed it was for the luxury of living there. If I didn't turn it over, they beat me, so really I was just paying to not get my ass whooped every week."

She shrugs, as if to say *oh well,* and all I can do is watch her.

"I discovered that I was a pretty good waitress, and I got good tips. I also got a night job as a cleaner for businesses. Offices and stuff like that. I really liked that job, and Mrs. Pitkin was super nice. She always slipped me an extra twenty bucks here or there because she knew I was saving up for a car."

I'd like to send Mrs. Pitkin a hundred thousand dollars and kiss her on the mouth.

"If it wasn't for Nate and Mrs. Pitkin, I honestly don't know what would have happened to me." Her voice has quieted again. "I know that sounds dramatic, but it's true. I've never been one to try drugs, but I can see why people do. Because for those few minutes or hours, you can forget how fucked-up your life is. You can just escape it all. That small amount of help from those two wasn't so small to me, and it gave me the edge I needed to try to make something of myself. Then, Nate and I got pregnant, and like I told you before, he wanted to marry me. Wanted to do the right thing. He didn't care that I'd been used and hurt or that I came from absolutely nothing. He just liked *me.* He loved me. We were kindred spirits and got along so well. We had a lot in common. His mom, however, hated me."

She frowns down at her fingers and then shrugs again.

"But that's a story for another time. I don't think I was ever touched in a kind way, sexually I mean, until Nate and I got together that night at his college party."

"You were a virgin."

She scoffs and shakes her head, but I take her hand.

"Abs, you were a virgin in every way that matters. What was done to you before...that wasn't sex; it was violence. It was *rape.* That's not the same thing, and you know it."

Her lip quivers, and then she nods. "I guess you're right. I never really thought about it like that. I was surprised, actually, that it felt good, and that we had fun while doing it. We laughed, and it was...*nice.* It wasn't passion. It wasn't an all-consuming burn that I suddenly couldn't live without, but it was nice. And I love knowing that Daisy came from that."

"Me, too," I whisper.

"Nate was not the love of my life," she admits with a whisper, "but he was my best friend, and he was so kind and *good.* He was really, really good."

It doesn't make me jealous to hear her talk about him. I'm grateful to him for taking care of her when no one else would, and I hate that he's not here for me to thank him.

"I'm glad you had him, Abs."

"Yeah." She nods and smiles, wiping her eyes again. "You would have liked him. Anyway, tonight's nightmare was a bit of all of that mixed together, and it always scares the shit out of me."

"You woke up screaming for Daisy, as if someone had her, and you couldn't reach her."

Something dark moves behind her eyes. "That happens sometimes, too. It's just more mind games. More fear. Because if something ever happened to her—"

She lets out a hiccupping sob, and I immediately reach for her, pulling her against me. "*Nothing* will happen to her," I promise as I bury my face in her hair and kiss her head. "Nothing. She's safe, baby. She's tucked away on the ranch right now, and she's perfectly safe. I won't ever let anyone hurt either of you."

"I know." She sighs into me, obviously exhausted, and I lean us both back so we're lounging and laid out on the couch, with Abbi's head on my chest. "It's just one of the reasons that I love you, Brady Wild."

"What are some of the other reasons?"

That makes her laugh the way I wanted it to. "I'm not going to inflate your ego."

"Come on. Give me three things."

"No."

"Fine. I'll go first. One, I love your cooking. Seriously, you're *damn* good in the kitchen, and I don't mean that to sound misogynistic."

She smirks, grinning up at me like a loon. "So noted."

"Two, when you come on my cock, it's the best feeling in the world."

She barks out a laugh. "Glad I can oblige. What's the third one?"

"You're the best mommy, Abs."

Now her eyes fill with tears again.

"Whoa, no more leaking. Come on, what are my three?"

"Okay." She sniffs and blinks rapidly, fighting back the waterworks. "One, I really love your ranch, and I don't mean that in a gold-digger way."

I bust up laughing at that one. "Okay."

"Two, that cock you mentioned, holy hell, it's talented."

"It's not the dick, sweetheart. It's the man."

She rolls her eyes at that. "And three, you're so kind, so good to us. Always."

"Always will be, Blue Eyes." I take a breath and kiss her hair. "Okay, let's nap. Just for a couple of hours."

"I guess I'm sleepy again." Her voice is soft, and soon, her breathing evens out, and for a long time, I stare at the ceiling.

Someone should have to pay for what was done to her all those years ago. Someone should suffer, and it pisses me off that no one will. Only Abbi, and she's the victim in all of this. I hate that it's bled over to Daisy, too, having to comfort her mama when Abbi is in the trenches with the nightmares.

It makes my heart sick thinking about it.

I *am* in love with her. If I could, I'd magically build a house—any house she wants—out here at the ranch and move us all in there tomorrow. I'd marry her, have more babies with her, and make a family. Daisy can have all the animals she wants.

I want to make a life with this woman. She deserves that.

She deserves everything.

"Wanna talk about it?" Remington and I have been out on our horses all afternoon, riding fence and checking on the cattle.

"Talk about what, exactly?"

"Whatever it is that's on your mind. You haven't said two words today, and usually, I can't get you to shut up. What's going on?"

I shake my head and pull out my needlenose pliers to work on a nail in the fence post. "Just normal shit, man. I have to go to Cheyenne in two weeks to kick off the season, and for the first time in my career, I'm not excited about it. We have a shit ton to do out here on the ranch before we brand and castrate in a couple of weeks, right before I leave."

"No," he says thoughtfully, pushing his hat higher on his forehead. "That's not it. Those are normal things. Whatever's going on with you isn't...typical."

I glare at my oldest brother. "Are you a shrink now, old man?"

"Observant," he counters. "I know you, maybe better than you know yourself."

"I know you're a pain in my ass."

He laughs at that, then passes me a fresh nail.

"Abbi confided in me the other day about some things in her childhood." I pause, staring at the fence-post. "I can't tell you what she said because it was in confidence."

"None of my business," he agrees.

"But it fucked me up a little."

"Enough that you don't want to see her anymore?"

"Fuck no." I stand, brushing my hands off. "Nothing like that. It just got in my head, and I know there's nothing I can do for her now. I can't go back in time to when she was fourteen and kill the asshole who hurt her, and I *want* to. I would do it in a heartbeat if given the chance."

"You can be there for her *now*," he says calmly. "None of us have a time machine. All we can do is the best we can with what we have, and I suspect that she just wants you to care about her now. Seems to me, you're pretty good at that."

"Yeah, well, that's the easy part."

"I would disagree. It's not *always* easy to love someone, not when you get down to the nitty-gritty, day in, day out of it all. It's not easy. But you choose it because the easy is the best part of your life. And the rest is worth the work."

"Says the experienced married guy." I grin at him. "Erin's been good for you."

"Better than I ever thought it could be," he agrees. "But it isn't easy. It's work. Probably more on her part because I'm an asshole most of the time."

"True that."

He glares at me, making me laugh.

"Thanks. I feel better."

"Good. We have a lot of fence left to fix."

CHAPTER FOURTEEN

ABBI

"Mommy!" Daisy's giggling as she pulls her marshmallow out of the bonfire and shows it to me. "It's on fire!"

"Blow it out," I tell her. "Like birthday candles."

She blows and blows on it, effectively extinguishing the fire, and we get to work building her s'more.

We spent all day out at the Wild River Ranch. There was branding and castration, vaccines, food, and a lot of hard work. The kids watched most of it from the sidelines, in between coming into the food tent for snacks and drinks.

I've never seen my daughter's eyes so big as when she watched what happened inside that pen. Assured that she would be just fine with Holly and Johnny, I spent most of the day in the kitchen tent with some of the other women, cooking and making sure that the ones doing the hard work were taken care of.

So many people from neighboring ranches came to

help, too. Erin said that that's normal and that the Wilds return the favor for the neighbors, as well.

God, I love it here.

I take a long, deep breath, enjoying the way the bonfire smells and hearing everyone's chatter around me. Brady's having a conversation with Ryan and Remington, and every now and then, I can hear him laugh, and it settles me.

I always feel so much better when he's nearby. I never thought I'd be the woman who depended on the presence of a man, but I never planned on meeting Brady Wild. It's not that I can't live without him; I know that I can do just fine for myself and Daisy on my own.

But with this man, I feel so much more at ease. As if I don't have to be hyperaware of every single thing. I can relax a little, knowing that he will protect us, no matter what might come our way, and for the first time since I was twelve years old, I feel like I can breathe a sigh of relief.

I don't ever want to lose that.

"What are you thinking so hard about?" Erin asks as she sits next to me. Daisy has run off to eat her treat with her best friends, and Erin takes my hand in hers and smiles over at me.

"I'm just...happy. Really, truly happy. And I sound sappy."

"And you're a poet." She winks at me and leans in to rest her head on my shoulder as we watch the flames. "I'm happy, too. Who knew that we'd have to come to the middle of nowhere, to this beautiful place, to find where we belong?"

"Not me," I admit and rest my cheek on the top of her head. "I'm in love with him."

"Oh, I've known that for a while. Does he know?"

"Yeah. He knows."

"Good. I'm really happy for you two. Also, if you end up getting married, we'll be sisters, and that makes me the happiest woman in Montana."

Married. Holy shit. "We haven't talked about that."

"You will. It's just a matter of time. When these Wilds fall in love, they do it for life." She pulls away so she can smile over at me, and then she sobers. "What's wrong?"

"He leaves the day after tomorrow."

Erin sighs. "I know. But just for a few days, right?"

"I guess so. I haven't asked him much because I think I've been in denial that he's leaving at all. And I knew that he was focused on getting through today so the ranch would be in a good place for him to go for a few days."

"He'll be fine. You know he will, Abbi."

I nod, sure that she's right.

"You're here!" Our heads come up at Jake's exclamation, and then we grin when we see him run over to Katie, who's walking his way, a huge grin on her beautiful face. He wraps his arms around her and swings her around before planting a kiss on her.

"He's *so* smitten with her," Erin says as I chuckle. "It's adorable."

"I hope Ryan had *the talk* with him," I reply, watching as Jake gets Katie set up with the makings for s'mores by the fire. She's so beautiful in a simple pair of wide-leg jeans and a black V-neck T-shirt. Her long red hair is down around her shoulders, and Jake brushes it back so he can whisper in her ear, making her grin.

"I hope so, too," Erin says with a laugh.

"I got everything closed up for the night," Katie says to Polly, who's sitting in a lounge chair nearby. Katie works for Polly at Polly's dress shop, Pocket Full of Polly. "There weren't any issues."

"Thank you, Katie. Now, relax and have some fun."

"This *is* fun," Katie says, smiling at Jake. "Did I miss the sad parts? With the calves?"

"Yeah, we did all that earlier."

"Good." Katie shivers. "I don't like that part."

Erin and I grin at each other.

"Are you two telling secrets over here?" I look up and see that Brady and Remington are standing behind us. Jesus, even upside down they're both movie-star gorgeous.

"All the secrets," I confirm with a grin, and Brady leans down to kiss me.

"You taste like chocolate and marshmallows," he says with a devastating grin. "Delicious."

"I'm stealing my girl," Rem says, taking Erin by the hand and pulling her to her feet. "Come on, Doc. Let's roast some marshmallows."

"Yes, sir, Grumpy." Erin winks at me, and then they're gone, and Brady joins me by the fire.

"What did you think of today?" he asks me, linking his fingers with mine.

"It was...a lot of things. Fun, interesting, a little disturbing sometimes when those poor babies cried." I glare at him, making him smirk.

"Aww." He kisses my temple. "Babe, you're a softie."

"I mean, you did a lot to them today, and they're just babies."

"They'll be okay, and everything we did was to keep them healthy. No one wants a sick ranch, Blue Eyes."

"No, I suppose not. I liked watching everyone work together. You can tell that you all have a routine down. A system. Like you've been working together for a long time."

"We have," he confirms. "We've done things this way since long before I was born."

"I do have a question, though."

"Shoot." He wiggles some marshmallows onto a stick and rests them in the fire. "Are you wondering about my stellar roping skills?"

"I mean, that *was* impressive." And it really was. The man has a way with a rope. "Also, sidebar, how are you with ropes in...other areas?"

His gaze whips to mine, his eyes narrow, and his voice is low as he leans in to whisper in my ear. "You want me to tie you up, babe?"

"Just asking a question. Your marshmallows are on fire."

"That's not all that's on fire," he mutters as he blows them out. "Ask your question before I haul you back to my cabin and fuck you, Abs." His voice is still low, and he's staring into the fire, but I can feel the lust coming off him in waves.

I swallow hard, my attention averted to way better things.

"*Abbi.*"

"Sorry." I clear my throat and then giggle when he nudges me with his shoulder. "I see that there are a lot of neighboring ranches here."

"Yep."

"But no Lexingtons. They're *right* next door, aren't they?"

"They are," he says, looking over his shoulder.

"Who are you looking for?"

"My dad. He doesn't like that name to be spoken on his property. No, they aren't here."

"Why?"

"You've heard of the rivalry."

"Yeah, I guess I didn't realize that it was a Hatfield and McCoy situation."

"Pretty much."

I frown, blinking at him. "Did you kill each other in the Wild West days?"

"Sure."

"Stop it. You did not."

"Rumor has it that they did. These days, it's been a bunch of lawsuits over property lines and moved fences. Bad attitudes, mostly from Old Man Lexington, who is a complete asshole. Neighbors help them out, and not because they feel any friendship or kinship to that old man, but because of the kids and the hands they have out there that need the help."

"But no help from the Wilds."

His eyes meet mine, glowing in the firelight. "No. Personally, I don't have a beef with Holden or his sisters. Never have, although I know something happened between him and Millie."

We both look over to where Millie's sitting with the kids, laughing as they tell her stories.

"There's something there," I agree softly.

"Like I said, no beef on my part. But my dad is old-school and still remembers some of the shit that happened when he was a kid, and it wasn't good."

"Maybe, as generations pass, things will change."

Brady shrugs and offers me a bite of his s'more.

"When do you leave, Brady?" Chase asks from just a little way away.

"Day after tomorrow," Brady replies. Instinctively, he reaches for my hand and threads our fingers together. "I leave before dawn for the airport."

Polly's watching me with somber eyes, but I smile, putting on a brave face.

"He's going to kick ass," I add, squeezing his hand. "Hey, is it televised somewhere that I can watch it?"

Brady's gaze whips down to mine, his eyes fierce, and I know that I've asked the wrong thing.

"You can *not* watch." His voice is almost desperate, full of panic. "Absolutely fucking *not*."

"I know you don't want anyone there in person, but—"

"It's his thing," Remington says with a shrug. "No watching, even on TV. We can watch after, though."

"There are all kinds of videos of his rides through the years on YouTube," Ryan adds.

"Oh." I blink up at Brady and see that he's still breathing hard, and it breaks my heart that I made him panic. "Don't worry. I won't seek it out and watch it. But I *might* watch some rides on YouTube."

He licks his lips and nods, then kisses my forehead. "Those we can watch together."

"Tonight?"

He laughs and nods. "Sure. Whenever you want."

I glance around, looking for my daughter, and find her huddled up with Holly, both of them with heavy eyes, watching the fire.

"I think Daisy should get home for a shower and bedtime."

Brady nods, pops the last of his s'more into his mouth, and stands, guiding me to my feet, as well.

After saying our goodbyes, we get Daisy into my SUV and head for town. We're not even on the highway when Daisy falls asleep in the back seat.

Brady's quiet as we drive in the darkness, so I settle back against the seat and reflect on the day.

The more time I spend out on the ranch, the more I love it. The views of the mountains, so tall and proud, reaching up into the sky, are absolutely stunning. We have amazing views in town, too, but there's something extra special out at the ranch. I know that today was damn hard work for everyone. Each and every person there had a job to do, even the kids, and no one sat idle. It was exhilarating. I loved the comradery and the sense of community, and that my daughter and I were a part of it, even if it was just a small part.

Daisy was enthralled. I could see on her face that she wanted to be in that ring, helping, wrangling calves, and doing what the cowboys do.

And maybe someday she will. My girl loves animals so much and has no fear of the horses.

Sometimes, that scares me. A little fear is healthy.

Before long, Brady pulls into my garage and lifts Daisy out of her booster seat and carries her inside.

"Baby girl," I croon, brushing her hair off of her face. "You have to wake up, baby doll. You need a bath before bed."

"Tomorrow," she whimpers, but I shake my head.

"No deal. You're too dirty to sleep like that. Come on, we can make it quick." I glance up at Brady. "You can set her down. She needs to walk up the stairs and wake up a bit."

Since our night in the cabin, Brady and I haven't spent even one night apart. He stays here every night, and I feel a little guilty about that because he works so early at the ranch and has to leave before the sun even thinks about coming up so he can do his early chores and then train.

Honestly, it would be so much better if we lived at the ranch.

"Come on, baby. Quick shower. I'll help you."

I get Daisy stripped down and under the warm spray,

and she just stands there like a zombie, so I get to work, scrubbing her down with a washcloth and then using the wand of the showerhead to spray the soap away.

I have to wash her long dark hair, as well, so I do, loving the way it feels in my fingers. She has such pretty hair.

When we're done, I towel her dry and help her into clean pajamas and then comb out her wet hair and secure it in a braid. It'll be nice and wavy tomorrow, and she'll like that.

"Come on, my love." I kiss her head and nudge her toward her bedroom, where Brady's waiting with a book on standby. It's become his nightly routine to read her a story or have her read with him before bed, and it melts my heart every time.

Tonight, though, he's not on the bed, but sitting in a chair next to it, because he's also filthy.

"You go get in the shower," he says with a smile. "I've got this."

"You're the *best*." I kiss his cheek, then Daisy's, and head for my own shower.

I don't remember the last time I was this dirty, and it kind of makes me laugh as I start the water and then get under the spray. Working at the ranch is hard, filthy work.

In less than fifteen minutes, after I've brushed out my own hair and put on my moisturizer, I pad over to Daisy's room and find the light off and Brady gone.

So, I walk downstairs, and there he is, in the kitchen, pouring me a glass of wine.

"You should grab a shower now," I say as I accept the glass from him. "You did the most work, and you're last to shower. Doesn't seem fair."

"My girls get taken care of first," he replies and kisses my lips softly. "Always. But I'll go do that and meet you back here."

"Deal." I grin, watching him walk away. The man fills out those Ranchers *perfectly.* And it's not lost on me that he has a bit of a limp and looks like he's sore.

All of his injuries play through my mind. Of course, he's sore. He has to ache more than he lets on, especially after a physically grueling day like today.

Hopefully, that hot shower feels good and helps soothe his poor body.

I grab a few ibuprofen and pour a couple fingers of whiskey and then settle on the couch with my computer.

Now that I know there are videos on YouTube, I can't wait to watch them.

I go ahead and open the browser, search his name, and gasp at the hundreds of videos that pop up.

Brady Wild Wins Second World Championship.

Brady Wild: an Extensive Interview with the Montana Bull-Riding Legend.

Brady Wild: What's Inside My Gear Bag?

Dave Fisby Talks to Brady Wild about His Near-Fatal Accident.

I swallow hard at that one.

A Look Into the Life of a Real Rodeo Cowboy: Brady Wild.

The list goes on and on. Interviews, a day in the life, and so many rides caught on film.

I could go down this rabbit hole for *days* and never see everything. But something at the bottom of the page catches my eye.

Death of Dirks Johnson, an Intimate Interview with Brady Wild.

Tears fill my eyes, and I can feel Brady move up behind me and lay his hand on my shoulder.

"Don't watch that one tonight," he says softly before leaning down to kiss the top of my head. "Not until after the season is over. Okay?"

"Okay." I sip my wine and gaze up at him as he circles around the couch and sits next to me. "I have ibuprofen and whiskey for you. Which do you want first?"

"Both." He pops the meds into his mouth and then swallows it down with the whiskey, making me cringe.

"I'm sure your body is grateful for that."

"It is," he says, laughing at my sarcasm. "I checked on Daisy. She's snoring."

I chuckle at that and reach up to push my fingers through his wet, dark hair. "She does that when she's overly tired. How long into the story did she last?"

"Roughly half a page." He grins down at me. His hazel eyes are heavy with fatigue.

"Do you get to sleep in tomorrow, or do you have to be at the ranch early?" I ask him.

"There aren't many days off with ranch life," he replies with a sigh. "Besides, I'll be gone for a while, and the guys will have to pick up my slack, so I'll be out there most of tomorrow, starting early."

"I'm sorry."

He scowls down at me. "Why the hell are you sorry?"

"Because you have to drive so far to get there every day. We'll have to figure something else out. Although, I'm not kicking you out of my bed, so staying apart isn't one of the options."

"Good." He settles me back against him, my back to his front, and kisses my hair. "Because that's not an option for me, either. Now, what do you want to see?"

"I didn't know that there would be so *many*," I admit.

"I've been doing this a long time. Fourteen years, professionally. So, yeah, there's plenty to watch."

"You won the world championship *twice*?"

"Three times," he says with pride.

"Where are all of your belt buckles and trophies?"

"In totes. I don't have the space to display them. I keep a couple out to wear when I'm working, but otherwise, they're just stored away."

I tip my head so I can stare up at him. "These aren't simple bowling trophies, Brady. This is a *big* deal. You should have those on display."

"You've been to my cabin," he reminds me. "Where do you propose I put them?"

I twist my lips and then turn back to the computer. "Someday, you'll show them off. Now, where should we start?"

"Do you want to see me ride?"

"Hell, yes. I want to see you ride."

He pages back up the screen and clicks on the *Brady Wild Wins Second World Championship* video. There is commentary, a little interview with him before, and he says, *"I want Bushwacker."*

He pushes away, places his cowboy hat onto his head, and the announcers start talking.

"Bushwacker again. That's the toughest bull out there, and Wild keeps choosing him, week after week."

"No one has conquered that bull sixteen times in a row. Wild wants to set another record."

I glance up at him, and his eyes are narrow, watching the screen, as if he's studying it.

"You're going to miss it, Blue Eyes."

I turn back to the computer, and now Brady's settling onto the bull, still behind a big gate. Men are around him, helping him, and then a buzzer sounds and the gate swings open, and that huge bull starts to buck and kick, trying to get the human off his back.

But Brady holds on, one arm in the air, his body jerking and bouncing. When the eight seconds are over —which feels like an eternity to me—he falls off, and the men hurry to him, helping him scurry out of the pissed-off bull's way.

"Wow," I breathe, my heart hammering. "That's intense."

He chuckles. "You should be on the bull."

"I think I'll leave that to you." I look up at him again. "That is scary as fuck, Brady."

"But *so* fun." He laughs and kisses my cheek.

"Your arm is limp as you run away."

"Dislocated it again," he says, as if it's no big deal. "It

happens. Twisted the shit out of my ankle on that one, too."

No wonder his body hurts and he has the walk of a man twenty years his senior.

"Oh, watch this one." He clicks on a link, and the noise of the arena is back. "I'm only about twenty-three here."

Before Dirks died. Brady's chatting with a man, laughing with him, before he walks to the microphone and says, "I want Bruiser."

"Do you always announce which bull you'll be riding that day?"

"Yeah, it's like a challenge to the bull," he says with a shrug. "Bruiser was a son of a bitch. Mean old thing. Not as bad as Bushwacker, though."

"Which one will you be riding this week?"

"I'll tell you when it's over." He kisses my head, and I frown up at him. "Call me superstitious, okay? When it's over, babe."

I sigh and go back to watching him, over and over again. He explains the point system to me, the importance of certain things, and why it's done the way it is, for the safety of the rider and the animal.

"Is that Dirks?" I ask, pointing to a handsome blond man, and Brady nods.

"Yeah, that's him."

He pushes play on one ride from last year, where he falls and has a huge gash in his head, bleeding badly, and I have to turn and bury my face in his chest, cringing away from the injury.

"And that's why I don't want you there," he murmurs as he closes the laptop and sets it aside. "You don't need to see me get hurt."

"You get hurt, in some way or another, almost every time."

"Usually," he agrees with a grin but then sobers when I frown at him. "It's not usually that bad, Abs. Mostly, what hurts the most right now is knowing that I'll be gone from you two for a few days."

"When do you fly home?" I ask him.

"Wednesday. But then I'll be back out on Sunday. That's how it's going to be for a few months. I'll be in and out."

"If it weren't for me, would you usually come home between events?"

"Usually, yes. I don't live on the road."

"And when is the season over?"

"End of October."

I let out a long, slow breath. "Okay, then."

He takes my chin in his fingers and makes me look up at him. "Are you okay?"

"I have to be." I smile up at him, but I'm trembling inside. "Because my man is a cowboy."

"Listen to me, Abbi. It's going to be a long summer, but it's going to fly by at the same time. I'll be here roughly half of each week. There will be weeks that I don't have to go anywhere at all, but most of the time, I will. I'll be in touch with you constantly."

"You don't have to explain—"

"Yeah, I fucking do, because I don't want you to

worry or wonder or come to any ridiculous conclusions because I didn't communicate with you. There will be women there. We call them buckle bunnies, but they're basically groupies. I haven't had anything to do with them in a decade, but you'll see them hanging around in photos, and because the media are assholes, they might try to say some shit about that."

"You're a rock star."

"In this world, yeah. I am. And that's not my ego talking. I'm flying out the morning before ride day, I'll be at the show, and then I'm flying right back home. *You* are my focus."

"No." I shake my head and shift on the couch so I'm facing him. "That bull needs to be your focus so that for the rest of the time, all but eight seconds of the week, we can be your focus. I just need you to stay safe. I don't give a fuck about the women, and I can be without you for a couple of days while you do what you love. I'm not insecure, and I'm not a clingy, whiny brat. I'm *proud* of you. I can hold down the fort here while you kick ass out there. So you focus on staying alive and healthy and whole, and I'll be here when you get home."

He frames my face in his hands, his thumbs brushing over my cheeks, his eyes so intense it almost steals my breath away. "I fucking love you."

I grin at him now. "I love you, too."

CHAPTER FIFTEEN

BRADY

"I'm riding Man Hater," I say into the microphone and push away as the audience cheers. The music is so fucking loud, it pounds through my body, but I don't hear the words. I'm focused, head down, pacing outside of the chute area.

I want to start the season right, with a win and a high score, and Man Hater is the highest-standing bull right now. He's going to help me get that score.

Finally, it's time to start. The bull is already in the chute, ready to go, and I go about my usual routine, looking him over in a split second, making sure the ropes and grips are where I want them. Holding onto the railing, I set my foot on his back, letting him know I'm here before I settle onto him, get my grip set, and tell my man to tighten the rope.

Finally, I nod, and they open the chute, and this son of a bitch takes off, bucking and throwing himself around like a fucking devil.

But I hold on, finding his rhythm, clinging to him until I hear the buzzer, and then I let go and fall, scrambling out of his way as Man Hater continues to buck and throw a fit.

I wave at the audience, who are going out of their minds, and then I take off my hat and gloves, ready to give interviews as we wait for my final score.

It's all a blur. It always is. I hope I sound somewhat coherent as I answer questions, but the adrenaline is rushing through me so fast I'm almost euphoric.

Ninety-seven point seven.

Not my best score, but with it being the first ride of the season, I'll take it. I have room to improve, but I'm also the highest-scoring rider of the night, and that feels fucking good.

Finally, after another hour of interviews and talking with friends that I haven't seen in a few months, I check my phone and see that I have a text from Ryan.

"I'm coming through Cheyenne to pick you up in my plane. I'll be waiting at the airport."

I don't have to wait for tomorrow morning's flight, and that sends relief through me. Because as exhilarating as the past thirty-six hours have been, I'm ready to go home to my girls.

I take a quick shower before I gather my things, and ignore the come-ons from the bunnies as I walk through the arena and find the ride Ryan has waiting for me to take me to the small, local airport.

When I climb the stairs onto the plane, I find my

brother sitting in a seat, staring down at his laptop. He takes off his glasses and grins up at me.

"How'd it go?"

"It'll get better, but I had the highest score. Rode Man Hater."

"That bull is a mean bastard," he says, shaking his head.

"Yeah, tell me about it."

"And how do you *feel*?"

The door of the plane closes, and the flight crew prepares for takeoff, so I sit across the aisle from my brother and fasten my seatbelt.

"Like I got tossed around by a pissed-off bull." I chuckle and sit back in the seat for a second, letting my system settle. "You didn't have to pick me up."

"You shouldn't have gone commercial," he counters. "If I'm home, you can take the plane. You'll get out and back faster, and I'm paying this crew whether I use them or not."

"You are?"

He nods, and I shrug.

"Hell, I'll take you up on that, then. This fucker is *fancy*."

The flight attendant asks me if I'd like something to drink.

"Do you have ibuprofen? And some whiskey. Maybe a bottle of water."

"Of course, sir," he says with a nod and turns to fetch it.

"Fancy," I say again to my brother, who just smirks. "Where are you coming home from, anyway?"

"I had to make a quick trip to New York for a couple of days for a meeting. I was on my way home, so we made a detour to grab you."

"Appreciate it." I accept the pills, and the drinks are set on the table in front of me. Now that the adrenaline is wearing off, the aches have set in. I'll be stiff as a fucking board by morning. I knock back the pills and the whiskey and then open the bottle of water and take a sip. "How's Polly?"

"The best thing that has ever happened to me."

I roll my eyes at him, making him chuckle. "Yeah, yeah, but how is she feeling?"

"She's tired most of the time. The third trimester is no joke. I felt the baby kick."

"No shit?" I grin and take a sip of water. "That's crazy. Wait, is it a boy or a girl? Why don't I know this?"

"We want to be surprised."

I stare at him for a hot second. "That's stupid. You need to find out because you know that all of the girls, including the moms, will want to buy all the shit in the universe. They need to know colors and stuff."

"There's a lot of gender-neutral options, you know."

"Leave it up to you to be difficult." I shake my head, but I can't keep the smile off my face. "It's exciting. Now, when are you going to marry her?"

"She set a date for early fall because she didn't want to have the baby bump in the photos. I was fine either way. I just want her to be happy, and I know she's mine for the rest of my life, so the legalities don't really concern me so much. We'll make it official before the end of the year."

"You're so fucking laid-back about it all. So calm and collected."

"There's no need to be worked up. Not anymore. Anyway, how are things with you and Abbi? You looked good at the branding the other day."

"Things are great," I confirm. "It's kind of a pain in the ass to drive from town to the ranch every day, but in the grand scheme of things, I suppose it's not a huge deal."

"I guess you're about ready to build that house, then." He lifts his eyebrows as we take off into the air, and I nod slowly.

"If they'll agree to ranch life, then yeah, I'm past ready. But her business is in town, and I don't love the idea of her making that drive every day."

"So is Polly's, but she makes the drive for it. It's really not that bad, Brady. The family's been doing it forever."

"Yeah, I know. I need to talk to her about it. She told me that she loves being out on the ranch, and I know that Daisy gets a kick out of it. The kid loves the horses. Actually, she loves all of the animals and wants a mini cow, so that'll happen."

"Where do you think you'll put a house?"

"That's the thing, I don't know. I've never really thought about it because the cabin has suited me fine. I guess there is space near the cabin that would be good for a house and garage, and it's close to my practice shed.

We could use the cabin for a guesthouse or an office if someone wanted to use it."

"I'm sure someone could find a use for it," he agrees. "Since Abbi's going to be living there, too, take her out and give her options. Find out what *she* wants."

I watch him, pulling on my bottom lip, and start to make a plan.

"You know, sometimes you have some good ideas."

"I have my moments."

It's late when Ryan drops me off at Abbi's townhouse. The lights are off, and I should probably just go out to the ranch for the night and see her in the morning, but I fucking miss her.

I haven't even been gone for two full days, and I miss her so much I ache with it.

After letting myself in through the front door, using the code Abbi gave me months ago, I lock it behind me and then pad upstairs to Abbi's bedroom, but I peek in on Daisy as I pass by her room.

She's zonked out, hugging Mr. Bunny close to her chest.

That girl is so fucking cute, I can hardly stand it.

When I walk into Abbi's room, I see the light on in the bathroom, and then she's walking out of it, wrapped in a satin pink robe, brushing her hair.

She jumps, clamps her hand over her mouth so she doesn't scream, and then glares at me.

"You scared the *shit* out of me." But then she's running right into my arms, hugging me close. "You're early, and it's *so* good to see you. You're okay? You're not hurt?"

"Shit, I forgot to call you." I bury my nose in her hair and kiss her head. "I'm not hurt. When I was finished, Ryan was waiting at the airport to bring me home, and all I could think about was getting here."

"Next time, a text would be nice because I've been going out of my goddamn mind."

I tip her face up and kiss her lips softly. "I'm sorry, baby."

"Apology accepted." She grins and opens her robe, revealing that she's completely naked underneath, and my mouth goes dry. "Come to bed. It's late."

She moves for the bed, and I close the door, making sure it's locked. When I turn back, already pulling my shirt out of my jeans, she's shucked the robe and is lying on her side, head braced on her hand, watching me lazily.

"Were you happy with your ride?" she asks as I strip out of my clothes. Fuck me, I can't get naked fast enough.

"That's going to be my question in about twenty minutes."

She tips her head back and laughs and then sighs when I take one nipple into my mouth as my hand journeys up the inside of her thigh.

"Lie back, baby. Let me make you crazy."

She doesn't argue. She shifts to her back, and her

fingers dive into my hair as I kiss down her torso, headed for the promised land.

And when my mouth lands on her core, she arches, lifting her perfect tits in the air, and I spend the next few minutes wrapped up in making her come with my mouth.

With one finger inside of her, I can feel her start to quake, and I immediately move up the bed and cover her with wet kisses.

"I missed you," I whisper into her ear, grinning when her hands land on my ass, urging me to push inside of her. "I fucking missed you so much, and I thought of exactly this more than I should have."

"Brady," she whispers into my ear. "I need you."

I push just the tip inside and growl against the skin of her neck. One touch, *one* inch, and I'm ready to explode.

"More," she says, and I give her what she wants, seating myself fully inside of her until we're both moaning in satisfaction.

"You have to be quiet, baby," I remind her with a grin. "We don't want to wake up a certain someone."

"Your fault," she says and bites my chin. Her hands are everywhere, and I know that if she keeps touching me the way she is, I won't last another minute.

"Hands on the headboard."

She frowns, and I lift an eyebrow, and then I pull out of her and quickly move to the side of the bed, reach for her robe, and pull the belt off of it before returning to her.

Those gorgeous blue eyes flare with interest.

Abbi's just full of sexy-as-fuck surprises.

When she mentioned the ropes the other night, it was all I could do not to carry her off caveman-style to fuck her senseless.

If she wants to play, we can play.

Without having to ask, Abbi touches the insides of her wrists together, holding them out to me willingly with so much trust and love in her eyes, it's almost more than I can bear.

"You're so fucking beautiful," I murmur against her lips before kissing her, and then I wrap the satin belt around her wrists and secure them to the wrought-iron headboard with a knot that I can easily pull free if she needs or wants me to. "You're in charge here, Blue Eyes. Don't forget that."

"This is *sexy*," she says and licks her lips. "And totally new. I don't want to know if it's new for you."

I kiss her again. No, it's not new to me, but it's new with *her*, and that's all that matters.

"Do you like it when I'm in control, Abbi?"

"Yes." There's no hesitation in her voice.

"Good." Now that she's lying before me, spread out for my pleasure, I move up to push my cock between her tits, watching her closely for any sign that she doesn't like this.

But this little vixen just sticks her tongue out, asking for the tip of my cock.

Who am I to deprive my girl of what she needs?

I offer her the tip, and she licks greedily, pulling on

the belt for leverage to get more of me in her mouth. I reach back and circle her clit with my finger; that little patch of nerves sends her body writhing, moaning around the crown of my cock.

"What a good girl," I croon, and those eyes burn as she stares up at me. I never realized that giving praise was my kink until the first time the words *good girl* slipped out, and she came apart at the seams with the words.

She *loves* it.

And I'll give it to her every single time.

She's straining against the belt, but not in a *let me go* kind of way, but in a *holy shit, this is hot* kind of way, and watching her suck my cock is going to send me over the edge.

I pull out of her mouth slowly, replacing it with my thumb, and she happily sucks the digit while I make my way down her body, settle between her thighs, and push inside of her.

"Ah, fuck, baby." With one hand, I jerk the belt free, and Abbi wraps those arms around my neck as I begin to fuck her a little harder, a little faster. "I never get enough of you."

She bites her lip and moans, and I pick up the pace, chasing that climax for both of us, and when I feel her shudder around me and watch her fall off that ledge, I follow her over.

"HOW BUSY ARE YOU THIS AFTERNOON?" I ask Abbi as she pours herself a cup of coffee and yawns.

"Not very," she says. "I'll be doing laundry and books this morning at the office, and then I should have a light afternoon until Daisy gets out of school at around three. Why do you ask?"

"I'd like you to come meet me at the ranch for a little while, if you don't mind."

"I don't mind. Are you going to tell me why?"

"Sure, when you get there." I grin and kiss her, enjoying the way she feels when she's all soft and warm from sleep. "Just head that way whenever you're ready."

"Okay. Do I need to bring anything?"

"Just you. I'd better go."

"Brady," she says when I turn to the door.

"Yeah?"

"How was yesterday? You never told me how you did."

"You didn't watch?" Remington and the others usually pull it up online as soon as I'm finished, and I assumed she did the same.

"No, I wanted to wait for you."

She's so fucking sweet. "It was a good ride. I ranked at the top when all was said and done, and I was happy with the way the season started."

She smiles, and her shoulders ease. "Good. I'm so glad. Not too banged up?"

I hurt like a motherfucker today, but I just smile at her and tuck her hair behind her ear. "Not too badly.

We'll watch it together later, and I'll give you a play-by-play."

"I can't wait."

There's no traffic at this time of day, so the drive out to the ranch only takes about twenty minutes or so, and I park at my cabin so I can change into clothes that can get fucked up before I head to the barn.

The hands are already out there to congratulate me on yesterday's ride, and then we're busy for the rest of the morning, cleaning the barn, exercising the horses, and the dozens of chores that never seem to end around here.

Several hours later, I hear a car outside, and then Abbi's strolling into the barn, and my heart catches at the sight of her. She's in jeans and a navy blue top with little yellow flowers on it that makes her eyes look even brighter than normal, which should probably be illegal in all fifty states.

"Hey, Cowboy," she says with a wink. "I was summoned, so here I am."

"Good. How do you feel about riding a horse?"

That stops her in her tracks, which makes me smirk. "*Today*?"

"I guess not." I tip her chin up and kiss her. "But one day soon, I'm getting you on one. Let's take the side by side."

She frowns but follows me out of the barn to the all-terrain vehicle that I pulled out earlier so it would be ready when she got here.

"I have a whole bunch of questions for you," I warn

her. "And when I ask, it'll be like a lightning round. Just say the first thing that comes to your mind."

"You're being quite peculiar today," she says slowly but then smiles wide. "Okay, I'm game. Ask away."

I'm heading in the opposite direction of the lake, toward the foothills of the mountains.

"Lakefront or foothills?"

"Uh, I don't—"

"Don't overthink it. Just say whatever comes to mind."

"Foothills, I guess. What about you?"

"I don't matter, sweetheart. Okay, two-story or ranch?"

"Ranch. Are we—"

"No interrupting." I take her hand in mine and kiss her knuckles. "Wraparound porch or patio?"

"Porch, of course."

"Landscaped or natural?"

She purses her lips. "A little of both."

"Fascinating. Four bedrooms or five?"

"Four, I think. Brady, why are we playing twenty questions about houses?"

I pull to a stop at one of my favorite places on the ranch. It's too close to the foothills for decent grazing land, and the views of the mountains in the opposite direction are gorgeous. It's only about a quarter of a mile from my cabin, but the views are way nicer.

I get out of the side by side and offer Abbi my hand and then lead her to a fallen tree and gesture for her to sit.

"This is a gorgeous spot," she says, looking around. She shields her eyes from the sun and stares out at the mountains. "It just never fails to take a girl's breath away."

"I don't want to live in the townhouse forever." The words just come tumbling out of me, and I swear under my breath as she turns her gaze to me and looks almost wounded. "I didn't mean for that to sound as jacked-up as it did. It's a nice place, and I love being there with the two of you. If that's where you want to be forever, I guess that's okay because I want you to be happy, but I really think we need to have a conversation."

I take a breath, and Abbi stands, walks a few steps away, and turns to me, wrapping her arms around her middle.

"I'm confused," she says. Of course, she is. I sound like an idiot. "I need you to just tell me what you want or what you're trying to say here."

I rub my hands over my face in agitation. "Why am I so nervous?"

"I don't know, but you're making *me* nervous. Are we breaking up, Cowboy?"

I'm off that log in a heartbeat, pulling her against me and kissing the hell out of her.

"No. *No.* Never. Jesus, that's not what I'm saying at all. I want to talk about the living arrangements, that's all, but I'm botching it up good. Okay, I'm just going to tell you what I want, in a perfect world, if I could snap my fingers and it just magically happened."

"Please do."

"I'd like to build a house out here for us. The cabin is *way* too small for a family. I want to build any house that you want and bring you and Daisy out here with me. I know that's selfish as fuck, but I can't help it. This is my home, but *you're* where my heart lives, so I'll go where you go. You want to live in Bolivia? We'll live in Bolivia."

"I'm partial to Montana," she murmurs, the panic finally gone from her eyes.

"Well, good, because I am, too. Specifically, *this* piece of it. All the siblings are entitled to acreage out here. Rem has the majority because he technically owns and runs the ranch. Chase claimed his land by the lake, and Ryan already has his own ranch, although if he ever wanted it, he could claim property out here, too.

"I don't know where Millie might want to be. And before you, I never really thought that hard about it, but I have been considering it over the past few days, and I am fond of this piece of land right here. Of course, if you'd like to be on the lake, closer to Chase and Summer, or anywhere else, really, we can do that."

She clears her throat and walks away from me, her back to me as she stares out at the ranch and to the mountains beyond, and I'm sure that I just fucked everything up.

It's too soon.

It's too much.

She turns to me with tears in her eyes, and I want nothing more than to pull her to me and take it all back.

"Brady Wild, are you telling me that you want to *build a house* out here, on this beautiful ranch that has seeped into my bones and embedded itself onto my soul, for me and Daisy?"

"Well, yeah. I am. I mean, if you want the ring and the fancy proposal and all the rest, you'll get that. I promise, you'll get it. I'm planning every minute of my life around you, around what you want and need and how I can make sure you have it. But this is something that I can start right away, even while I'm traveling."

She's swiping at tears, and it just about brings me to my knees.

"Ah, baby, don't cry."

"I should tell you that it's too much and that I can't accept it." She turns to look at the view again and shakes her head. "But I can't because I want this, with you, more than anything."

The relief is swift, and it propels me to her, and I wrap my arms around her from behind.

"Thank God. I was convinced that I was screwing everything up." I kiss her hair, breathing her in. "It'll mean a lot of driving for you to and from work."

"I don't care." She sniffs and turns to me, reaching up to cup my cheek. "My townhouse was perfect for Daisy and me. It's what I needed for us when we moved here, but it's okay that it's time for us to move on. It'll be someone else's safe place to land."

"We'll still be there until the house is finished, probably for about a year or so."

"I can be patient." She boosts up onto her toes and kisses me softly. "But I have to change one of my answers from earlier."

I lift an eyebrow. "Which one?"

"With a view like this, we need two stories. I want the main bedroom on the second floor, with huge windows so I can look at that view every single morning as the sun comes up."

"You can have whatever you want, baby." I kiss her back, relieved that I didn't ruin the best thing that's ever happened to me. "We'll get started right away."

"Wait." Her face falls. "We're going to need a mortgage, and I don't know if my credit—"

"We don't need a mortgage," I reply with a smile. "You really *don't* pay attention to the rodeo stuff, do you?"

"Uh, no. I'm sorry, I don't."

"Trust me. No mortgage needed."

"Oh, I can't ask you to just pay for everyth—"

I cut her off with my mouth and pick her up, sit on the log, and settle her in my lap. Finally, I pull back and smile at her.

"I've got this, Abs. Trust me, okay?"

She sighs and leans into me, turning her head so she can stare at her new view.

"If you insist, I won't say no."

"Good. I insist." I kiss her shoulder and watch the view with her. "It's a damn good view, isn't it?"

"The best one I've ever seen."

I look up at her gorgeous face and smile. "My thoughts exactly."

CHAPTER SIXTEEN

ABBI

The Iconic Women's Collective ranks in the top five things that I'm most proud of in my life. Together, with my four best friends, we founded this collective to help other women in business, whether they already own their own company or want to or simply need mentorship, and it's done so much more than we ever anticipated.

We meet monthly for a two-hour lunch at a local restaurant to network and listen to a guest speaker. It's my favorite day of the month, and it couldn't have come at a better time.

With Brady in Santa Fe for the next couple of days at his second show, I need the distraction.

"It's *so nice* that the rooftop is open for the season," Summer says, tipping her head up at the sunshine as she takes a break from setting out flower arrangements on the tables.

Old Town Pizza is one of my favorite restaurants in

town. The plaque on the door says that they've been here for forty years, and they recently went through a renovation, adding a rooftop area for the warmer months.

Since it just opened, we decided to hold our monthly meeting up here, and we couldn't have chosen a better day for it.

"Montana is so interesting," I comment as Erin and Polly join me. Millie's on the other side of the patio, making sure the microphone works, but she can hear me. "The seasons are so *distinct.* As soon as the calendar turns to the solstice, it's like the Universe flips a switch and that season is off and running."

"It's true," Erin says with a laugh. "In Washington, it's usually just rain or sun. Mostly rain. So it was interesting to adjust to the change of seasons here, but in the very best way."

"Exactly," I reply with a nod. "Anyway, this is a fun change for the luncheon. And this way, Heather can join us."

Heather and her family have owned this restaurant since its inception all those years ago, but she usually can't attend our meetings because she has to be here.

This time, we brought the meeting to her.

"I'm *so* excited for today's speaker," Polly says with a little shoulder shimmy. "Sophie Montgomery-Harrison is a *powerhouse* when it comes to social media advertising, and she's gorgeous, *and* she's married to the hottest quarterback in the league. Talk about an overachiever."

"And she's my cousin," Erin reminds her with a

laugh. "They should be here soon. I know that she and London were on their way this morning."

London is married to another of Erin's cousins and is the owner of the team that Ike Harrison plays for. Erin's family is *intimidating*. Full of celebrities and wealth that I can't even dream of, and we've met most of them. Everyone I've spoken with has been kind and welcoming and funny. They're also good at putting people at ease, so I know that Sophie will be a great speaker today.

"We're still good on time," Millie says, checking her phone. "We have almost an hour. You guys, I'm *exhausted.*"

She sits in a chair and braces her chin on her hand, blinking slowly.

"Are you *finally* going to tell us if you've been screwing around with Bridger Blackwell?" Summer demands. "Because if you and Bridger *are* visiting Pound Town on a regular basis, *good for you.* That fire chief is smokin'."

"For fuck's sake." Now she drops her head on her arms. "*No.* I'm not screwing around with Bridger. We've been friends for a million years, and he needs my help."

"Help with what?" Erin asks, pulling out a chair and sitting across from Millie. The rest of us follow suit, wanting to be front and center for this tea party. "Come on, Mill. You've been at his place on the regular for *weeks.* Maybe months. We all know that he has his daughter, but what's really going on? He's been a single dad for a while now."

I didn't realize that Bridger Blackwell was a single dad.

Millie lifts her head and sighs. "I'm not supposed to tell anyone."

"We're not *anyone*," I remind her. "We're the cone of silence. Maybe it's something we can help with, too."

"If any of you breathes so much as a *syllable* about this to anyone, I will skin you alive," she warns us and then pushes her fingers through her long, chestnut-brown hair as we all make the *cross my heart* motion over our chests. "So, we all know that Angela left Bridger more than two years ago, before Birdie was a year old."

"Sidebar," I put in, getting their attention. "I love how everyone in that family has a B name. Even Birdie."

"It's maybe the sweetest thing ever," Polly agrees. "Okay, continue."

"Okay," Millie says, leaning forward. "Angela didn't want to be a mom. Hell, she just wanted to bang Bridger, and, as we've all discussed, who can blame her? He may be my bestie, but even I can admit that he's a hottie."

"Right?" Erin says, nodding.

"But lately, Birdie's been really sick. Not with anything contagious. We don't really know *what* it is, and it's not cancer, that's for certain. But it's been bad enough that Bridger doesn't want to leave her with just anyone, and he has to work. He's the *chief.* He's been pulling mostly night shifts the past couple of months to help out his crew, so I go and stay with Birdie so she can sleep in her own bed. It's not that big of a deal because she sleeps 90 percent of the time I'm there, but she needs medicine, and damn. I shouldn't have told."

"Poor Bridger," I breathe, not able to fathom the thought of my baby being sick and not knowing why. "And poor Birdie."

"You're a good friend," Polly says, reaching out to cover Millie's hand with her own. "We already know that, of course, but seriously, Mill, you're a *good* friend."

"Bridger and I were always tight," she says with a shrug of her shoulder. "He's a couple of years older than me, but we got along. Aside from you guys, he might be my *best* friend, and I can't tell him that I won't help him out just because I'm not getting enough sleep. He's coming off of nights soon, though, and then he'll have to find help during the day."

"She could come to the ranch," Erin says, thinking it over. "But I'm pretty busy with the event center. He probably wants someone more full time."

"He'd like to be able to put her in preschool this fall, with the other kids her age. She turned three last month. Hopefully, they can figure out what's going on with her, and she can go. She's just the sweetest kid. His family's been helping, too, of course." She yawns hugely. "Anyway, that's the skinny on that. No Pound Town for me, and let me tell you, I could use an orgasm or two."

"Holden?"

Millie narrows her eyes at Erin and growls. "Don't start on that guy."

"You know," I say, tapping my finger against my lips, "I have a toy that I never got around to using, since I'm now getting dick on the regular, and you're welcome to it."

"First of all," Millie says, scowling, "ew. Second of all, absolutely not."

"I'm so sorry that I'm almost late!" The five of us turn as Sophie and London bustle onto the terrace, both looking absolutely gorgeous.

London's in a pink summer dress, her dark hair pulled back from her face, and she makes a beeline for Polly, giving her a big hug before rubbing Polly's belly.

Sophie is tall, also dark-haired, and absolutely gorgeous in her signature activewear—orange today—and crisp white sneakers.

Sophie has built an entire brand around wellness, from the inside out, at any size, and that's something that I really respect about her because I'm a curvy girl, too. Not only does she talk about nutrition and exercise, but also skincare and fashion, and because we're close to the same size, I've often felt like I can identify with her.

So, when she comes over to say hello to me, I can't help but hold on to her hand for an extra beat.

"Thank you," I say softly, only for her ears, "for what you do. And for being here."

Her beautiful face softens, and she leans in to hug me. "It's truly my pleasure, Abbi. It's *so* good to see you again. You look fabulous."

She pulls back to smile at me, and then her gaze narrows.

"Are you using a new skincare routine I should know about? You're glowing."

"Yeah," Erin replies for me, "it's called regular sex with a hot cowboy."

Sophie's grin spreads, and then she laughs and hugs me again.

"That'll do it. Good for you, girlfriend. Sex is good for us. Now, when does this party start?"

Over the next half hour, attendees begin to pop in. There's lots of mingling and chatting, and servers bring up the first of the pizzas for the buffet.

"There are gluten-free options here at the end," Heather announces. "Go ahead and grab it while it's hot, if you're hungry."

The pizza here is the best I've ever had, and she doesn't have to tell these girls twice. People dig in and then return to their seats to eat and talk.

"Abbi," Jackie Harmon, the owner of The Sugar Studio, says as she walks past. "How is Brady? Is he back on the road right now?"

I blink at her and then frown. "He's fine. Why are you asking *me*?"

Jackie grins. "Honey, I know it's relatively new, but this is a small town. Do you think that everyone doesn't know that you two are together? Silly girl."

I know that she doesn't mean anything bad by it. Jackie's the sweetest lady.

"Small towns," Millie says with a wink. "They get you every time. Where is Brady this week, anyway?"

"Santa Fe," I reply, suddenly feeling nervous and shy. I don't like being the center of attention. "He rides later today and should be back late tonight."

“We sure are proud of him,” Jackie says with a smile before she sits down with her pizza.

I’m proud of him, too.

There’s no reason for me to want to shut down at the idea of all of Bitterroot Valley knowing that Brady and I are a couple. I love him. He’s it for me.

But I’ve never loved being the one under a microscope. Since I lost my mom, it’s been in my nature to blend in and not make waves.

To not be noticed.

“It was rather sad when I heard the last Wild brother was scooped up,” someone says. I don’t know who because now I’m staring down at my hands. “They’re all a bunch of hotties—no offense, girls. I guess we all hoped it would be a local to catch Brady’s eye. That’s one fine cowboy.”

There’s laughter, but I feel my cheeks heat.

I want the floor to open up and swallow me.

With that one statement, I am reminded that I’m not *a local.* I don’t really belong here. And I don’t deserve someone as amazing as Brady Wild.

“Stop,” Erin whispers in my ear, clasping my hand in hers. “No one means anything by that.”

I take a breath and force a smile.

“I mean it,” she continues. “You pick your chin up because Brady is obsessed with you, you’re absolutely gorgeous and wonderful, and you’re not doing anything wrong.”

I clear my throat and nod, my smile more genuine when I turn it on her.

"Thank you for that."

"I love you," she says, and that alone just about brings tears to my eyes.

They love me.

And I love them.

"Okay, let's not make you wait any longer to hear from our *spectacular* speaker today," Summer says as she jumps up to introduce Sophie. "This woman really needs no introduction, but I'm going to give her one anyway. Sophie Montgomery-Harrison is a multi-million dollar entrepreneur in the health and wellness industry, but we all know that she's so much more than that. She inspires women to love themselves, just as they are, and she gives awesome advice on home décor, skincare, and even gardening. There's nothing this woman can't do. Give it up for Sophie Montgomery-Harrison!"

We don't just applaud. We stand and hoot and holler, and down below, someone honks their horn in response, making us laugh.

"Well, that'll make a girl blush," Sophie says with a laugh and takes the microphone, moving the stool out of the way. "If you don't mind, I'm going to stay standing so I can come to you and wander as I talk. I guess I'll tell you a bit about me and how I got started in this business, and then we can just chat."

We all nod at that, and she begins.

"I come from a physically *beautiful* family. Like, there are literal movie stars and athletes in my family, you guys. And when I was a teenager, I thought I was fat. Thus began my struggle with food and eating in general.

When I lost my best friend at thirteen—she died of a heart attack from being anorexic—I knew that I wanted to do something with my life that helped shift the way we think about ourselves. So, I became a nutritionist and a health coach, and yes, I'm still a size sixteen. I run, I lift weights, I'm mostly vegetarian and eat no sugar, and my body is naturally this size. It's who I am. My husband thinks I'm hot as fuck, and, well, so do I. And, because I was born in an age of social media, I've been able to reach a lot of people with my message of self-love and health."

We clap for her, and Sophie continues to speak about her company and what's worked for her to grow her brand, and then she opens it up to questions.

"I have a question," Charlie Lexington, Holden's sister, says, raising her hand.

"Yes, ma'am." Sophie jogs over to Charlie and gives her the mic.

"Can your husband introduce us to his single teammates?"

Sophie laughs at that and takes the mic back.

"You know, it's funny, because London and I were talking about bringing the team out here at some point for a couple of days of R&R. Anyone who wanted to come, that is. So, you never know. But be careful what you wish for." She winks at Charlie and then takes the next question, which is thankfully back on topic.

For the next hour, I listen raptly and take notes on my phone about branding and social media ideas. I know that my business is vastly different from Sophie's, but I think I can implement a lot of her ideas into my business to help it continue to grow.

Finally, Erin joins her cousin and gives her a big hug.

"Thank you so much," Erin tells her. "Please come back anytime you want, even if it's just to sit in on a meeting or for a visit. I miss you."

"I miss you, too. London and I were *also* talking about bringing the cousins out for another vacation. It needs to happen sooner rather than later."

"Bring everyone," Charlie shouts, making us laugh again, and people start to stand and file out, headed back to their jobs and schedules.

When it's just the five of us once more, with London and Sophie already saying their goodbyes and headed to London's condo at the ski resort, Millie turns to me and wraps her arms around me for a big hug.

"Hey," I say, awkwardly patting her back. "You're not a big hugger."

"I know, but you need one." She pulls back, my shoulders still in her hands, and smiles at me. "You're a good woman, and you're perfect for my brother. I don't care what those jealous women said earlier. I know they didn't really mean to be snarky, but they kind of were anyway. And even though I think they're gross, I know that most girls think my brothers are hot."

She gags at that, making me giggle.

"I'm okay," I assure her as Erin takes my hand. "For...*reasons* in my past, I'm not good at being the center of attention. That's what makes me the most uncomfortable. And I guess that I didn't realize that being with Brady was going to make that happen sometimes."

"You co-founded this whole thing," Polly says with a frown. "We're the center of attention a lot."

"*We* are," I stress to her. "As a group. In photos and at events, we're together as a unit. It's not just me singled out. I'm proud to stand with you guys, but I'm not usually the spokesperson, if you think about it."

"No," Summer murmurs. "You're not. And that's okay."

"It's totally okay," Millie agrees. "We've got you. And let the jealous types roll off your back. Brady's is the only opinion that matters anyway. And from the gross looks he sends your way, I'd say he's pretty much in love with you."

"Yeah." I can't help the giddy smile that spreads over my face. "We're going to build a house at the ranch."

"WHAT?" they all exclaim at once.

"You've been holding out on us," Polly says, rubbing her belly.

"Hey, are you okay?" I ask her.

"No, you're holding out on us. Spill it. Everything. Tell it all."

We take our seats once more, and I fill them in on the few hours Brady and I spent at the ranch and the property we chose.

"He was *so* nervous that at first, I thought he was trying to dump me."

"Men," Summer says, rolling her eyes.

"Right? He scared me for a minute. It's so beautiful

there, and he wants to get started on the house as soon as possible. First, we have to talk to whoever the people are who design those things and get the ball rolling." I turn to Polly. "Brady mentioned that Ryan knows all about that stuff."

"Oh, he knows," she says with a nod. "And he will happily take that whole project over if you let him. He's obsessed with building things and renovations. This will give him a new hobby to see to. Not that he needs one."

"My brother is good at it," Millie agrees. "He has expensive taste, but Brady can afford it."

"I didn't think Brady should have to pay for it all," I admit. "I mean, I have some money from my late husband, but—"

"Trust me," Millie says, shaking her head. "Brady can handle it. I'm *so* excited for you guys. All of you. I couldn't have asked for better sisters."

That strikes us all speechless, and then I can't help the tears that come.

"He hasn't proposed or anything—" I begin, but then I'm swept up in a group hug, and I just shut my mouth. Because whether or not Brady and I ever tie the knot, these four women are my *sisters*.

"We're really cool," Summer says after wiping away a tear. "I love being in this club."

"Same," Erin says with a laugh. "Best club ever."

"Daisy, I love you, but if you don't stop whining, I'm going to take away dessert tomorrow."

At that, my darling daughter flings her head back on the couch and continues to whine. I know she's testing me. I know she's grouchy because she's overly tired, and she had horseback riding lessons this afternoon, but if there was ever a day that I could use a short vacation, it's today.

"You're the *worst*," she cries just as my phone rings, and I frown when I see that it's Brady's friend, Amy Johnson. She and I have chatted when Brady's been on the phone with her, but we don't usually have private calls.

And then fear pierces through me. Brady rode this evening, and I haven't heard from him. Shit, was she watching? Did something happen?

"Hello?" I can hear the fear in my voice, and Daisy must, too, because she stops whining and listens to me. "Amy? What's wrong?"

"Oh, shit, I'm sorry, Abbi. Nothing's wrong, I was just calling to check in with you and see how you're holding up."

I sag against my kitchen counter. "You're not calling because you watched him ride and he's hurt?"

"No. God, no. I don't think he's ridden yet. I was just thinking about you and thought I'd call to chat. I know this is only the second time he's gone this season, and he won't let you go with him."

"No, he won't. And I really couldn't even if I wanted to because I have Daisy. I'm doing fine; I just worry most of the time until he's back home. Last week, he forgot to call or text to let me know he was okay. I'm waiting to hear now."

"Let me do a quick search." I can hear her tapping on a keyboard. "He just finished a few minutes ago, and it looks like all is well. He's talking to an interviewer."

"Thank God." I close my eyes and let out the breath I've been holding all day. "How am I supposed to do this for another six months?"

"You'll do it," she says, reassuring me. "Because he loves it, and you love *him.* I will say, though, that I'm glad this is his last year. It's time for him to retire. He doesn't have anything else to prove, you know."

"I agree, but it has to be up to him."

"That it does."

Her accent makes me want to fall into *my* old accent, so I clear my throat, careful not to.

"Have you and Hugh set a date for the big day?" I ask her.

"We're looking at a wedding around New Year's. At first, I wanted to do Christmas in the Smoky Mountains, but it's hard for people to leave their families at Christmastime, so now I'm thinking New Year's. I want snow. Is that weird?"

"You're talking to a woman who lives in Montana," I remind her with a chuckle. "That doesn't sound weird to me at all. It'll be beautiful."

"I think so, too. But, back to why I called, you're really okay?"

"I'm okay. Especially now that I know he's safe."

"If you ever want to talk, you just call me. Your

friends and family will think that they can relate and try to understand, but no one gets it like we do. So you call if you need me."

"Amy, you're so sweet. Thank you for reaching out. And I know that I've never had the opportunity to say this, but I'm very sorry about Dirks. I'm very, *very* sorry. I lost a husband, and I know what that feels like."

"You and I are part of a club that no one should have to join," she says, her voice soft. "And I'm sorry for your loss, too. Kiss your sweet girl for me, and let's stay in touch, okay?"

"I will, and yes, please. I think that's a great idea."

"Goodnight, Abbi."

"'Night."

I hang up and set the phone down, but then my screen lights up with a text.

Cowboy: I'm okay. All went well. Wanted to let you know. I'll be home by midnight.

I smile and type out my response.

Me: Thank you. Glad it went well! Can't wait to kiss you. <heart emoji>

I glance at the couch and see that Daisy has fallen asleep, so I kiss her on the head and then cover her with a blanket.

I love my girl to pieces, but she is the *grouchiest* person when she's tired. I grab my book and sit in the chair to read. Brady will take her up to bed when he gets here.

I can't wait to see him.

CHAPTER SEVENTEEN

BRADY

"Right here." I'm standing with all my siblings and my parents, showing them where I'd like to build the house, and they're all just smiling at me like I'm...*cute*.

It's a little unsettling.

"Did you guys hear me?"

"Oh, Bubba," Mom says, linking her arm through mine and then looking out over the land. "It's the perfect spot for a home."

"Why aren't they talking?" I ask her, gesturing to the others.

"I never thought I'd see the day," Remington says with a shrug. "I mean sure, you've got it bad for Abbi, but I didn't think you'd take it this far."

"I'm in love with her," I correct him, holding his gaze. "I want a life with her, and yeah, I'm taking one hell of a chance because the season has barely started and anything can happen, but—"

"Life's short," Dad puts in, cutting me off. "If you love the girl, *love* her. I think it's great. You don't need our permission. The land's yours, Brady."

"Well, I need to make sure that Rem doesn't have plans for this piece and that neither Millie nor Ryan had their eyes on it."

"I don't need it," Rem says right away.

"Me neither," Ryan agrees, grinning at me. "Mill?"

"Nope," she puts in. "Looks like it's all yours, big brother."

I let out a breath, feeling nervous all over again as I rub my hands together and try to keep the butterflies under control.

It's not working. The butterflies are suddenly mutants.

"You'll need to have power and water brought out this way," Dad says, thinking it over. "And a septic. It's raw land, but it's doable."

"Do you have an architect?" Ryan asks.

"No, but I bet you have several."

"Yeah, I have people we can use," he agrees and pulls out his phone to make notes. That's Ryan, always ready to put a plan into action.

"I'm *so* happy for you," Mom says again and squeezes my arm. "When are you getting married?"

I frown down at her. "I haven't asked her yet."

Mom's eyes narrow. "Are you telling me that you asked her to build a house with you but didn't say anything about marriage?"

"No, I told her that she'd get the ring and all the romantic stuff later."

Dad barks out a laugh, my siblings all shake their heads, and Mom smacks me on the back of the head.

"I raised you better than that," she says with a scowl.

"You're in *trouble*," Chase snickers, and I glare at him, but he doesn't lose the shit-eating grin on his face, obviously enjoying the hell out of this.

"How *romantic* of you," Millie says, shaking her head in disgust. "I'm sure that was a thrilling conversation for Abbi. *Hey, I don't want to marry you or anything, but let's shack up. I'll even build you a house on my property, but don't get any ideas about the legalities.*"

"Fuck you. That's not what I said."

"Watch your mouth," Mom says and cuffs me on the back of the head again, making my brothers laugh even harder.

I hate all of them.

"It *was* a nice moment," I stress, suddenly feeling like an asshole as I replay what I said to her in my head. Jesus, I was fucking nervous, and I was saying all the wrong things. And yet, she still said she wanted to live here.

I must not have fucked it up too badly.

"Don't be that guy," Rem says as he tries to catch his breath. "The one that shacks up with his woman for *decades* and doesn't marry her."

"I have no plans on doing any such thing. I *am* going to marry her. Hell, I want to adopt Daisy and have more kids, and everything else that comes with it, but I wanted to start here, on the house. Get that going because the summers are short, and I don't want it to take years to finish."

I sigh and shove my hands into my pockets. Maybe I *did* fuck up.

"It's a beautiful spot for a house," Ryan says with a nod, the laughter calming down. "The views are amazing right here."

"She cried." I give my sister the stink eye. "In a *good* way, smartass."

"I didn't say anything." Millie holds her hands up, her eyes wide as if she's innocent, but I know better. "I'm *rooting* for you, moron."

"Okay, well, since no one objects, I'll get the ball rolling on things. Thanks, guys."

We shuffle about for a few more minutes, talking about where I'd like to put the garage, a chicken coop, and a small barn for Daisy's mini cow, which makes my dad laugh in surprise.

"All the cattle on this ranch, and that little spitfire wants a *mini* cow."

"A *Highland* mini cow," I add as I check the time. "I have to admit, they're cute. Speaking of Daisy, I have to pick her up from the babysitter."

"What's Abbi up to today?" Millie asks as we all walk to our vehicles. "I haven't talked to her since our IWC lunch the other day. When some of the girls were idiots."

That has us all pausing.

"She's working late. She had some people quit, and she's just busy with the business. So, I'm taking Daisy out on a date. Why were the girls idiots? Abbi didn't say anything."

Rem, Chase, and Ryan all shuffle their feet and look down, and I know that something's up.

"What happened?" Dad asks, also scowling.

"I have a big-ass mouth," Millie mutters and presses the heels of her hands to her eyes. "They didn't mean to hurt anyone's feelings."

Now I'm getting pissed off, and I narrow my eyes at my sister. "What. Happened?"

"Girls are dumb," she whispers. "They were saying that the Wild brothers are all hot." She makes a gagging noise. "And someone—I think it was Robin Healer, that girl who owns the travel agency downtown—said that they were hoping that it would be a *local* girl who snagged Brady, and then people laughed and made stupid comments, and we could tell that it made Abbi feel bad. So, after everyone left, we gave her the pep talk of all pep talks and made sure that she knew that you adore her, and we all love the shit out of her, and she needs to let it all roll off her back."

"Take a breath," Chase advises. "And yeah, people can just be thoughtless."

"She seemed fine when I got home," I reply, but I hate that anyone made my girl feel inferior for even *one* second. I'll make sure she knows that there's no one else in the world for me, no matter what anyone else says.

"Thanks for letting me know. I really do have to go get Daisy."

"You're welcome to bring her out here," Rem says. "Come have dinner with us."

"I appreciate it, but I thought she'd like to go out to a restaurant for a treat. I'd like some time with her before I head to Wyoming in a couple of days."

"Makes sense to me," Ryan says, clapping me on the back. "Have fun. I'll email you the contact info for the architects."

"And I have the info for the utilities," Chase adds. "I had to do the same not long ago. Oh, and the guys who laid the driveway."

"Right." I nod, already a little overwhelmed. "I guess we'll need that. Thanks, guys."

I climb into the 4Runner and make my way into town, looking forward to some one-on-one time with Daisy. I feel like I've hardly seen her since the season started back up again. By the time I get home after a ride, she's already in bed, and then I'm off before she wakes up, out to the ranch.

I park in the driveway of the townhouse and walk next door to Merilee's place. She's the nice older lady who keeps Daisy whenever Abbi needs a sitter, and I've met her several times. Daisy adores her, and I can tell that the feeling is completely mutual.

Of course, what's not to love when it comes to that little girl?

When I knock on the door, I can hear the two of them laughing inside, and when Merilee opens the door, they're both covered in what looks like...flour?

"Hello, ladies. Do I need to call an ambulance?"

Merilee laughs again and shakes her head. “We were baking cookies, and *someone* dropped the whole bag of flour.”

“It was *heavy*,” Daisy says with a giggle. “And then we sneezed and sneezed so much!”

“I bet you did. Can I help clean up?”

“No, I’ve got this,” Merilee says. “But little miss here might need to be tidied up before...well, before anything else.”

Date night with me is a surprise, so I wink at Merilee and nod.

“We can make that happen. Come on, Princess. Say thank you.”

“Thank you,” Daisy says and wraps her arms around Merilee’s middle, hugging her tight. “See you after school tomorrow.”

“Have a good day,” the older woman says, and then Daisy and I walk over toward the other townhouse.

“We have to get you cleaned up,” I tell her. “Because I have a surprise for you tonight.”

“What is it?”

“A *surprise*.” I boop her on the nose. “And it’s a good one. Let’s brush as much of this flour as we can out of your hair and dust you off while we’re outside.”

Before we go through the front door, I brush Daisy’s clothes off and shake out her hair, making her laugh.

“Okay, let’s go in and change. Those clothes go right into the washer.”

It only takes me about fifteen minutes to get her ready to go.

"Your mom has to work late," I inform the little girl as she puts her pink sandals on. "So, you and I are going to do something fun together. How would you like to go out for dinner? On a date, of course."

"Wow, yes, please." She stands and claps her hands with excitement. "Where are we going?"

"You get to choose. Where would you like to go?"

"Hmm." Her eyebrows pull together as she mulls it over. "Pizza?"

"Is that what you want?"

"If I can have breadsticks, then yes."

"You're a girl after my own carb-loving heart." I kiss the top of her head. "You can have whatever you want. Let's do it."

"Wait. We're going on a date, and I'm not wearing a pretty dress."

"Sometimes, you can go on a date in casual clothes."

"You can?"

"Sure. You don't always have to get fancy. I think you look beautiful no matter what you wear."

That makes her smile and her cheeks darken with happiness. "Okay, then, I'm ready."

"Me, too. I'm *hungry*."

"I could eat a whole *house*!" She hops along beside me as we walk out to the 4Runner, and I get her settled in her seat before I take off from the house, headed the short distance to Old Town Pizza. Abbi told me that the new rooftop area is great, so I'll see if we can get seated up there.

"Well, hello, you two. No Abbi tonight?" Heather asks

when we step inside. She smiles down at Daisy, who holds my hand and suddenly gets shy, pushing her face into my side.

"Not tonight. I'm on an important date, so I was hoping we could sit on your fancy new rooftop."

"Well, of course, you can," Heather replies with a bright smile. "I have just the perfect table for the two of you. Follow me."

She leads us up some stairs to the rooftop area. Abbi was right. It's great up here. There are sunshades to keep the hot sun at bay, lots of tables and chairs, and a bar at one end.

It's pretty busy up here, but Heather leads us to a table with a great view of town.

"Here you go, you two." She sets the menus in front of us. "What can I get you started to drink?"

"Can I please have a Shirley Temple?" Daisy asks shyly.

"Absolutely. And you?" Heather turns to me.

"Sweet tea sounds good. Thanks, Heather."

"You betcha. Melody will be your server tonight." Heather winks and then bustles off, and I smile over at Daisy.

"It's really nice up here."

She nods, looking around. "I can see my school. Can we see all the way to the ranch from here?"

"I don't think so." I shake my head and point down the street. "Wait, come here so I can hold you up, and we'll look."

Daisy hurries around the table, and I bend down so

she can hop onto my back, ignoring the way my knees sing when I stand up, and I walk closer to the edge.

"Do you see Millie's coffee shop?" I ask, pointing down the block.

"I see it. Is that Grandpa walking out the door?"

"I think it is," I confirm with a grin. "He must have come into town for a coffee. Oh, there's Grandma following him."

"I love them," she says, resting her chin on my head.

"Me, too. There's Polly's shop over there."

She's patting my head, but in a soothing way that makes me grin. Being with Daisy feels natural. I don't feel like I'm babysitting her at all, but more like I should have been with her all along.

She's mine, just as much as her mother is.

"Can I interrupt just for a minute so I can take your order?"

I turn at the sound of Melody's voice and smile. "Sorry, we were taking in the view."

I bend down so Daisy can hop off of my back, and then we take our seats, and I order us breadsticks and pepperoni pizza before Melody leaves to put our order in.

"Brady?" Daisy's eyes are suddenly serious as she studies me.

"Yeah, Princess?"

"Do you think that maybe someday I can call you daddy? Maybe if you marry my mommy and stuff?"

And just like that, my heart just explodes.

"I know you got mad the last time I said that, but—"

"I wasn't mad," I assure her, leaning on the table. "I

was just surprised. Sweetheart, I plan to be with you and your mommy forever. For as long as I'm still alive, I want to be with you guys. I'd like to marry Abbi, and I'm working out the details of asking her, but you have to keep that a secret between you and me, okay?"

"Like a good secret?" she clarifies. "Like a surprise?"

"Yes, that's right. If your mom says yes, then you can absolutely call me Dad. I would be so honored and proud to be your daddy."

Her whole face lights up at that. "I won't tell Mommy. I love you, Brady."

"I love you, too, Princess."

"Pizza time," Melody announces in a sing-song voice as she sets the steaming pie in the middle of the table. "I brought lots of ranch for dipping and *lots* of napkins," she says with a wink.

"Thank you," I reply and scoop a piece onto Daisy's plate. She's already put a bite of hot cheese into her mouth and closes her eyes on a sigh, as if she's never tasted anything so good.

"Yum."

When we were finished eating, we took the leftovers over to Abbi's office so she'd have something for dinner, too.

She looked fucking exhausted, but she put on a brave face for Daisy and me, giving us hugs and kisses, and even took a minute to scarf down a piece of pizza before she gently shooed us out so she could dive back in.

She was buried in white sheets and towels and had her computer screen up with a big calendar that she was swearing at.

"How many people are you down?" I asked her.

"Three," she murmured. "Too many during this season. I'll figure it out."

"I can clean," I offered with a shrug. "I'll buddy up with you."

"I can clean, too," Daisy agreed, and to my horror, Abbi's eyes filled with tears.

"Okay, I love you two, but I have to get to work so I can come home tonight. Thank you for dinner."

I pulled her to me, my hands on her sides, and pressed my lips to her forehead. When she sighed, I tipped her chin up and gently kissed her lips. "I'll see you soon."

She nodded, and then I brought Daisy home.

We made it through the bedtime routine just fine, and then I got her settled into her bed and read her three stories before those pretty brown eyes drooped closed.

And now, it's eight-thirty, and there's no sign of Abbi.

Me: How's it going there?

The bubbles bounce on the screen as I sit on the couch.

Blue Eyes: Just finishing up. I'll do the last of it in the morning. Is Daisy in bed?

Me: Just put her to sleep. Come on home, baby, and I'll take care of you.

She sends back the heart emoji, and I get to work upstairs, getting her favorite lounging clothes together and making sure there's a big, fluffy towel waiting by the shower.

When Abbi walks in, her shoulders are slumped, her pretty blonde hair is in disarray, falling out of a low ponytail, and her eyes look...*defeated.*

"Oh, baby." I pull her against me and hug her close as she sighs and hugs me back. "I'm sorry that it was a rough day."

"Me, too," she murmurs. "I know that I'm going to have turnover, but it's so inconvenient during the busiest months."

"Are you hungry?"

"A little."

"I have a plan. How about a nice, hot shower, and then you can come down here and have a snack, and I'll rub your feet. Or anything else that needs to be rubbed."

She tips her head back, giving me a fake scowl. "Is that an innuendo?"

"It wasn't, but it could be." I relax a little when she smiles. "That's my girl. Come on, shower first."

With her hand in mine, I lead her upstairs, and her face softens when she sees that I have everything ready for her.

"You're the *best*," she whispers before I start the water, letting the stream warm up.

"I'm just a mortal man, in love with the most beautiful woman in the world." I kiss her forehead before I pull her dirty T-shirt over her head and toss it into the hamper. Then I make quick work of her jeans and underwear, tossing them into the hamper, as well.

God, she's fucking gorgeous. I know she's self-conscious of her curves, but I can't get enough of them.

However, now is not the moment for sex. That's for later.

"Come on, my hard worker. Into the shower for you."

"Thank you," she says, lifting up on her toes to kiss my chin before she steps under the hot spray. "Oh, God, this is heaven."

I grin at her and then shut the door of the shower, giving her privacy.

"I'll be downstairs when you're done."

"I won't be long."

"Take your time, Blue Eyes."

Once downstairs, I pop some popcorn and add Abbi's favorite seasoning to the top, then arrange a plate of cheese and crackers and pour her a glass of wine, then I turn the A/C down a bit to make it colder in here and start the fireplace.

I don't know what it is with women wanting to make a house feel like the arctic tundra, just so they can curl up in blankets and start a fire, but I've learned that it's a thing.

And I want my girl to relax tonight.

I hear the creak of the stairs and turn to find Abbi descending them, and when she sees the food and the fire, she grins.

"This is *so great.*"

"Come on," I instruct her, holding out my hand. "Let's get you off of your feet."

"Yes, please." She takes my hand, and I kiss her knuckles as I lead her to the couch and get her settled.

"I have food for you. Hold on."

After grabbing the goodies from the kitchen, I return to her and watch her sigh in happiness.

"Let's start with wine and popcorn," she says, and I pass her the bowl and the glass of wine, then pop a cracker and cheese into my mouth. "This is a great way to end a shitty day."

"Do you want to talk about it?" I ask as I pump some lotion from the bottle I set on the end table into the palm of my hand and then lift her foot onto my lap and start to rub. "Or do you just want to relax?"

"Holy Christ on a cracker, you've been holding out on me if you can rub feet like that." Her smile is soft and sweet, and then she shrugs a shoulder. "There wasn't anything *terrible* that happened, aside from the fact that three people quit on the same day, didn't give me notice, and now I'm severely short-handed. I just got all of the positions filled, and I thought I'd be able to coast through the summer, but no. Not to mention, now I have an odd number of employees again, and I won't let anyone work alone, so that means that I have to help until I can get someone else in. Which means that laundry gets stacked up."

She pops some popcorn into her mouth and chews.

"I'll figure it out. It's just a pain in the ass and long hours. Thank God for Merilee and my hot cowboy."

I fucking *love it* when she calls me *cowboy*.

"Did you and Daisy have fun?" she asks me.

"There was pizza with a view, so of course, we did. She's great, Abs. No worries there."

"Good. And you're right, I *do* have a great kid. Where do you head off to next?"

I frown down at her foot. I'd rather not have to talk about leaving again, but this *is* our life for the next few months.

I can't avoid it forever.

"Wyoming." My thumbs move up the outside of her foot and circle her ankle, making her groan with pleasure. And that little groan makes my dick twitch. "Give me your other foot."

She sets her bowl and wine aside and then shakes her head. "I have a better idea."

CHAPTER EIGHTEEN

ABBI

"You do?" Brady asks, his eyebrows climbing as I crawl over the couch and straddle his lap. His hands land on my ass as I wrap my arms around his neck and lean in so I can bury my face against him. "And what is that, sweetheart?"

"I need you inside of me." I'm too tired to flirt and play games. I've had the shittiest of shit days, and right now, I want my man, naked, inside of me, making me forget all about it. "Not that the massage isn't nice, but—whoa!"

I'm cut off when he simply stands, hands still on my ass, and carries me up the stairs. He groans a bit, and I pull back to see his face.

"You're hurting."

"I'm fine," he says and kisses me firmly. "And as much as I want to fuck you until your legs shake and all of Bitterroot Valley knows my name, I can't do that with your daughter asleep upstairs, so I'm taking you to a room that I can lock."

"Smart. You're a smart man, Cowboy."

He grins, closes and locks my bedroom door, and then sets me on my feet.

Without hesitation, I strip out of my clothes. "No games tonight. I can't take the time to flirt and be...*cute*. I just need you, Brady."

"You're always cute." He unbuttons his shirt and tosses it aside, and my mouth goes dry at the sight of his fucking *stellar* torso.

Muscles for days and smooth skin make my mouth water.

The scars remind me that what he does for a living scares the shit out of me.

"Keep looking at me like that," he growls, watching me with hooded eyes, "and I won't last ten seconds."

"You usually last at least eight."

He smirks at that, and then we're naked and on my bed, lying facing each other with my leg hitched up on his hip and his hand in my hair, holding me where he wants me so he can kiss the ever-loving *fuck* out of me.

No one kisses like Brady Wild.

His lips are soft, but he's confident and sure about what he wants from me. His tongue isn't too aggressive and slides against mine, making everything in me tighten with need.

"I'm going to make you want to scream," he whispers as he kisses his way along my jawline. "I'm going to make sure that you never forget exactly who you belong to."

Holy shit.

Belong to him? *Belong* to him. The feminist in me, the independent woman, should bristle at that and remind him that I belong to *myself*, thank you very much.

But his hand glides down my spine to my ass, pulling me more firmly against him where the hard length of his need presses against my stomach, and I know without a doubt that if I've ever *belonged* to anyone in my life, it's to this man.

I am Brady Wild's, and he'll have my heart until the end of the time. It's as simple and as scary as that.

He rolls us so I'm tucked under him, and then he kisses his way down to my breasts.

If I've learned anything about this cowboy, it's that he's a breast man, without a doubt. And I *love* the way he molds them with his hands, nipping and kissing at the already pebbled nubs until my legs scissor, and I want him inside of me *now*.

"Brady." My hands are in his hair, holding on as *his* hand finds my center, and he groans.

"Jesus, you're so wet for me, baby."

"Always." I have to swallow hard. "God, I'm always ready for you. Brady, I need you. Right now."

But he shakes his head and journeys farther south. I don't *want* him to kiss me there now. I want his gorgeous, big cock filling me up, reminding me how completely we fit together and how amazing it feels when we're together.

As soon as his lips fasten on me, and he hollows out his cheeks, sucking the tenderest of flesh inside of his mouth and using that magical tongue, all thought flies right out the window.

"Ah, goddamnit." My words run together, and I have to hold on to the pillow on either side of my head, gripping until my knuckles feel like they might break. "Holy fuck, Cowboy."

He moans and then pushes two fingers inside of me, making that *come here* motion that hits that perfect spot, and he's right, my legs shake, and I see stars, and I have to turn my head into the pillow to swallow my screams.

Someone's kissing up my body—I hope it's Brady—and then he's cradled between my thighs, the length of his heavy cock resting along my center, and he kisses me, brushing my hair off my cheeks.

I can taste myself mixed in with his desire, and it's enough to fuel my hunger for him again.

"Brady," I whisper against his lips.

"Yes, my love?"

"I. Need. You inside. Of me." I cup his face and nibble on his bottom lip. "Right now. Okay?"

That slow, devastating smile spreads over his lips as his hips rear back, and then he slides inside of me quickly, stretching me and burying himself to the hilt.

"Goddamn," he mutters, bracing his forehead against my own. "So fucking tight."

His fingers find my clit, and as he begins to move, he circles that bundle of nerves until I'm right at the precipice of falling off the edge again.

"Now," he growls. "Fucking come. Open your pretty eyes and come for me, Abs."

I couldn't defy him if I wanted to, but I absolutely *don't* want to. My gaze clings to his as he hurls me right off of that cliff and into oblivion, falling with me. I *want* to scream his name, but he covers my mouth with his and kisses me until the climax has wrung us both out.

And later, after we've cleaned up and tidied up downstairs before climbing back into bed, Brady pulls me against him and brushes his mouth back and forth on the crown of my head.

"I love you." I sigh with it, so relieved that I can say those words whenever I want to. "So much that sometimes it scares me."

"I've got you." His voice is heavy with sleep, and his arms tighten around me. "And I love you, too, baby."

"We're here," Erin announces as she and I walk into Polly's house on Friday night. Our kids are with Joy and John for a sleepover, and we've decided that we all need a girls' night out.

But Polly is *very* pregnant and much more comfortable at home, so we brought all the fun to her.

"We're having virgin huckleberry margaritas," Summer informs Polly. "And those three can get hammered if they want to."

"And you can all stay out here so that no one is

driving," Polly adds, clapping her hands. "This is *fun.* And probably a good distraction for you, Abbi."

I nod and pour the bag of corn chips into a big bowl. "Yeah, I could use a distraction while Brady's out of town."

"Ryan's gone, too," Polly says with a sigh. "It's his last big trip out of the country before the little one arrives. He'll be spending the next few months at home with us, so he has to wrap up some business first. He had to go all the way to Amsterdam."

"That's a long way," Millie says.

"Way farther than Wyoming," I agree and lean over to pat Polly's shoulder. "I'm sorry, friend."

"Me, too," she says. "Because it means that Brady has to fly commercial on his way home, and that delays things for you."

I hadn't thought of that. My stomach sinks, knowing that Brady will now be gone for another day, but there's nothing I can do about it.

He'll be home again before I know it.

"Okay, no being sad," Millie decides. "We have each other, and we're going to have a good night. We can play pool and listen to music and gossip about all the tea happening in Bitterroot Valley."

"I want to hear the tea," Erin says, waggling her eyebrows. "Yes, please."

We have the *best time* making enchiladas with chips and salsa in Polly's massive, amazing, *gorgeous* kitchen, and then we take our drinks and dessert of lemon cupcakes from The Sugar Studio to the game room, where some of us play pool and others lounge on couches.

"Why are my feet so swollen?" Polly asks the room at large. "Like, they're *huge*. And it's not hot outside or anything. It's dumb."

"Because you're going to have a little baby," I remind her and smile at her bump. "Tell me again why we don't know the sex?"

"Oh, there was sex," Erin says with a wise nod, making me snort with laughter.

"Jesus Christ," Millie mutters, making me grin.

"Because we want to be surprised," Polly answers and rubs her belly again. "I don't care if it's a girl or a boy, as long as it's healthy."

"Yeah, yeah," Summer replies, rolling her eyes. "But there are certain *besties* who would like to buy pink or blue shit, Poll. If that's a girl in there, I want to buy frilly things. Like, *all* the frilly things in the world. You're stealing that from me."

"No, I'm not," Polly says with a laugh. "You can buy things after it's born. Besides, we don't need anything. I don't want you guys to spend your money on us. Ryan—"

"He may be rich," I say, interrupting her, "and that's great for you, but honey, we're your friends, and we want to buy stuff for you. Because we're your village, and that's what we do."

"Don't make me cry." Polly rests her head back on the

couch. "For the love of God, don't make the waterworks start because it's hard to make them stop."

"Did you have a huge baby shower and a million gifts when you were having Daisy, Abbi?" Millie asks, stuffing a cupcake into her mouth.

And suddenly, all of the laughter leaves me, and I'm reminded of what Daisy and I didn't have before we came here.

"No." I shake my head and pour myself another margarita. "No gifts."

"Not *one* gift?" Erin demands.

"I didn't have family," I remind them. "And Nate's family wasn't exactly pleased that I got knocked up and was trapping him into marriage."

"Bullshit," Millie bites out, clearly pissed on my behalf.

"It's fine. Nate and I were able to buy everything we needed. But *you*," I turn to Polly, "have people, and those people love you."

"I know," she says, blowing out a breath. "And I love you all, too. Summer, are you guys going to find out what you're having?"

Summer grins and rubs her own smaller baby bump. "It's a boy."

"Oh, my God!"

My eyes sting with tears as I grin at my friend. There are hugs and smiles, and then Polly breaks down into tears.

"What's wrong?" I ask her.

"Well, now I want to know, too."

I can't help but laugh at that. "But Ryan wants to wait?"

"No, *I'm* the dumbass who said we should wait, and Ryan just gives me whatever I want. I'm a complete idiot."

"You can call them in the morning," Erin reminds her, "and ask them. I'm sure they've already noted the sex somewhere, because although they didn't tell you, they still saw it."

"That's true," Millie says. "Just call them."

"A baby boy," Erin says, reaching for Summer's hand. "That's so exciting. Do you know what you might name him?"

"We have a list of things that we don't hate. So far, we're thinking about Devin, Lincoln, or August."

"Oh, I like all of those," Millie says and sips her margarita.

I'm feeling fuzzy. More than tipsy but not shitfaced.

And that means that I'll probably want to fall asleep soon.

"You guys, I hate to do this, but I think I need to go to bed."

"I didn't want to be the first one to tap out," Erin says. "The pregnant girls beat us!"

With a snort, we stand and walk through the house to the wing of guest rooms. Yes, the *wing of guest rooms.*

This house is ridiculously big.

When I'm tucked inside of my little room, I pull out my phone and call Brady.

"Abs?" He sounds sleepy, and I kick myself for not texting first. "You okay, baby?"

"Yeah, sorry." I sound a little slurry. "I shoulda texted, but I'm drunk."

He sniffs, and I can hear the bed rustling. "You're *drunk*? Where's Daisy?"

"Hey, I'm not a bad mom. She's with *your* mom, if you must know. We had a girls' night at Polly's house, and I'm staying here because I can't even walk a straight line."

"Oh, good." I can practically hear him relax. "I'm glad you're safe. Did you have fun?"

"It's always fun when we're together. What are you doing? I bet you look hot, no matter what it is."

He chuckles. "I was sleeping, remember?"

"Oh, yeah. I woke you up. You should go back to sleep and ignore me."

"Not a chance. I can't ignore you; you're too important."

And just like that, I'm a pile of goo. "Did you know that sometimes you say things to me that make me feel really good?"

"It would suck if I made you feel bad, Blue Eyes. How much did you have to drink?"

"Don't know. We kept pouring from the pitcher." I roll onto my side, cradling the phone to my cheek. "I miss you."

"I know. I miss you, too."

"And this time, you don't get to come home in Ryan's plane."

"Heard about that, did you?"

"Yeah. Sucks. How first world are we?"

"I know, but it *does* suck. It means I won't get home until Sunday evening."

Almost a whole day later than usual.

"Oh. Okay. It's okay. You're working and stuff. How do you feel?"

"Like I just recovered from *last* week." He chuckles in my ear, and my eyes feel heavy. "But it'll be okay. This time tomorrow, the ride will be over."

"Are you excited?"

"Hell yeah. It's an incredible feeling to ride a bull."

"I know." I snort-laugh. "Tell me about it. I think *I've* just recovered myself."

"You *are* drunk."

"And sleepy."

"You're sounding sleepy."

"And horny. Man! I should have brought my toy with me. Fail."

"Wait. Are you telling me that you use that thing when I'm not home?"

"Uh, no?"

"Abbi. Tell me the truth." His voice is hard and it makes me squeeze my thighs together.

"I mean, I *haven't*, but now I think I will. Because you're gone, so I can't have the real thing. I think you'd get mad at me if I went out looking for a replacement."

"Be careful, Blue Eyes." His voice is almost lethal now, like he clearly didn't find that funny.

"I make bad jokes when I'm drunk. It's either you or plastic for me, Cowboy."

"Don't use that fucking toy until I'm home. Do you understand me?"

I bite my lip. Shit, he's hot when he gets all bossy and growly like this. "If you're home, I don't *need* the toy, remember?"

"I'm going to use it on you myself."

"How?" I frown into the darkness. "How does that even work? *Brady.* My back door is exit only. You're not going to—"

Now he's laughing his ass off in my ear, and I can't help but grin.

"No back door play for you, Cowboy."

"That's not what I was planning on, but I bet we could have fun with that."

"Nope. No way. Nuh-uh." I shake my head and squeeze my cheeks together. "But if you want to turn it on vibrate and push it against my clit while you're inside of me—"

"*Abbi.*"

"What?"

"I can't have this conversation with you when you're a thousand miles away."

"Why? Are you hard? Are you horny, too? Man, this is bad timing."

"You're killing me."

"If you were here, we could do all kinds of fun things. Well, maybe not *here*, in your brother's house, but you know what I mean."

"Abs?"

"Yeah?"

"I love you."

I smile and hug myself around my middle. "I know. It's so crazy. I love you, too."

I'M SO HUNGRY.

My stomach growls really loud, and I push my hands over it, as if I can cover the sound with them. I haven't had any food in three days. Only water.

Because I'm a bad girl. And I'm fat.

I don't mean to be either of those things. I don't eat too much, only what I'm given, and that never even fills me up all the way.

I have to sit in the living room, perfectly still on the couch, while the family I live with gets to have dinner in the dining room. This house is the biggest one I've ever lived in, with tall ceilings that make footsteps echo on the tile floor. It's cold in here all the time.

I can smell the roasted chicken from the oven, and my stomach growls again. I feel so sick. *Nauseous and empty and shaky. This morning, I was dizzy.*

I just need a piece of chicken. Just a couple of bites, and I'll be okay.

I can't help the whimper that comes out of my mouth, and I hear everyone stop eating.

Oh, no.

"You want food, fatso?" It's the oldest son who yells it, a laugh in his mean voice. "You can have the scraps."

"No, she doesn't get anything," the daughter says. God, I hate her prissy voice. She's so mean to me, and I have to share a room with her. It's humiliating when she laughs at me when I have to change my clothes. "She's fat; she won't starve."

There's more laughter, and I have to fold my lips in so I don't cry out. At least no one in this house has tried to rape me.

They just humiliate me here. And withhold food from me.

I'm always so hungry.

I can hear them scraping the silverware over the plates, and then they get up and start to take their finished meals into the kitchen.

I wish I could just have whatever they didn't finish. I'd be happy with anything at all.

The youngest child, a girl about the age of eight, is the last to leave the table, and she looks around the room, then walks to me and holds out a big chunk of chicken that she must have hidden in her napkin for me.

"Hurry," she whispers, and I snatch it out of her hand and shove it into my mouth. But as I chew, the mom comes in and sees what's happening.

"Go to your room, Elizabeth."

"Mama—"

"To your room."

The mom hasn't raised her voice, but the girl swallows hard, gives me a sympathetic look, and then slinks away up the stairs.

I've just finished swallowing the chicken when the mom

walks calmly to me, rears her hand back, and slaps me across the face so hard that I see stars.

I cry out, so she does it again.

And then a third time.

Then she grips onto my face, her fingertips digging into my flesh. "You eat when I *tell you to eat, you hear me?"*

I can only whimper a response.

"You're a gross, fat pig, and I'm going to get all of this fat off of you. You don't want to be fat, do you?"

More whimpers.

"Now you have to go another two days."

No. God, no. I'm so hungry.

I sit up in bed, gasping, tears coming down my face. At first, I panic because I don't know where I am. Am I in another foster home? Oh, God, will they hurt me here?

But then I remember that this is Polly's house, and I'm with my friends.

I'm okay.

Everything is going to be okay.

I miss Brady, and I reach for my phone, but it's not even dawn yet, and I woke him up late last night. He has to ride today, and I don't want him to be distracted or too exhausted.

"You're okay." I set the phone down and pad into the bathroom, where I splash some cold water over my face. "You're fucked up, but you're okay."

I look at myself in the mirror and remember the young woman I once was, and feel the tears well for her. She didn't deserve to be treated like that. Hell, no one does. People can be so cruel, so evil and mean, and I just don't understand that.

I was a good kid. I was a *nice* kid. And still, I was brutalized mercilessly by the people who were supposed to help me. And why? Because I'm not naturally thin? Because they *could*? It's so fucked-up.

I shake my head and splash the water once more and then pat my face dry with a thick, soft towel.

And then another memory hits me. In that same fucked-up house, they didn't let me dry off with a towel after bathing.

I had to use my own dirty clothes.

"Enough." I shake that off and pad back to the bed. That's not where I am anymore. My life is amazing. I have friends who care about me, my daughter is safe and happy, and I have the love of an amazing man who is what dreams are made of.

There's no need to dwell on the past. I wish my subconscious would catch up to the rest of me.

I have no intention of falling back to sleep, but I lie down anyway and take a long, deep breath.

I've had a sinking feeling in my gut all fucking day. Of course, I'm hungover, but that's not it.

I did end up falling back to sleep after the nightmare, but still rose early and chatted with Polly over coffee in the kitchen. Everyone else was still asleep when I left to go home to shower and change my clothes and then go to work.

I'm working seven days a week right now. Sometimes, I take off earlier than I should, but for the most part, I'm spending a *lot* of hours working. I usually go out in the field in the mornings to help clean some of the units, and then I go to the office in the afternoon to get laundry underway, work on the schedule, and run errands for more supplies, as needed.

To say that I'm busy is a massive understatement.

I helped clean four units all before noon today, and then I came back to my office to do that laundry, but all day, I felt like something bad was going to happen.

"Please don't let it be Brady."

I've texted him more than usual today. I'm never this needy when he's gone, but something isn't right.

I don't mean between us. Brady and I are solid. But there's *something* in my gut that won't shut up. The poor man has texted me back twice, reassuring me that everything's normal and absolutely fine on his end, trying to put my mind at ease. I need to let him focus and do his thing so it stays that way.

The dryer signals the end of a cycle, so I walk back to the laundry room and realize that I'm sloshing through *water.*

About two inches of it.

"Shit."

It occurs to me that the washer obviously isn't running anymore either, and it appears that it has a leak.

Great.

One more thing to worry about and deal with when I have *no* time or brain space for this.

At least I have *two* washing machines, so I'm not completely dead in the water, so to speak. It takes me thirty minutes to find a plumber who has time to come take a look at it today, and then I find out that it's not an easy fix.

Because of *course,* it isn't.

No, that would be too easy.

Maybe this is the thing that was making my gut feel weird. I take a second to take stock of my feelings and realize, *nope.* That's not it.

"I have to order a couple of things," Peter the plumber—I can't make this shit up—says with a sigh. "We can't get much overnighted out here, but it shouldn't be more than a couple of days."

"A couple of *days*?" I blink, staring at the mountain of laundry. "I'll be here all night."

"I'm sorry. I just don't have it in stock at the shop. I'll see if I can get it FedExed overnight, but inevitably, it will take two days."

"The joys of living in the boonies." I force a smile and then shrug. "Ah, well, looks like my daughter and I will be hanging out here tonight. Thanks for your help, Peter."

"I'll keep you posted, Abbi." He walks out, and I give the busted washer the stink eye.

"Today of all days?" I demand, as if it'll talk back to me. With a deep sigh, I go find a mop and a bucket and then decide to use the wet vac because that'll pull the water up faster. It's noisy, and I swear I can hear ringing, and when I turn it off, I find that I'm right.

My phone is ringing, and I don't recognize the number.

"Hello?"

"Hey, Miss Abbi, this is Lucky out at the barn."

My stomach churns. Daisy's out at the barn today for riding lessons.

"Hi, Lucky. Do you have bad news for me?"

"Well, I don't want you to panic because Little Miss is fine. Or, she will be. She fell off the horse this afternoon and hurt her wrist."

"Crap," I whisper. "Is it broken?"

"We don't think so, but I think it'll make everyone feel better if she gets an X-ray. What do you think?"

"I agree. I'll come out right away and get her and take her to the ER."

"I'm real sorry about this, ma'am. It's never fun when the little ones fall off."

"It's not your fault. I'll be there soon."

I click off and then turn and stare at the mess that I haven't finished cleaning up, but then throw my hands up in the air.

My daughter is the most important thing.

So, I send a text to my crew to fill them in on what's happening, and then I lock the door behind me and drive out to the ranch, straight to the barn.

"I think she's fine," Erin assures me as I get out of the car. "But she's favoring her wrist a bit. Scared her more than anything."

"I bet. It would scare me, too." I smile at her and then look over to where my baby is sitting with Holly and Johnny. "Hey, baby. I hear you took a fall."

She nods and then starts to cry again, and I inwardly roll my eyes. She'd already calmed down, but now she has to turn the tears back on for my benefit.

Which is fine.

"Come on, pretty girl. We're going to the doctor."

"She wasn't going too fast or anything," Johnny says as he and his sister walk with Daisy. "It happened so fast. I don't know what went wrong."

"Sometimes, people just fall," I tell him and pat him on the shoulder. "There wasn't anything you could have done."

He's just like his dad and uncles, wanting to protect everyone. He's the cutest kid, and I'm so glad that Daisy is growing up with him and Holly.

I get Daisy buckled into her seat and then wave as I leave the ranch.

"Does it hurt, babes?"

She nods, holding the wrist against her chest, and that makes me frown. Maybe she *did* break it.

I guess we'll find out soon enough.

The emergency room isn't busy when we walk in, and to my surprise, we're whisked right back to a little room where a nurse takes Daisy's vitals and then asks her what happened.

"I was riding a horse, and I fell off."

"Well, that'll do it, won't it?" The nurse smiles up at me. "Dr. Blackwell will be in very soon."

That's right. I remember the girls saying that one of the Blackwell brothers is a doctor. If he looks anything like Brooks or Bridger, he's hot with a capital H.

Was *this* what put the pit in my stomach all day? It's not gone, but then, I'm sitting at the hospital with my injured daughter, so it makes sense that I'm still a little off.

"Did you tell Brady that I fell?" Daisy asks me.

"Not yet." I don't know if I should. He rides in just a couple of hours, and I don't want to take his focus away from that bull and doing what he needs to do. "I think we'll wait until we know for sure what's wrong, okay?"

Daisy nods. "I miss him."

"I know, baby. He'll be home tomorrow night."

"Hello, I'm Dr. Blackwell."

Yep. Hot with a capital H. Jesus, do they just breed hot men in Montana? Is it in the water?

"Hi, I'm Abbi Kastella," I reply, shaking his hand. "And this is Daisy."

"Abbi," he says with a smile. "You help run the Iconic Women's Collective."

"Yes, I do. I know your sister, Billie."

"Billie loves what you're doing. She talks about it all the time. Now, let's focus on Daisy, shall we? What happened?"

We tell him the story of Daisy falling off the horse, and he nods as he gently takes Daisy's arm in his hands.

She winces but doesn't cry out when he moves her hand side to side and up and down.

"Well, I suspect that it's just sprained and bruised up,

but I want to get an X-ray to make sure, okay? That means we're going to take a picture of your bones."

"Do you have to take them out of my body?" Daisy's eyes are wide with horror, and Dr. Blackwell chuckles.

"Nope, the machine can see through your skin. You won't feel a thing."

"Okay," my daughter replies, her shoulders sagging in relief. "Good."

Less than thirty minutes later, he comes back with the film in his hand and puts it on the lit-up screen.

"Well, Daisy, I don't see any sign of a broken wrist or arm. That's excellent news."

"Thank God," I mutter in relief.

"Looks like it's just banged up really good from that fall. I want you to wear a brace for a couple of weeks so you don't move it around too much. This way, it'll heal faster." He turns to me. "You'll want to give her the children's dose of ibuprofen for a couple of days to help with swelling. Ice will be good for it, too."

"Does that mean that I can't ride again?"

"Just until the wrist heals," he assures her. "I get it. I don't know what I'd do if I couldn't ride my horse. But don't worry, you'll be back in the saddle in no time."

"Thank you, Dr. Blackwell."

"Call me Blake," he says with a wink. "Are the rumors true that you and Brady Wild are an item?"

"Yes," Daisy says with a big smile. "He's our Brady."

"Well, then," Blake says with a laugh. "My loss. Have a good day, ladies."

It's always flattering when a sexy, successful man

shows interest, but I definitely only have eyes for my man. And it seems that my daughter shares in that sentiment.

With Daisy's injury only being a sprain, I decide to wait to tell Brady about it until after his ride. There's no need to distract him with anything happening around here.

Besides, that pit is still sitting heavily in my stomach.

It takes another hour to get the brace and other things we need before we get home, and then we're both exhausted.

Going back to the office tonight just isn't going to happen, but I have *so much* laundry to do. So, I call Millie.

"Hey, is Daisy okay?" she asks when she answers.

"News travels fast in this town. Yes, it's just a sprain, but it'll take a couple of weeks to heal up. Hey, I need a favor. There's a ton of laundry at my shop that I need to have brought to me so I can do it here at home. Do you mind grabbing it? Or come over and hang with Daisy while I go get it? Shit, I should have just called Merilee over."

"Swear jar," Daisy calls out, and I roll my eyes.

"We've got this," Millie assures me. "Why don't I come chill with Daisy, since I don't have a key or know what you need from the shop, and you can do that piece of it?"

"Thank you. Yes, thank you, that would be awesome."

"Okay, I'll be there in fifteen."

I hang up with her, relieved that I have a plan B for

work, and then my phone rings again with a number I don't recognize. With a frown, I accept the call.

"Hello?"

"Abbi Kastella?"

I can hear commotion in the background, and every hair on my body stands on end. "Yes?"

"This is Dr. Stephens calling from Cody, Wyoming. I have some bad news about Brady."

CHAPTER NINETEEN
BRADY

I've never been so fucking pissed off in my life.

I can hear the goddamn doctor talking to Abbi, and if I wasn't seeing two of him, I'd punch him in the mouth.

"Give me the phone," I growl.

"As his emergency contact," he continues, as if I didn't say anything at all, "I need to let you know that Brady's suffered an injury. He has a concussion, and he separated his shoulder again."

"Let me fucking talk to her," I say, louder this time. Jesus, I didn't even have time to tell her that I added her as my emergency contact. And this phone call is going to scare the fuck out of her. "Doc, I swear to God, if you don't hand me that phone..."

"Yes, he's going to be fine," he says, not looking at me.

"Calm down," Dan, a fellow rider, says. He's standing

next to me, and I glare up at him. “You know this is how they do it. If you didn’t want her called, you shouldn’t have listed her as the fucking emergency contact.”

“Yeah, well, I didn’t plan on getting hurt.”

Dan scoffs at that. We *all* get hurt, all the time.

But I forgot to tell her, and that makes me feel like a son of a bitch.

Finally, the doctor hangs up the phone.

“You didn’t let *me* talk to her.” But my phone rings with an incoming FaceTime call, and I immediately answer. “Baby, I’m okay.”

“Brady?” Her eyes are wide with worry and fear. “My God, are you sure you’re okay?”

“Yes, I’m going to be just fine,” I tell her. Sure, it hurts like hell now, and I feel like I’m going to throw up, but I’ll heal from this.

I always do.

“I’m sorry I didn’t tell you that I added you as my emergency contact. It totally slipped my mind.”

“It’s okay,” she assures me, holding the phone close to her, as if she wants to wrap her arms around me and hold on.

Not gonna lie, I could use that right now.

After I’m done throwing up.

“Hey, don’t scare her like that.” My sister nudges her way onto the screen. “You gonna live, big brother?”

“Looks that way, but I can’t fly home.” I wince as the nausea rolls through me. “Not with a concussion.”

“I’m coming to get you,” Abbi announces. “I’ll leave right now. Millie, you stay with Daisy.”

"You can't," Millie interrupts her. "Honey, you have *so much* to take care of for work, remember? The shit-tastic day you just had?"

Abbi sighs and closes her eyes. What shittastic day? What the fuck happened at home while I was gone, getting pulverized by a pissed-off bull?

"You stay here," Millie continues, "and I'll leave right now to get him. He's eight hours away, so if I leave now, I'll be there by morning."

"I don't want you driving overnight by yourself," I tell her, getting her attention. "Mill, call one of the brothers and have them come with you."

"I'll take care of it," she tells me. "Don't worry about me. Go find a soft spot somewhere and start recovering. Send me the address of where you are, and I'll be there as soon as I can."

"Brady," Abbi says, her face coming back on screen. It absolutely *destroys* me to see the tears in her eyes and the fear on her face. "I want to come get you so bad. If it were literally any other day, I would drop everything—"

"Baby," I interrupt her, keeping my voice calm and soothing. Jesus, I need to get off the phone. "It's okay. Millie will take care of it, and I'll see you before dinner tomorrow. Don't worry about me, okay?"

"Uh, not gonna happen, Cowboy." She tries to smile. "Do everything they tell you to do. Don't be stubborn. Hydrate."

"Yes, ma'am." God, she's fucking adorable. "I'll see you soon. I'll call you in the morning and keep you posted on our drive back, okay?"

"Yeah." She licks her lips. "Yes, please do that because I'm going to be a nervous wreck. I love you so much."

"I love you, Blue Eyes. Don't worry so much. I'm *fine*."

"Text me the info," Millie reminds me. "I'm on my way."

"Call Chase or Rem to come with you," I instruct her again, but she just rolls her eyes.

"Don't worry about this. Hang tight. I'll keep you posted."

She clicks off, and I reach for the barf bag and let my stomach empty itself.

"I have anti-nausea pills for you," Doc says. "Take them every six hours as needed. Tylenol for the headache. Get some rest. It's not a severe concussion, so you can safely sleep. I recommend you go back to the hotel and rest until your sister gets here."

"I'll help him back to the hotel," Dan says. "Come on, buddy."

"I fucking hate all of this."

The hotel is nearby, and once in my room, I take the Tylenol, press an ice pack to my shoulder, and call my agent.

I need a shower, but I want the ice more, and I can talk to Sandy while I ice down.

"Hey, Brady," she says. "It's late."

"Not in Wyoming," I reply. "I want to retire *today*."

She's quiet for a moment, obviously stunned speechless. "What happened?"

"Nothing that hasn't happened before, but damn it,

I'm over the fucking concussions and torn shoulder. And I terrified my girl tonight. I'm over it. I'm ready to be done."

"Brady," she says with a sigh. "You *can't* just quit. Here's the thing, I understand that you're ready to retire, and I don't blame you. Your poor body has taken one hell of a beating over the years. But you're under a contract, and you have sponsorships."

"None of which say that I don't get paid if I get injured and have to step back."

"If it's a career-ending injury, yes. But no doctor is going to say that this is career-ending. Am I wrong?"

I close my eyes, so fucking frustrated that I want to punch my fist through the wall.

"No. They wouldn't sign off on that."

"So, here's what you're going to do. Are you listening to me?"

"I'm here."

"You're going to take the next few weeks off, or however long you were told you need to heal, and then you're going to finish out this season. If you win, you get one hell of a fucking bonus, but either way, you're going to finish it. We'll announce the day after championships that you're retiring, and you'll get the big party and induction into the hall of fame, and more sponsorships because brands eat that shit up. I'm setting you and your family up for the rest of your life here."

"How do you know that I have a family?"

"Because the Brady I've worked with for more than a decade would *not* willingly quit. I figure there's a woman involved here, and you're the one who mentioned her in the first place. That concussion is fucking with you."

I blow out a breath but don't confirm or deny.

"Yeah, that's what I thought. I'm your voice of reason here, honey. I don't need the money. I want you to remember all the hard work you've put in, all the beatings you've taken, and how much you love getting on that bull, and *then* tell me that you want to quit."

She's right. I don't ever *want* to quit, but seeing how torn up Abbi was broke my fucking heart.

I can't love her as much as I do and continue to put her through this much worry. But I don't want to quit.

I *can't* quit.

"Okay," I say at last. "I'll finish it. The doctor said I need three weeks for the head and the shoulder to be okay enough to ride again."

"Then you take those three weeks. I'll put you on the injured list, and we'll reevaluate you before you get back into the arena to make sure you're healthy enough. Don't rush it, Brady. I want you healthy for the rest of the season."

"Thanks, Sandy. I'll be in touch."

"See that you are."

She hangs up, and I toss the phone onto the bed before walking into the bathroom for that shower.

For the first time in my life, I hate my job.

My head is pounding again by the time we get to the townhouse. Millie was a stubborn ass who didn't have one of the brothers go with her, and she got an earful when she arrived.

Not that she cared.

My sister is so fucking stubborn, she drives me nuts.

But I'm home, and that's all that matters.

"I've got your bag," Millie says as we climb out of her truck. "You go on inside."

"This is one time that I'll take you up on that."

I open the front door and already feel better. Abbi's head pops up from the kitchen, and then she's sprinting toward me, but comes to an abrupt stop about two feet away.

"Why'd you stop?"

"I don't want to hurt you."

"Get over here." My voice is deep, and my good arm is open wide as she steps gingerly into my embrace and lays her ear against my chest, listening to my heart as I hug her close. "I promise, I'm okay. Nothing that a couple of weeks of rest won't heal."

"Scared the shit out of me," she whispers before pressing a kiss over my heart and then stares up at me with wet blue eyes. "Don't you *dare* do that to me again, Brady Wild."

"Yes, ma'am." I grin and kiss the top of her head. "Where's Daisy?"

"I'm here." We turn to the stairs where Daisy's grinning, but my eyes narrow in on the brace on her right wrist.

"What the fuck happened?"

"Swear jar," Daisy announces, but I ignore her and hurry over to where she stands on the fourth step from the bottom, my heart in my goddamn throat.

"What happened?" I repeat, frowning into her sweet face.

"I fell off of Good Girl yesterday." She shows me her brace.

I whirl to Abbi, and it makes me dizzy for half of a second. Millie's coming in with my bags.

"Why didn't you tell me that she got hurt?"

"Because *you* got hurt, too." Abbi props her hands on her hips. "And I didn't want to tell you before you rode because you would be distracted. It's not broken. If it *had* been broken, or if something worse had happened, I definitely would have told you."

I narrow my eyes on her and then turn back to Daisy and cup her little face in my good hand.

"How do you feel today, Princess?"

"It's sore," she says. "But Mommy gave me medicine. We match!"

I look down at the sling that I'm wearing and then smile at her. "Looks like we do. Your mom has her hands full with us."

"And her broken washing machine," Daisy adds.

Now I slowly turn back to look at my woman, who's biting her lip. Millie's laughing her ass off.

"I have to get over to the coffee shop," Millie says and hugs Abbi close. "Don't worry, he was his grouchy, annoying self all the way home. Totally fine. Call me if you need me."

She grins at me, and then she's off.

"What happened to the washing machine, Abs?" And why the hell don't I know about any of this?

"One of the big machines at the shop broke and leaked water everywhere." She sighs, and I can see the fatigue in every line of her gorgeous body. "Come on, let's have the tacos I made, and I'll fill you in on everything. And *I* want to hear about what happened yesterday, too."

"That's fair." I pick Daisy up with my good arm and kiss her cheek, making her grin, and carry her to a stool at the kitchen island. When she's seated, I bury my nose in her hair and breathe her in. "I'm starving."

"Me, too," Daisy agrees as Abbi fixes her plate. I wander around the island, into the kitchen, and do the same for myself, having a hell of a time doing it one-handed.

"I can do that for you." Abbi moves in to reach for the spoon I'm holding.

God, she looks so tense. Every muscle in her body is tight, and her jaw is clenched, so once she's set Daisy's plate in front of her, I take the spoon from her, set it aside, and just pull Abbi to me, hugging her close and rocking her back and forth.

"Let it go," I whisper into her hair and feel her sag against me. "Let it go, baby. Everything's okay."

She lets out a sob, and then she's crying in earnest, clinging to me almost desperately. I look over at Daisy, who hasn't touched her taco and is watching us with serious brown eyes.

"It's okay," I murmur, still looking at Daisy so she knows that I'm talking to her, too. I nod at her reassuringly, and Daisy's lips tip up into a hesitant smile. "Your mama's just overwhelmed, sweetie. It's okay."

"I'm sorry," Abbi cries against me, sniffling. "It's just been the worst two days of my life. Or, at least, close to that. And then I got that call last night, and I—"

"They shouldn't have called you." I kiss her head again and rub my hand up and down her back. "It wasn't that serious."

"Yes, it was," she disagrees, "and they should have called, but I'd just gotten home from the hospital with Daisy, and it was just bad timing. I didn't handle it well, and I'm sorry."

"You don't need to be sorry."

"Yes, I do." She pulls back and stares up at me with tears running down her sweet cheeks, and it makes my heart ache. "Because you don't need me to be hysterical when *you're* hurt. I need to be the strong one. I need to pull my weight when you can't."

"You're allowed to be scared and worried," I remind her. "And it's okay to cry. I'm just fine."

She nods and wipes at her tears. "I'm not very hungry. I'll fill you in while you eat."

I don't like that she's not going to eat with us, but I'll get something in her later. So, I finish building my taco and sit next to Daisy. Before I pick up my dinner, I lean over and kiss Daisy's head, breathing in her fresh shampoo once more, as if to reassure myself that the kiddo really is safe and sound.

I hate that she got hurt when I wasn't here to help.

"Don't worry, okay?"

"Okay," she says and bites into her taco.

"Tell me what happened yesterday," I say to Abbi as I pick up my taco and take a bite.

"Well, it all started with a freaking nightmare. Then the stupid washing machine." She tells me about finding the flood in her shop and the plumber coming out to take a look. Having to wait for days for parts and then getting the call about Daisy. "I knew she was going to be okay. Lucky didn't sound panicked at all, and I knew that if something catastrophic had happened, Erin would have either called an ambulance or brought her into town herself. So, I didn't panic. I really just felt bad that she hurt herself."

"Falling off of a horse hurts," I say, turning to the little girl, who nods. "They're really tall."

"I *know*," she says. "It felt like I fell forever. And then I reached out with my hand and *owie*."

I nod, understanding all too well what that feels like. My shoulder twinges at the memory.

"Dr. Blackwell was great," Abbi continues.

"I think he liked Mommy," Daisy adds.

"Why do you think that?" I ask as Abbi bites her lip. My eyes narrow on her.

"Because he asked her if she really was with *you*. He smiled at her a lot. He liked her. But I told him that you're *our* Brady, and he was okay with it."

"Why do you sound so grown up?" Abbi asks her.

"Blake Blackwell *hit on you*?"

"Stand down, Cowboy. I only have eyes for you." She smirks and then pulls a piece of meat out of the bowl and pops it into her mouth. "He was *nice* and totally fine when I assured him that I am, in fact, in a committed relationship."

"Good."

"So, all of this was happening, and I still had laundry piling up at the shop, and my original plan of bringing Daisy back with me while I did it was thwarted because she needed to be at home to rest, so I decided to do it all here. I called Millie and asked for her help, and she was awesome about it. But just before I was about to head out the door to collect said laundry, I got the call."

Her gaze falls to the countertop, and the smile from a moment ago is gone.

"And it scared ten years off my life." She clears her throat. "I had a sinking feeling in my gut all day. Like something bad was going to happen, and it was driving me nuts. After each thing, I'd think, was *that* the thing? But no, the feeling never left. I guess things happen in threes. Four, this time, if you count the nightmare."

"I'm sorry, sweetheart."

"It's not your fault. Okay, your turn. What the heck happened out there?"

"Yeah," Daisy echoes. "What happened?"

I push my empty plate away. "Can we sit in the living room? It's more comfortable."

"Oh! Of course. Do you need some ice for that shoulder?"

"That would be good."

"I need ice, too, Mama," Daisy says, and for the next ten minutes, Abbi gets us situated in the living room with ice packs. "Sit with me, Brady."

Daisy snuggles up with me on the couch, and Abbi sits across from us in the rocking chair. It's then it hits me that I'm so *relieved* to be home.

"Okay, tell us the story," Abbi says.

"Well, it all started with a bull." I grin at her, but she doesn't smile back. "I didn't have my rope with me. I forgot it in the truck, so I had to use someone else's."

"All of this because of a *rope*?" Abbi demands.

"We have routines. I have a rope that I prefer. I feel confident in how it feels in my hand. It's familiar."

"Okay, I get that."

"I knew as soon as that chute opened that it wasn't going to be a good ride. You always know. I was right. I made it just under five seconds before I lost my grip and was thrown off. I couldn't roll the way I wanted, and my shoulder and head took the brunt of it. Knocked me out for a second, and the cowboys had to pull me out of the way of the bull."

Abbi covers her face with her hands. *This* is why I don't ever want her near an arena. She doesn't need to see that.

"Still," she says after taking a breath, "five seconds is a long time."

"Anything less than eight seconds is failure," I reply,

sounding harsher than I mean to. “My standings are still fine for now, but I’m not happy. I have to sit out for at least three weeks.”

“*Only* three weeks?” she asks.

“You don’t get it. I’m not even allowed to practice for those three weeks while I heal. I’ll be rusty, and my body won’t know what to do. This isn’t good.”

“Muscle memory is a thing,” she reminds me.

Daisy’s snoring against me, and I grin at Abbi. “We bored her.”

“She’s tired. She was uncomfortable all night with that brace on.”

I frown and kiss Daisy’s head. “In the future, if either of you gets hurt while I’m gone, I want to know *immediately.*”

“Brady—”

“No argument. You two are my world, and if something’s wrong, I need to know. Not after I ride and not the next day. Understand?”

She lets out a gusty breath but reluctantly nods. “Yeah.”

“And if you have a bad feeling, just talk to me, baby.”

“I already felt like I was too needy yesterday, texting you all day.”

“You’re never too much. I want to know what’s going on in that gorgeous head of yours. I’m always available to you, no matter where I am or what I’m doing.”

She smiles softly. “Thank you.”

“Now, tell me about the nightmare.”

Her eyes widen, and she almost shrinks into herself, against the chair.

"Baby, tell me."

She swallows hard. "There was a home I was in that refused to let me eat."

You have got to be *fucking kidding me.*

"Because I'm fat," she continues softly so she doesn't wake Daisy.

"You are *not* fat."

"I've always been curvy, to different degrees. I'm bigger now because of being pregnant with Daisy and hormones, but anyway, I was a larger kid. And this particular house didn't like it. So, they withheld food. Oh, and I wasn't allowed to use towels in the bathroom."

It takes me a second to wade through the red-hot fury swimming in my head before I understand her last sentence.

"Wait, what? What in the hell were you supposed to use?"

"My clothes." She shrugs, her eyes so fucking sad that I want to pull her close to me. But I have Daisy in my arms.

"Abbi." I clear my throat. "You will never have to worry about anything like that ever again. Never."

"I know," she says with a nod.

"Even if something happened to *us*, I would make sure that you're safe and taken care of."

Her throat works as she fights tears. "I know that it's all in the past. It just fucks with me. And then I woke up in a strange place, and—"

"Why didn't you call me?"

"Because I woke you up in a drunken stupor six hours before that." She tries to smile at me. "You were working and needed to sleep."

"You're *always* the most important thing."

"I love you, too. Okay, enough about that. So, we get you for three whole uninterrupted weeks?"

"Looks that way."

"I'm not mad about that."

CHAPTER TWENTY

ABBI

"It's been a goddamn week," Brady grumbles in that sexy, sleepy voice he gets in the morning. His face is pressed to my neck, and he's kissing me right where he knows that I can't resist. My core tightens, and I want to push back against his hard cock, but I control myself.

"*Only* a week," I remind him and shimmy around to face him so I can look into his gorgeous hazel eyes. "Your shoulder isn't ready for vigorous activity, horny man."

"Fuck my shoulder."

I smirk and cup his cheek, loving the way he's looking at me. "No, that's not the part that I'd like to fuck right now."

Brady groans. "You're killing me, Blue Eyes. I." He kisses my nose. "Want." Kisses my forehead. "You."

I bite his chin and urge him onto his back. "If we're going to do this, *I'm* doing the work."

"That's not how I like things to roll, and you know it."

“Take it or leave it.”

He narrows his eyes at me, but he doesn’t stop me as I kiss my way down his hard, sculpted torso and grip his already hard cock in my fist, pumping up and down. I know that Brady likes to be in control when we make love, but I won’t take the chance of his shoulder being hurt more than it is. The bruising on it is startling, but it’s finally fading to a sickly green.

Which tells me that the rest is helping.

“Baby, you touch me so good.” He drags his thumb across my bottom lip, and I lick it before pulling it into my mouth to suck on the tip, making his jaw clench.

“Mm,” I agree and rub my nose around his navel. “Love touching you, Cowboy.”

The word *cowboy* has his cock twitching in my hand, and I grin against him. His good hand is in my hair, brushing through the strands as I kiss his hip, and then drag my tongue down that long line that makes one side of the V at his pelvis.

That V makes my mouth water.

“Shit,” he mutters. “Ride me, baby.”

“You’ll hold on to me,” I reply, slowly shaking my head. “And we can’t have that.”

“I will spank your ass if you don’t ride my cock, Abbi.”

I grin up at him and, without further ado, lick over the crown of his cock, and Brady sucks a sharp breath through his teeth.

“Ah, fuck.”

"Still gonna spank me?" I sink over him, taking him all the way to the back of my throat.

"Yes." But his hand fists in my hair and holds me where I am. "Later. Much later."

I moan around him and work him up and down. His hips move with me, and he's making the most delicious noises as I take my time with him.

"I'm going to come, baby." He pulls on my hair, trying to get me to move off of him, but I stay firm and tighten my lips around his shaft, wanting to taste him. "Ah, shit, Abs. Shit."

He comes, letting go in my mouth, and I lap him up. And then, as he's panting and watching me with bright hazel eyes, I pad into the bathroom to wash my hands.

When I return, he's sitting on the edge of the bed, watching me.

"I don't just want you to blow me, babe. Not that it isn't the best fucking blow job of my life, and you're a goddamn goddess for doing it, but I need to be inside of you. I need *all of you.*"

"I know, but you're too...*active* when we have sex, and you have to take it easy. I need you healthy."

He wraps his arms around my legs, his hands cupping my ass as he pulls me to him.

"And you should be wearing your sling," I add, but he leans in and plants a kiss on my belly, and my hands instinctively dive into his hair. "How's your headache?"

"No more headache," he murmurs against my skin. "And tonight, I'm making love to you. I'm going to sink inside of you and feel you come on my cock. We'll make it work."

I grin and bend over to kiss his hair. "Okay. I miss you, too. What are you doing today?"

"Daisy and I are going to the ranch."

"Brady—"

"Don't start," he says, shaking his head as I back away. "We're not going to work, and neither one of us will get on a horse, but we miss it out there, okay? And I need to check in with the utilities people for our property."

Our property.

Those words send a shot of electricity through me, and I feel giddy. I can't *wait* to live on the ranch with Brady and my daughter. On *our* property. Not Brady's family's homestead, where Daisy and I get to live, but *ours*. It's the best feeling in the world, and it's something that I never dared to wish for. People like me, where I come from, don't get to live on beautiful ranches with the best views in the world.

"What just went through that gorgeous head?" Brady asks.

"Nothing." But I smile at him, and he tips my chin up so he can cover my lips with his. "You promise you won't do anything stupid?"

"Of course, I won't do anything stupid. Daisy will babysit me."

I smirk at that and lean down to kiss him. "I don't mean to be a nag. I just want you better."

"You're not a nag." He chuckles when I lift an

eyebrow at him. "Okay, you're not *much* of one. I'd do the same if the tables were turned, which they'd never *be* turned because I would lose my mind if you were injured."

I kiss him again and then pull away to get ready for work.

I'm still swamped and buried in the never-ending laundry, but at least I was able to fill the empty housekeeping positions, so I can stay at the shop and focus on catching up. Hopefully, I'll be recovered from the chaos in the next day or two.

Daisy wanders down the stairs, rubbing her eyes, as I pour myself a cup of coffee and pull together some things for lunch.

"Good morning," I say to her as she wraps her arms around my waist and hugs me close. "How did you sleep, babes?"

"Fine," she says. "Can I have cereal?"

"Sure."

"I've got this," Brady says with a wink. "You head off for work."

"You sure?" He smirks and turns his back on me to pull a bowl down for Daisy, and I shrug a shoulder. "I guess you're sure. Give me a kiss."

Daisy tips her lips up, and I press them to my cheek, and then Brady's there, offering me his lips, too, which I buss with my own.

"Have a good day, Blue Eyes."

"You guys, too. Stay out of trouble."

THERE'S a light at the end of this wet, dark, annoying tunnel.

For the first time in almost two weeks, I have the last load of sheets in the dryer. My arms are so *sore* from all the lifting and moving and sorting, not to mention the folding, but I've reached the bottom of the pile. Finally getting the washer fixed a few days ago made all of the difference.

Of course, my crew is about to get here with today's dirty laundry, but it'll finally be a manageable amount that, with my machines, should only take a couple of hours.

And I can do that in the morning.

At last, I'm back on schedule! It feels so good, I could cry.

With the work day almost finished, I clean the office, both the front area where my desk is and the workroom, with the washers and dryers, tables for folding, and all the shelving where the linens sit, waiting for the next day.

After my crew drops off their supplies and today's laundry, they head out for the day, and I'm just about to lock the door when a woman comes sauntering in.

She's beautiful. Taller than me, with long dark hair and olive skin. Her eyes are also dark, and her complexion is flawless. She's willowy thin and is wearing tight jeans with a tucked-in cami, and her laser-sharp gaze finds mine.

"Wow," she says, looking me up and down. I wouldn't say she's watching me with appreciation.

I instantly don't like her.

"Uh, hello. Can I help you?"

"I wanted to come in and see you for myself." She nods as she walks closer to my desk. "That Rancher ad is impressive, and I can see that they did you justice."

What Rancher ad?

I frown up at her and purse my lips.

"Ah, you haven't seen it yet," she says with a smug smile. "Don't worry, it's a good one. Of course, Brady looks good enough to eat. He always does. That man is *delicious,* with a cock that makes a girl just about beg for it."

"Who are you?" I'm no longer perplexed. Now, I'm pissed.

"Jen," she says and doesn't hold out her hand. "And you're the bitch he dumped me for."

My mind whirls and then goes back to that night before Christmas when Brady came to the house and admitted that he'd been to his fuck buddy's place before he found his way to me.

And all I can do is grin.

He came to *me.*

"From what I hear," I say as I prop my hands on my hips, "it wasn't really a *dumping.* I didn't think fuck buddies could be *dumped.*"

Her eyes narrow, and her lips firm in agitation before she looks me up and down again, disgust written all over her face.

"If he wanted to leave my bed and move on to a fat-ass like you, I guess that tells me all I need to know about his taste."

Yeah, it hits the mark. But I just laugh at her again because this bitch will never see that she hurt my feelings.

"You know, it occurs to me that he stopped fucking you months ago. Why are you coming in here now? Our relationship isn't a secret."

Jen doesn't lose that look of disgust. I suspect it's on her face all the time, not just when she's looking at me. "I didn't buy that it would last. Then I saw the ad."

With one last look, she spins on her heel and strides away.

As soon as the door closes behind her, I open my laptop and search for the newest ad and sit back, watching it.

I remember not long after the shoot, they set Brady up in a sound booth and asked him to record some lines for it so they could play his voice in the background. And I'm surprised to see that the ad runs for a minute and thirty seconds.

That's a long-ass commercial.

"Here in Montana, we do things a little differently," Brady's voice fills the room as images from the ranch come on screen. The men fixing the fence, laughing with each other. Brady leading Blackjack around the arena, smiling up at him.

Of course, there are plenty of images of his ass in those jeans, and that makes my mouth water.

Brady doing just about *anything* makes my mouth water, but he looks particularly hot in this commercial.

"Family isn't just meeting up for Thanksgiving dinner or saying hello at a wedding. Family is a way of life. A promise."

And now, I'm choked up as Brady and his dad fill the screen, and then his siblings, all sitting on the fence line. *Here at the Wild River Ranch, we take pride in our history. Of how our ancestors worked this land, long before we were here. They paved the way for us to succeed, far beyond their wildest imaginations. I like knowing that we live on the wild side here, taking what comes and not letting the small stuff bother us too much. It's a quiet way of life that we plan to pass on to those who come after we're long gone.* With twenty seconds left to go, my tears dry up, and I stare in shock as I watch myself walk over to Brady in the arena, and he bends down to kiss me. His arms flex as they come around my waist, and he's watching me with eyes so full of love that it takes my breath away.

I don't remember taking his hat and putting it on my head, but I do, and now we're laughing together.

"We live this life because we love it, who we are because of it, and those who care about us despite it. Bitterroot Valley, Montana is where my heart lives."

The image shifts to the barn at the end of the day as soft music plays. Brady's brushing Blackjack, then leads him into his stall and kisses his nose.

And there is my daughter, running to greet Brady. Every part of me goes cold.

"Please don't show her face," I murmur, watching

closely. "Please, for fuck's sake, do *not* show my daughter's face."

But she turns and smiles up at me, and there she is. For all the world to see.

For all the goddamn world to see.

And my heart starts to hammer in my chest. Without another thought, I pick up my phone to call Brady. To rail at him. How could he do this without checking with me first? He has no idea the danger he just put us in.

We have to move, is all I can think. I have to go straight home and pack our things and get us the hell out of here.

Before I can dial his number, Erin's calling.

"Hey," I say, trying to act casual. "I can't talk long."

"You need to come to the ranch," she says. "We all just saw the commercial, and everyone is pissed off. No one gave permission for them to use you, Daisy, or anyone else's faces in the ad, and the men are on the warpath."

Thank God. Brady didn't know.

"I just saw it." I swallow hard, trying to calm down despite the panic making its way through my body. The panic attack is *right there*, and I need to keep it at bay. "It's a beautiful commercial, but yeah. I wasn't expecting that."

"We're all here, Abbi. Even Chase is leaving work early to come here. We're making a big dinner, and we can all be together to discuss the next steps. Trust me, this wasn't on purpose. As a mom, I'd be freaking *pissed*."

"Yeah. Yeah, okay." We'll be safe on the ranch, and

then I can figure out what to do next. "I'll be there in thirty."

I lock the door and hurry out to my car, and as I'm driving out to the ranch, Brady calls.

"Hey," I say as I answer.

"Baby, I'm *so sorry*. I didn't know that they were going to put you and Daisy in that fucking commercial."

"We'll talk about it when I get there." I swallow hard. Shit, I'm going to have to tell them everything. I don't have a choice. "It's going to be okay."

But I don't believe that. I don't believe for a second that everything's going to be okay after this.

"Wait. How did you know about it?"

I clear my throat. "Your old pal *Jen* came into my office to check me out and told me about it."

"Fuck." His voice is tired and irritated. "I'll take care of her."

"She was also sure to make it clear that you left *her* for a fat-ass bitch."

He snarls as I blink quickly, fighting the tears that want to come.

"Quite a nice girl you had there, Cowboy."

"Fuck that and fuck her. I'll take care of her, baby."

"I did that myself. She won't make any more trouble."

"Are you almost here?" he asks.

"Yeah, five minutes."

"Okay, babe. Love you."

He clicks off, and I want to succumb to the tears. He *loves me*. And I love him so much, I can't think straight. I don't want to leave him. I don't want to give up this life that Daisy and I have worked so fucking hard for.

But I don't see any other option. Janet will find us, and she'll take Daisy away from me, and that can never happen. It won't happen.

Because I'll disappear again.

I pull up in front of the farmhouse. Before I can even open my door, Brady's rushing out the front door and down the steps to me.

I step out, and then I'm in his arms, and he's holding me tightly, kissing my head.

"I'm so sorry." He kisses my forehead. "About the whole situation, but especially about Jen. She's a mean bitch, Abs, and I'll make sure she knows that she fucked with the wrong girl."

I pat his back, already trying to mentally distance myself from him. God, this is going to be the hardest thing I ever do. "I don't really care about her and her jealousy. It's actually a really beautiful commercial and makes this place, and your family, look amazing."

"But they showed you and Daisy," he murmurs, anguish in every word. "And I didn't say they could do that. Abbi, *I didn't know.*"

"I'm glad to hear that." I step out of his arms, already missing him so much, and try to smile up at him.

"Why are you looking at me like that?" He scowls and frames my face in his hands. "Talk to me, Blue Eyes."

"Let's go inside." Again, I step out of his grasp. "We'll talk everything through."

"Baby, I understand being upset. I know how you feel about Daisy's face being shown."

You don't know. I want to scream it at him. But I just nod and walk ahead of him into the house, where everyone else is already waiting.

"Abbi," Joy says with a bright smile. She hurries to me and wraps me in a hug, and I just want to lean into her and sob.

But I don't.

"We're going to sue the fuck out of them," Ryan says from across the room. His hazel eyes, so much like his brother's, are feral with rage. "By the time I'm done with them, I'll own that entire goddamn company."

I believe him. He will.

"A lot of money is going in the swear jar today," I hear Johnny say to his sister and Daisy, who both nod.

I do believe Ryan, but the damage is already done. I have to hurry up here so I can rush home and get Daisy and me ready to leave. I have no idea where we'll go, but I can't stay here.

It's not safe.

My phone rings, and when I pull it out of my pocket, I see that it's Jerome, my P.I., and I swallow hard but answer.

"Someone fucked up," he says in my ear. It's loud enough that Brady can hear.

"Who is that?" Brady asks, but I shake my head.

"I know," I reply softly. "I'll handle it."

"You need to get the fuck out of there, Abbi."

"Who the *fuck* is that?" Brady demands.

"I'll handle it," I say again and click off, just as Chase approaches me, his face hard.

Oh, God.

"Abbi," Chase says, but Brady puts his hand on Chase's chest, holding him away.

"Mommy?"

"Jake," I say, without taking my eyes off Chase. "Would you please take the little kids outside? Don't go far, okay? And don't take your eyes off of them. That's very important."

"Sure," Jake says. "Come on, you little turds. Let's go find some trouble."

When they're gone, Chase shakes his head at me, and Brady's watching both of us.

"Abbi," Brady says, his voice hard. "I need you to tell me what the fuck is going on."

"First," Chase says, holding up his phone. There's a *Missing Child* image on the screen, with Daisy's smiling face on it. "Tell me what the fuck this is about." His voice is all cop. All ice.

Brady's gaze whips to me, and he backs away as if he's been burned.

My life is falling apart around me, and the panic attack wants to surface, but I swallow and then look around the room.

Erin and Remington, all of my friends, and their husbands. Millie. Their parents. They're all staring at me, waiting for me to talk.

"Did you *kidnap* Daisy?" Brady demands.

"No." It's a whisper, and I rub my hands over my face before Joy jumps in.

"Come on, everyone," Joy says. "Let's sit in the dining room and talk this out. Abbi, it's okay, darling. Let's sit."

I follow the others, and I sit at the end of the table so I can see everyone.

If I have to tell those who mean the most to me that I've been lying to their faces, I'm going to look them in the eyes while I do it.

Brady sits next to me, but he won't touch me. He's iced me out, and that alone shatters my heart.

"I'm going to tell you this story," I say, my voice not wavering, my chin up. "And then I'm going to leave. Daisy and I will disappear."

"Like. Fucking. Hell." Brady's voice is hard, bordering on mean. I reach for his hand, but he pulls back, out of reach.

"Most of you know that my mom died when I was young. I spent my teen years in foster care. It was *not* easy. I was emotionally, physically, and sexually abused."

"Jesus," Chase whispers as Polly covers her mouth with her hands.

"In high school, I made a friend named Nate Channing. He was from the other side of the tracks, so to speak, and he was super smart and really nice to me. Anyway, we were friends all through school. He'd help me with money, especially after I turned eighteen and left the foster home I was living in.

"This is relevant, trust me. When he was in college, we ended up getting pregnant." I swallow hard. "On accident, of course. He wanted to do the right thing and marry me, and I agreed. His parents did *not* like me. Not at all. Not even a little."

"Assholes," Millie mutters.

"What I haven't told you is that Nate had an older sister, Natalie. She died before he was born, but that death kind of sent his mom into a bad mental space. And when I had Daisy, my daughter looked a lot like Natalie."

"Oh, shit," Ryan says.

"Yeah. She was convinced that Daisy was *her* daughter. She went mad with it. She'd steal Daisy away and wouldn't give her back, and we'd have to call the police. She tried suing us for custody several times. If it weren't for Nate's dad, she would have yanked all the money out from under us so we'd have no choice but to come to her for help."

"She's a fucking peach," John says, his eyes narrowed.

"It gets worse." I have to stand and pace, ignoring the look on Brady's face as he watches me. He's not cold now. He's *livid.* And hurt. "Nate got sick right before Daisy turned two. Pneumonia that turned septic and killed him. The last thing I promised him was that his mother would *never* get her hands on our daughter."

I look at the others again.

"She tried. When I was at the hospital with Nate, as he was *dying*, she showed up at the daycare center and tried to take Daisy. Thank God the girls there knew the situation, and she didn't get away with it. I didn't even get to attend my husband's funeral because I was too busy packing what little we had and fleeing. I hired a PI —that's who called just now—who fills me in if things change with Janet, and every time she starts to figure out where we are, I change our last name and move."

"I don't even know your name," Brady says with hot steel in his voice. "Jesus Christ, I love you. I want to build a *life* with you, and I don't even know your goddamn name."

"Abbi *is* my name. It would get too complicated to change our first names all the time."

But he lifts his eyes to mine, and the devastation there almost brings me to my knees.

"You told me," he says and then has to swallow hard, "that if you ever didn't feel safe, you'd tell me and let me help you."

"I wish I could do that." I lick my lips and turn my attention back to Chase. "I didn't steal Daisy. She's mine, and I've never lost custody of her."

"Then why run?" Summer asks with a frown. "If you legally didn't do anything wrong, why run away?"

"You don't understand." With a sigh, I sit heavily back in my chair. "Nate's parents weren't just wealthy, they were *fucking rich.* I had a little money from Nate, but Janet has millions at her disposal, along with a small-town sheriff and politicians, and I'm...nobody."

"I'll fucking bury her," Ryan says, and it makes my chest warm. "I'll make her wish she was never born."

"This isn't your fight." I smile sadly and turn to Brady. "I'm very sorry for the lies. I wanted to tell you, but I couldn't risk that she'd find us. That's why I never share photos of Daisy. I look a lot different than I did back then."

"How so?" Erin asks.

"I let my hair go back to blonde. This is my natural color, but Nate liked it dark. And I've gained some weight. Before the baby, I was smaller. Add in hormones and a baby, and well..." I shrug. "I'm curvier. I don't really dress the same. But Daisy is Daisy, and it's not like I'm going to make her dye her hair or something."

"I can't believe this." Brady leans forward, rubbing his forehead with his fingertips. "I don't know your goddamn *name*."

"He's malfunctioning," Chase says to Rem, who just nods slowly.

"Abbi Sue Palmer is my maiden name," I reply. "Kastella was my grandmother's maiden name."

"You've been my friend for a while now," Erin says. "You know that this family, my family in Seattle, we all would have helped you. She may have money, but so do *we*, Abbi. Have you met Ryan? My father? Just about everyone in this room? Hell, even London Montgomery. You have resources."

"This is *my* mess," I insist, but she just rolls her eyes. "I know it's hard to understand. I was scared of her. I *am* scared of her. Terrified, actually."

"Is this what you have nightmares about?" Brady asks, interrupting, his eyes hot. God, I fucking *hate* the way he's looking at me. "When you wake up screaming, in a panic, and you say you can't find Daisy?"

I nod and press my lips together, and Brady's chair scrapes back as he shoves to his feet.

"I need a minute."

"Brady—"

He puts his hand up and looks me in the eye now. "I love you, but I need a fucking minute."

He slams out of the house, leaving silence in his wake.

Finally, I clear my throat. "I need to go."

"You're not running away," Ryan says, his voice hard but calm.

"Not a chance," Chase agrees, while the others nod in agreement.

"Yeah, I am. Listen, I love you all." Now the tears come, and I swallow hard again. I can't dislodge this lump in my throat. "I love your family so much, and the last thing in the world I want is to have to say goodbye to you. But I can't lead her to your doorstep. You may be able to fight her, but she'll cause so much chaos in the process that I just can't do that to you. She's not just mentally ill, she's...evil."

I stand now and wipe the tears from my cheeks.

"Thank you for everything you've done for us."

I turn and walk out the back door, looking for my daughter. She's playing with the other kids, laughing and singing with them. God, she loves it here so much. These are her best friends. This is *her* family.

"Come on, babes. We have to get home."

"But we haven't had dinner," she says with a frown that reminds me so much of her father's.

"I know, but I'll feed you at home."

"Is Brady coming?"

"No. Come on, and don't sass me. I'm not in the mood."

Daisy frowns, but she doesn't say anything as I lead her to the car and help her get buckled in. I'm not usually short with my daughter like that, but I *have* to go before I break down into a sobbing mess and accept any help that the Wild family is willing to give me. Before I scream for Brady to hold me and tell me that everything is going to work out.

Because it's *not* going to work out. I *want* to accept their help. I know that they all have more money than Janet and that they could squish her like a bug, but I don't know how to depend on people like that. I've always depended on myself, and it's time that I remember that.

We're quiet in the car on the way into town, and once we're in the house, I tell Daisy to go to her room and choose her favorite things to pack.

"No." She watches me with wide, brown eyes. "No, Mama."

My girl is smart, and she remembers more than I give her credit for.

"Baby, we have to go." I don't know what I'll do about this house and the business, but I'll figure it out when we get wherever we're going.

"No." She shakes her head, and tears fill her sweet eyes. "We need to *stay*. I don't want to move again. Please don't make us go. We have Brady. What about Brady?"

I close my eyes and sigh. I should have known better than to get too comfortable. To fall in love and let my daughter fall in love, too.

I've royally fucked all of this up.

"Daisy, I'm sorry. I'm *so* sorry my love, but it's not safe for us here anymore."

"Brady will protect us," she says, propping her fists on her hips. "We're safe with him."

Before I can argue, the doorbell rings.

It has to be Brady. I don't want to see him and have to tell him all over again that we can't be together. It's only going to make this so much harder. Jesus, I don't know if I can recover from this.

With another heavy sigh, I walk to the door and open it.

"Oh, God." Crazy eyes stare back at me.

"Where's my daughter?"

CHAPTER TWENTY-ONE
BRADY

"You've got to be fucking kidding me," I mutter as I brush Blackjack. "She's been lying to me since the day I met her, boy. How can I even know her, *really* know her, if I don't know her name?"

He blows out a breath and nudges my shoulder, hoping for an apple.

"Exactly, I can't. I've held her while she screams and cries and has a breakdown about night terrors that I thought were about the bullshit she went through as a teenager." I shake my head and move around to the other side of the horse. "And maybe there was some of that laced in there, but it was really about shit that I didn't even know about. Because she didn't tell me."

My heart won't quit hammering. From the minute she got out of that car this afternoon, my heart has been hammering like a jackhammer. And when I saw that missing person's poster on Chase's phone, I thought I was going to come out of my skin.

"How am I supposed to help her, when I don't even know what's going on? I can't protect her like this. What else is she hiding from me, for fuck's sake?"

She told me that she had secrets. She never lied about that, but I thought that over the past couple of months, we'd worked our way through them.

We've been living like a motherfucking *family* for weeks. I have house plans, and the septic has already been dug and set where I plan to build her a house, for the love of God.

Everything I've done has been with her in mind, and she's been *lying*.

"Sure, she was scared," I concede as I pull an apple out of a barrel and hold it out for the horse to munch on. "And I get that she could have some trust issues with the past that she has. But Jesus Christ, this is *me*. I'm supposed to be her safe place. I'm supposed to be the one that she can count on for anything.

"I thought she was that for me, and now I don't know. I felt so guilty over that stupid commercial, and now my whole fucking world has fallen apart." I lean my forehead on Blackjack's neck and take a breath. "She talked about leaving, and I can't have that happen. Because as fucking pissed off as I am right now, I love her. I can't do this life without her. We'll figure the crazy lady out because she is *not* leaving."

I hear footsteps behind me, and hope fills me that it might be Abbi, but when I spin around, I find Rem, Ryan, Chase, and Millie watching me.

"I know," I say before they can speak. "I shouldn't

have walked out, but I was about to say some shit that I couldn't take back, and I needed a minute."

"I get it," Millie says. "As long as you're not going to do something stupid and give up on her or something."

"No. I don't think that's possible. She's my heart, beating outside of my chest."

I look at the four of them and shove my hands into my pockets.

"I've already figured out who this *Janet* person is," Ryan informs me. "It'll be taken care of."

"You're kind of scary, Ry."

"I know." He doesn't smile at me.

"If she'd just said something a year ago, it would all be over by now," Chase says, shaking his head.

"She doesn't trust people very easily. Even when she loves them," Remington replies. "And, with all of the shit she's been through, I can see why. We'll just have to keep showing her why she *can* trust us."

"How is she?" I ask, kicking a rock. "Is she okay? Is she crying? Shit, I should get back in there."

"She's gone," Millie replies. "She scooped up Daisy and left."

"What the fuck do you mean, *she's gone?*"

"She's pretty insistent that she doesn't want us to help her," Ryan says. "She says that she won't bring that mess here, so she's planning to skip town with Daisy and run."

"And you *let her go*?" I stare at Chase. "You fucking let her go?"

"She hasn't done anything wrong," he replies. "The missing person's bulletin is trash. So, she changed a name here and there; it's not illegal. She is free to go wherever she pleases."

"Fuck that." I push through them, ready to go to war to make sure Abbi does *not* leave. "I have to go get her."

"Good luck," Millie calls after me.

"I'll be behind you," Chase adds. "I have to stop at the station and then get Abbi's official statement so I can resolve the missing child bulletin that was sent here."

I've never driven into town so fast, and I curse a blue streak when I get stopped at a red light in town, but then I'm off and running again and pull into Abbi's driveway behind her SUV.

I ring the doorbell, but no one answers.

"Come on, Blue Eyes," I call out. "Answer this door!"

Still nothing, so I unlock it and walk right in.

And then feel my blood go cold. Standing in the middle of the living room is a middle-aged woman with wild eyes, holding on to Daisy as if she's a lifeline.

Daisy's crying, and Abbi's face is sheet white.

"Sorry to interrupt," I say, keeping my voice casual. "I didn't realize you had company."

"You *bitch*," Janet bites out as she cradles Daisy and runs her hand down the little girl's hair. "How *dare* you steal my daughter?"

"Mommy," Daisy cries.

"Shh," Janet says. "I'm right here. Mommy's here."

That only makes Daisy cry harder.

"Hello?" I walk around the woman so she has to look at me. "Hi. I'm Brady. You must be Janet. I've heard a lot about you."

Sure, it's all recent, but I've heard a lot, nonetheless.

"Good, you're here," Janet says. "Call the police. I've finally found my daughter, and this little bitch needs to be arrested."

She's pointing at Abbi.

"Janet, you know that isn't true," Abbi says, keeping her voice soft. "You remember that Nate and I had a little girl, Daisy. This is *Daisy*, not Natalie."

"You're *lying*!" Janet screams, and Daisy wails with her. "This is my baby. My little baby."

I hold my hand out without looking her way, and Abbi slides her hand into mine, palm to palm, and closes her fingers tightly.

"Janet, a policeman will be here shortly to help us straighten all of this out."

"Do you know what she is?" Janet asks, gesturing to Abbi with her chin. "She's a lowlife. She trapped my son into a marriage. He didn't know what he was doing. She used her tits and her cunt to lure my poor boy in."

Janet's crying now, and I'm seeing nothing but red.

"That's not true," Abbi whispers.

"Chase is coming," I murmur to her and squeeze her hand reassuringly.

"And now she's found herself another rich man," Janet continues. "A *rodeo* god. What a joke. You're all a joke. And I refuse to let you have my daughter for even a moment more."

Daisy is just whimpering now, not even fighting to get away from Janet. I don't care if the crazy old bitch talks all night now that her grip on my kid has loosened.

"Janet," I begin and lick my lips, "would you mind if we set Daisy on the couch where she'll be more comfortable?"

"No." Her grip tightens, and Daisy whimpers. "You'll take her. You're all trying to take her."

"Janet." My voice is hard now, no more Mister Nice Guy. Her head whips up as if I slapped her across the face. "If you don't take your motherfucking hands off of my daughter right now, you're going to regret it."

Janet blinks and then frowns down at Daisy, but her grip has loosened, and she looks back at me. "Who are you?"

"I'm her daddy. Now, please hand her to me."

"Oh." With a scowl, she crosses over, and I take Daisy from her, relieved when the little girl buries her face in my neck and holds on. My shoulder *sings* from the weight of Daisy, but I don't give a flying fuck. "But she's *my* baby."

"No." Abbi's voice is full of rage now that Daisy is safe. "This is *Daisy*, your granddaughter. Not Natalie."

Janet is crying hysterically and sinks onto the floor, her arms wrapped around her middle, rocking as if to soothe herself.

And Chase walks through the open door.

"Just in time," I tell him. "That's Janet. She was trying to take Daisy."

"I just want my baby," she cries. "I want my Natalie. Where's my baby?"

"Jesus." Chase pulls his hand down his face. "I'll call for the ambulance. She'll be going to a psych ward."

"You've got this?" I ask him.

"Yeah," he says with a nod. "Get them out of here."

With Abbi's hand still in mine, and Daisy in my arms, I march us outside to my 4Runner.

"I'm taking you to my cabin."

Abbi crawls into the back seat with Daisy, cuddling her as close and as hard as she can while I drive us back out to the ranch. I keep checking them in the rearview mirror, and as Abbi has a small panic attack, Daisy holds her tiny fingers up so Abbi can blow them out like candles.

It's the sweetest and most heart-wrenching thing I've ever seen in my fucking life.

"Do you want the cabin, or do you want Erin?" I ask her after she takes a long, deep breath.

"Cabin," she whispers. "Please."

With a nod, I turn toward my little place and get them both inside and onto the couch, where they stay huddled up together.

"Baby." I press my hand against Abbi's cheek. "It's done. She can't hurt either of you ever again. I'll make sure of it. It's all done."

Abbi watches me with wide blue eyes brimming with huge, unshed tears.

"How can that be? It happened so fast. I've been protecting Daisy from her for *years.*"

"I know."

Daisy's face is pressed to Abbi's chest, and it looks like she's fallen asleep, likely from the exhaustion of everything that's happened over the last hour.

"I'm so s-s-sorry." Abbi dabs at the tears on her cheeks. "I wanted to tell you so many times, but I couldn't risk her. I just couldn't, Brady."

"Hey." I lean in and press my lips to her forehead, breathing her in. "I asked you before if your secrets would hurt my family."

"I don't have any more secrets," she assures me.

"But you lied."

That has her stopping and staring at me. "I didn't lie about that."

"Yes, you did, because this secret *did* hurt my family. You and Daisy *are* my family. You're part of *my whole* family, too, and this hurt all of us."

"Brady." Her voice is a whisper as she grips my shirt. "I guess you're right because you're *my* family, too. You're ours. But when I promised you that, we weren't what we are now."

"Maybe not for *you*." I grin when she gulps. "I know you well enough to understand why you couldn't tell us, but, baby, that was one hell of a bomb to drop."

"Yeah. Pretty dramatic, huh?"

"Pretty fucking dramatic."

"Swear jar," Daisy whispers, making me chuckle. She doesn't even open her eyes or move away from her mom, but she's obviously been listening.

"Would you have really left me?" I ask her as I drag

my knuckles down her cheek, then brush her soft blonde hair behind her ear.

"Yes." Her lip wobbles. "If it meant keeping Daisy safe, I would have. Although, Daisy and I were fighting about it when Ja—*she* rang the doorbell because Daisy was having none of it."

"That's my girl." I brush my hand over Daisy's hair. "My sweet princess. I want you to know that I would have followed you, and *I* would have found you. There is no world where you run from me, Abbi. You're it for me. You are the love of my life, and I plan to make a home and a family with you out here. No crazy broad is going to ruin that for us. Not today or any other day."

She sniffs and turns her face so she can kiss my palm. "I panicked. I can admit that now. I'd let my guard down for so many months and had become so comfortable in our life here, and when that threat showed up again, every instinct told me to run, to protect my girl."

"And from now on, you run *to me*, and we figure it out together, no matter what it is. You do *not* run away from me."

Abbi nods. "Cowboy?"

"Yes, Blue Eyes?"

"I love you. Forever. And I won't run ever again."

"Good." I kiss her cheek and then her lips, and I slip beside her, pulling her against my side so I'm snuggling both of my girls, and this is where we stay for quite a while.

Until Chase comes calling, and then chaos ensues once more as we're called back to the farmhouse so my girls can be fussed over, and Chase can ask Abbi some questions.

"It's over," Chase informs Abbi. "She'll be moved to a psychiatric hospital in North Carolina. Her husband is on his way to collect her."

"He doesn't want to see Daisy, does he?" Abbi asks, fear moving over her face once more as she looks at the ceiling, where Daisy is in Holly's room, playing.

"No," Chase replies, shaking his head. "He didn't say a word about Daisy."

"What will happen to them?" Joy asks. "If she's as mentally unstable as you say, Chase, what will happen next?"

"They'll escort her to her home state, and she'll be admitted. I'm no doctor, but based on what I saw, it wouldn't surprise me if she's committed for the rest of her life. But, just in case, we'll file a restraining order, and if she does ever come out of the hospital, she'll face charges of trespassing, attempted kidnapping, and a whole host of things. Basically, she'll spend the rest of her life pretty miserable."

"Good." Abbi deflates in relief. "I'm sorry for all the drama, you guys."

"Are you kidding?" Millie grins as she sips her beer. "We love some good drama. We'll be telling this story for generations."

"So, Abbi," Remington says, catching our attention. "Do you still plan to move away?"

I start to speak, but Abbi shuts me up by pressing her hand to my mouth, making my family laugh.

"No," she finally says, as if she's really thinking it over, and then she grins. "I'm already home. Right here, at this ranch, with these amazing people."

I kiss her palm and then move her hand aside. "Damn right, you are."

CHAPTER TWENTY-TWO

BRADY

"Where are my girls?" The townhouse is still as I push inside and then drop my bag on the floor by the front door. I had to stay the night in Oregon last night, rather than heading right back home, but it's Saturday morning, and they should be here.

So much has happened in the past month since everything came to a head with Janet, and Abbi's past was finally put to rest.

The man who attacked Abbi in the condo all those months ago is officially back in federal prison, where he belongs. He won't have the possibility of hurting another woman for more than twenty years, and Ryan made sure that the father wouldn't be able to pay off another judge.

Rancher Jeans was sued by Wild Industries, and they settled out of court for two million dollars, and, in exchange, they got to keep the commercial. Every dime from that settlement went into a trust for Daisy.

I'm back to riding and don't actually feel too bad. I'll

get through the rest of the season, and then I'll propose to Abbi. I need to officially close that other door before I can ask her to take that last step with me.

But our house is framed in and should be finished by spring.

Now, I just need to see my girls.

"Ladies?" I call out, but the house is quiet.

There's no one here.

My gut tightens, and I pull out my phone, dialing Abbi's number. She answers on the third ring.

"Hello?"

"Where are you guys?"

"We're at the ranch. Wait, where are *you*?"

I shake my head and walk back out, headed for my 4Runner. "I'm at home, Blue Eyes."

"Well, shit, I wasn't expecting you for a few more hours."

"Swear jar," I hear Daisy say, and it makes me grin.

I've already pulled out of the driveway and am headed to the ranch when I say, "Are you at the farmhouse?"

"Huh? Oh, no. We're at *our* house. There's no crew today because it's Sunday, so Daisy and I brought a picnic breakfast up here."

My heart stalls in my chest. Just when I think I can't love her any more than I already do...

"Baby, you're having breakfast at the new house?"

"Yeah. We love it here, Cowboy. Hurry up and join us. There's plenty to go around."

"I'll be there soon."

It actually takes me nine minutes to pull up to a stop in front of the house. The driveway has been built already, so it's easier to get out here than it used to be.

The house is just a frame, but my girls don't mind. Abbi has spread a blanket on the ground about twenty yards from the house, and there's a big basket open beside her. It looks like they're eating bagels and cream cheese.

"Daddy!" Daisy jumps up and runs to me, launching herself into my arms. "You're finally home."

"Yeah, I am." I kiss her sweet cheek. God, I love her. Since that day a month ago, Daisy has called me Daddy.

And I'll never tell her to call me anything else.

"Hey," Abbi says with a sweet grin as she stands to greet me. "I'm sorry we didn't wait for you."

"I'm just happy you were still here." I set Daisy down, kick off my boots, and join them on the blanket. Abbi pours me some juice and passes me half of her bagel, and then the three of us chew while looking out at the mountains. At the land. The cows and the red barn off in the distance. I plan to see this exact view, every day, for the rest of my life, with Abbi by my side.

I glance her way and find her smiling at me.

"What?"

"You look so good out here. Such a cowboy, right at home on his ranch."

"I look good here because *you're* with me. Both of you. You're my home."

Daisy smiles and reaches over to pat my arm.

"When can we sleep here?" she asks me.

"Not for a long time. Probably next spring. But we can come out here whenever we want to."

"Okay." She shrugs a shoulder and eats her last bite of bagel. "Where will we put my cows?"

"One cow," Abbi says, but I just chuckle.

This girl can have all the damn cows she wants.

"We'll build a small barn with a fenced-in pasture over there." I point to the south. "They'll live there."

"That's right by our house!" Daisy is obviously happy with this plan. "Can I have chickens?"

"Sure."

"*Brady.*"

I look up at Abbi. "What? She can have whatever she wants. Do *you* want a cow?"

"No." She frowns. "But maybe..."

"Maybe what?"

"Maybe a horse of my own."

I tug her to me and nuzzle her ear. "Anything you want, baby. You can have anything you want."

CHAPTER TWENTY-THREE

ABBI

Five Months Later...

"God, I'm so nervous." My hands are wringing in my lap, my knuckles white. The whole family, and I do mean *the whole family*, including Amy, Sierra, and Hugh all the way from North Carolina, are here with us. We even have two little babies here. Polly and Ryan's three-month-old daughter, Charlotte, and tiny August, Summer and Chase's one-month-old, are here to cheer on their Uncle Brady.

We're at the world championships in Vegas, and my man is riding tonight. Of course, none of us are allowed to be in the stands watching. We can't go out there until he's finished.

"He's going to be great," Amy assures me, squeezing my hand.

Amy and I have become good friends over the course of this year. No one understands the life of a bull rider's woman like another bull rider's woman, and she's been invaluable for my mental health.

In addition to the concussion and separated shoulder earlier this season, Brady suffered broken ribs and a pulled groin, which really pissed him off.

No sex for a month was *not* easy on my cowboy.

But despite all the injuries, he came into this championship at the top of the standings, and he's favored to win tonight.

There was no way that his family would stay away for this. I made it *very* clear that wild horses couldn't keep me away.

So, this is the compromise we made.

"There's not even a TV in here so we can watch," Jake grumbles.

"That's the point, son," Ryan reminds him with a laugh.

"He's about to start." Hugh, the only one allowed to have video in here, is watching his phone. "It won't be long now."

I close my eyes and hang my head. *Please let him be okay.*

"My daddy is gonna win," Daisy announces. "He's gonna *win.*"

She's been calling him *daddy* for months, and it's so adorable. Brady melts every single time, and Daisy knows it.

My very *not* innocent daughter has been getting away with murder. She even managed to talk Brady into not one, not two, but *three* mini Highland cows.

Because, as he said, why shouldn't he make all her dreams come true?

"He's done," Hugh announces. "And he's running out of the arena."

"Thank God," Joy whispers, and looks over at me with tears in her eyes.

That's it. Brady's bull-riding career is over. He's officially retiring.

We jump up and run out of this stuffy room, headed for the arena. He was the last rider, and it's been announced that he's the official world champion, and I *can't see him.*

"Over there," Chase shouts, pointing, and then I see my cowboy. "He's already giving interviews."

I make my way through the crowd, with Daisy's hand firmly in mine, and before we can reach Brady, I see that motherfreaking Jen sidle up next to him. Brady scowls, and I can't hear him, but I can read his lips when he says *Fuck off.*

That's right, bitch, you can fuck all the way off.

When Brady glances our way, his face transforms into the biggest smile.

"Excuse me, I need to hug my family." He rushes to us and pulls us in. He's sweaty and filthy—it's amazing what only eight seconds on a bull will do—but I don't care.

"I'm *so proud* of you," I yell into his ear. "So damn proud of you, Cowboy."

"Thank you," he says and kisses me right on the mouth, for the whole world to see. I don't pay any attention to the cameras flashing around us. "I love you so much."

"I love *you*."

"Me, too!" Daisy's jumping up and down. "Me, too, Daddy!"

Brady lifts her in his arms, and then we're surrounded by the rest of the family with hugs and congratulations.

"Come on," Brady yells out. "I want my *whole* family on that stage with me."

"Aren't you Dirks Johnson's widow?" I hear behind me as a reporter approaches Amy. "Ma'am, I'd love to get a word from you."

"Later," Amy says. "I'll stick around to talk after the ceremony."

"You don't have to talk to them," Brady assures her, but she just smiles and shakes her head.

"I want to. Dirks would be *so proud* of you, Brady. I should say something on his behalf."

It's not often that I see Brady at a loss for words, but Amy has managed to render him speechless.

The next hour is a blur of excitement. And when Brady is finally awarded the trophy and the coveted gold buckle, along with the million-dollar check the size of a couch that makes Daisy's eyes bug out, the arena quiets so they can hear his speech.

"Wow," he says and takes a deep breath, looking out at the crowd. "You guys have been with me for a long time. Through a lot of injuries and a lot of heartache. Some great rides."

He waits for the applause to die down.

"This season was a roller coaster ride, but I'm grateful that I managed to stay healthy enough to make it through to the end. As always, I need to thank the fans, who never fail to wow me with their dedication to this sport. My family is truly the best. I love them with all my heart, and I'm grateful for their support through what is always a chaotic season."

He turns to me and grins, and I get butterflies in my stomach.

"This lady right here is the best thing that's ever happened to me, and I can't thank you enough for everything you bring to my life every day."

He thanks Daisy in the cutest way ever that has tears coming to my eyes, and then he pauses and looks over at Amy, swallowing hard.

"Someone is missing here today. When I started this sport, I met a guy named Dirks Johnson."

The arena explodes in applause, and Amy wipes a tear from her cheek.

"He was my best friend. Probably the best damn bull rider that I've ever seen. That man was *talented.* But more than that, he was a good man. A devoted husband and a loving father. The best friend I'd ever had, aside from my brothers. Dirks was the kind of guy who gave 100 percent of himself in everything he did, and that included getting on a bull. And it cost him. He's not here with us today as I stand here to accept this honor and to announce that this was my final ride."

He has to stop talking as the deafening noise

surrounds us. Finally, he gestures for everyone to quiet, and they do.

"I'm stepping aside so that young riders can do what they love, and that's how it should be. How it's supposed to be. I wish my friend was here to retire with me so we could have a beer and talk about the old days." He smiles faintly, then shrugs a shoulder. "Thank you for an amazing career, for allowing me to do what I love for so many years. This was one hell of a way to go out."

He passes the microphone back to the announcer and then wraps his arm around my shoulders and buries his lips in my hair.

"Let's go," he says. "I'm starving."

After celebrating with the family for a while, Brady and I decided to take Daisy back to our suite to order room service and relax.

He needs to ice the ribs that he tweaked again. Of course, he was stoic and didn't let on that they were killing him.

My stubborn cowboy.

"This is a good burger," Daisy says as she takes a bite.

We're all sitting cross-legged on the king-sized bed, our plates in front of us, enjoying our meal.

"I almost forgot something," Brady says and walks out of the room for a second.

Daisy and I share a look, but she shrugs as if to say, *I don't know.*

When he returns, he sits on the bed again and grins at me.

"What are you up to?"

"I love you more than anything in this world." He sets our plates back on the table by the bed and takes my hand in his. "I've been waiting a hell of a long time for this. I didn't want to make this one last promise to you until after the season was over. I *couldn't* make this promise to you until I knew without a doubt that I'd never ride another bull again."

His thumb brushes over my knuckles as he stares into my eyes.

"I promise you that I will love you, no matter what, for as long as there is breath in me."

I bite my lip and feel the tears spring to my eyes. *Holy shit.* We're doing this. Right now.

"You are the reason for everything in my life. You are the light and the goodness that I didn't know was missing. I can't wait to move into our home, to make more babies, and to live this life with you, every day, knowing that no matter what happens, we choose each other."

He reaches into his pocket and pulls out a sparkling diamond ring, and Daisy starts to jump on the bed with glee.

"Will you marry me, Abs? Will you make me the happiest man in the world?"

I look up at Daisy, and she giggles. "I already said yes, and he made me keep this secret until tonight. *Please* say yes, Mom."

"You already asked her?"

"Well, yeah. If she wasn't in on this, there was no way you would be." He reaches out and catches a tear on his thumb. "Don't cry, baby. I can't stand it when you cry."

"Happy tears. Of course, I'll marry you, Cowboy."

He slides the ring onto my finger and then kisses me long and slow and deep until Daisy makes a choking noise.

"Do we get to be Wilds now? For real?" Daisy asks.

"Yes, ma'am," Brady says with a wink and then turns back to me. "Wild will be the last name you ever have."

I can't help but laugh at that. "Sounds like a plan to me."

"Hey, what if *I* get married?" Daisy asks, and Brady's face goes pale.

"Absolutely *not.*" He shakes his head. "No way. Not happening."

I take his face in mine and kiss his lips. "Breathe, Cowboy. We have a few years before we have to cross that bridge."

"I love you, Blue Eyes."

"I love you, too."

EPILOGUE

HOLDEN LEXINGTON

Today is going to be a son of a bitch, and if I'm going to get through it with my sanity intact, I need some coffee.

And maybe I need to see her.

Okay, mostly, I need to see her. So sue me.

I push my way into Bitterroot Valley Coffee Co., and the smell of coffee and sugar assaults my nose. At first, I don't see Millie Wild behind the counter, and I consider turning around and walking back out, but then she bustles through a side door, a smile on that drop-dead gorgeous face as she carries a couple of sleeves of cups behind the counter. Her long, chestnut-brown hair is up in a high ponytail to keep it out of her way. She's in a branded T-shirt and jeans, with a signature orange apron tied around her waist.

It's the middle of the morning on a weekday, so of course, it's busy in here. I hang back for a moment and take her in before she sees me. She smiles and jokes with her customers, and I love seeing this carefree look on her face.

She glances my way, and the ice seeps into her eyes, and those walls come crashing down around her.

Not that I don't deserve it. I abso-fucking-lutely do. But it still pisses me off.

"Hey," she says with a polite smile as I approach her. God, I fucking hate it when she looks at me with indifference. I'd almost rather the blatant animosity that shows up more times than not than the cool indifference. "What would you like today?"

"My usual."

"And that is?"

I narrow my eyes at her. This woman has half the town's *usual* memorized, and I know she knows mine, too. She's just being obtuse to be a brat.

I wish I could take her over my knee and spank her pretty little ass.

"Coffee. Black. One sugar."

"Ah, yes, that's right." She taps the screen of the computer. "What are you up to today?"

"Headed to the lawyer's office," I say as I tap my card to the screen. "Will reading."

Her hazel eyes—no, *gold*, flecked with green—soften on me. "I'm sorry, Holden."

"Yeah, well. Have to get it over with."

"I was sorry to hear about your dad."

She wouldn't be if she knew the absolute *fuckery* that man caused. For both her and me. But she'll never know, if I have anything to say about it.

I simply nod at her, and she turns to pour my coffee, adds the sugar the way she knows that I like it, which makes me grin, and then snaps the lid on and turns to pass it to me.

"Thanks."

"You're welcome. Good luck."

When she softens like this, it's almost my undoing. So, I turn and walk out of the coffee shop and down the street to Jameson and Jameson, Attorneys at Law. When I walk inside, I'm shown into a conference room where all four of my sisters are already seated. I take the chair right in the middle of them.

I *love* my sisters. My father was a son of a bitch who didn't give a rat's ass about anyone with a vagina, so I'm quite sure he's going to find a way to hurt them today, even from beyond the goddamn grave.

"Hey," Dani says, rubbing my back.

"I should have brought you all coffee," I say with a frown. "Sorry about that."

"We're fine," Charlie assures me. "Let's just get this day over with so we can get on with our lives."

Darby and Alex haven't said a word, but I know they're nervous.

"No matter what happens here today," I assure them all, "we'll make it right. I promise."

I look at Dad's attorney and nod.

"Thanks for meeting me today," he says, after clearing his throat. "This shouldn't take too long. I'm going to read the will, and then I'm happy to answer any questions."

He clears his throat again.

"I, Lawrence Lexington, being of sound mind and body, do declare this my last will and testament. I leave each of my four daughters, Danielle, Darby, Charlie, and Alex, each ten thousand dollars."

Each of my sisters gasps, and I already want to punch a dead man.

"To my son, Holden, I leave the rest of my worldly belongings. My ranch, livestock and equipment, the buildings and land, in its entirety, valued at five million dollars. I also leave all of my bank accounts, valued at three million dollars."

I'm shaking my head, pressing my fingertips to my eyeballs.

"With the following stipulation."

Now my head comes up again, and Charlie takes my hand in hers, giving it a reassuring squeeze.

"Holden must marry within sixty days of the reading of this will and stay married for one year. If he fails to do so, the entire inheritance will be sold, and the money will be donated to the following charities."

He reads through a list of bullshit charities that no one has ever heard of, and I'm just shaking my head.

That son of a bitch.

That motherfucker.

That pitiful excuse for a human being.

"Do you have any questions?" the attorney asks.

"No." I stand, and my sisters stand with me. "Do we need to sign anything?"

"Yes, there is paperwork, but each of you can come in when it's convenient for you to finish up."

"Great." I turn to my sisters and try to offer them a smile. "Team meeting?"

"Right now," Charlie says, nodding. "Sir, can we use this room?"

"Of course, take your time." He gathers his papers and leaves, closing the door behind him.

"That son of a bitch," Dani says, shaking her head.

"I'm going to make sure you each get a hell of a lot more than ten grand."

"We don't care about the money," Darby says with a scowl. "Dad didn't give a shit about us. I'm surprised he left us anything at all."

"He left what we'd consider an *insult*," Alex says with a smirk. "And he's right. It is. Fuck his money. He can go to hell."

"Hopefully, he's burning down there," Charlie agrees. "But to demand that Holden has to get married in order to inherit what's rightfully his? That's insane. He can't do that."

"Pretty sure he can," I reply grimly.

It's just another way for him to dick with me. To make me pay. Hell, to be in control. He probably thought that I'd never marry, so I wouldn't inherit, and I'd be shit out of luck.

And he could be right.

There's only one woman in this world that I'd ever consider marrying, and she'd rather smother me in my sleep than say a nice word to me.

Thanks to him.

"We're going out for lunch to talk about this," Darby decides. "Are you coming, Holden?"

"Nah, you guys go on. I'll catch up with you later." I smile and pull Darby's dark curls. "I'm fine. Really, go ahead."

"If you're sure," Charlie says. "Call me later."

"Will do." I wait until the four of them are gone and then blow out a long breath.

Well, hell, I have to talk Millie Wild into marrying me.

WOULD you like to read Sophie Montgomery and Ike Harrison's story? Get The Score here: https://www.kristenprobyauthor.com/the-score

KEEP READING for a preview of She's a Wild One, Millie Wild and Holden Lexington's story! https://www.kristenprobyauthor.com/shes-a-wild-one

SHE'S A WILD ONE PREVIEW

PROLOGUE - HOLDEN

Eight Years Ago...

It's been the best fucking month of my life.

I've spent every spare minute with Millie Wild and all her young, innocent beauty, since I ran into her at the farmer's market. She's home for the summer from college, and like a moth to an inferno, I couldn't stay away from her.

She's too young for me. All my instincts scream that at me daily.

She may be an adult, but I'm pushing thirty, and I should stay away from her. At nineteen, she's *too young*.

Not to mention, she's the only daughter and youngest child of John Wild, my father's arch nemesis. Our families have a hundred-year-old feud to maintain, so the likelihood of either of our parents sitting back and agreeing to this match is less than zero.

But I'll be damned if I can stay away from her.

"I don't want to go back to college," Millie says with a sigh. We're not on either of our properties, in the off chance that we'd get caught. Instead, we're sitting on a blanket at my friend Brooks Blackwell's ranch. The sun has gone down, and the stars are starting to come out.

"We still have a week," I remind her. Her head is in my lap, and I'm brushing my fingers through her long, soft chestnut-brown hair. "We'll do whatever you want before you go. Name it."

"Except, we can't actually *date*." She narrows her eyes up at me. "This family feud shit is stupid. So what if our great-great grandparents hated each other? Get over it already."

"I couldn't agree more." I drag my fingertip down the bridge of her nose. A coyote howls somewhere off in the distance.

I can't stop touching her. For a month, it's been impossible to keep my hands to myself. Whether I'm holding her hand or touching her hair or sitting like this, memorizing her gorgeous face, I need to be in constant physical contact.

But I haven't slept with her. Because once we do that, there's no going back, and I don't want to push her too far before she's ready. I don't ever want to do anything that might make her pull away from me, or run in the other direction.

"Holden?"

"Yes, Rosie?"

That makes her smirk. She told me a couple of weeks ago that her favorite flower is a wild rose, and now, that's how I think of her. My little wild rose. It's appropriate, given that her last name is Wild.

And when I want to see that sweet smile, I call her Rosie.

"I'm not going to see you for a while, am I?"

I sigh, not wanting to think about what's going to happen after she returns to Bozeman to go to school next week.

"I wish I could come out there every week, but I have to be here for my sisters."

She nods, understanding in those amazing hazel eyes. "I know. I'm sorry that your dad's so mean."

She doesn't know the half of it. I shudder to think what would happen to my four little sisters if I wasn't here to run interference.

"But I'll see you when you come home for holidays," I remind her. "And I'll talk to you every day. We can video chat before bed."

"Yeah, I'd like that." She sits up and moves to straddle me, planting her knees on the blanket on either side of my hips.

And just like that, my cock is on high alert.

"Mill—"

She covers my mouth with hers, so gently, so sweetly, that it tugs at my heart.

"Millie," I try again, stilling her hands when they roam over my shoulders and kissing them both. "Baby girl, if you keep this up, I won't want to stop."

"Who said anything about stopping?" She grins and leans in closer, pressing herself against my hard-on, and

I can't help the groan that slips out of my throat. "Holden, I want this, especially before I have to leave and not see you for *months*."

I cup her face, and then my hand glides down to her cheek and over her jaw, until I'm holding onto her throat, gently, but still holding.

"You need to be completely sure."

Her tongue pokes out to her lip, and with her eyes boldly on mine, she lifts her sundress over her head and discards it to the side.

Jesus Christ, I can't look down. She's not wearing a bra.

My girl is mostly naked, straddling me in the middle of nowhere, offering herself to me with utter love and trust shining in those golden eyes, and it's almost more than I can take.

"Holden," she whispers as she tips forward and rests her forehead on mine. "Make love to me, okay?"

And that's all I can take. Christ, who could say no to this sweetness?

I take her lips, kissing her the way I've learned she loves, and then I pick her up and move her so she's lying on her back on the blanket. My eyes haven't left hers.

"Before I look at all of you, I want you to tell me how you like to be touched."

She frowns and bites her lip. "Uh, what do you mean?"

"How do you want it?" I ask and drag my nose up her cheek.

"I don't know." She swallows hard, and I pull back so

I can see her face in the waning light. "I've never done this before."

Fuck me sideways.

"Oh, baby." Jesus Christ, I'm gonna go to hell for what I'm about to do.

And I don't fucking care.

"But I'm *really* sure," she assures me and grips onto my T-shirt, tugging it high on my torso. "I want to see you."

"Me first."

For the first time since she stripped off that dress, I let my eyes move down, and my mouth goes dry.

My cock has never been so hard.

Her skin, all smooth and bronze from the sun, feels like velvet under my hands, and her nipples are already hard little nubs, just begging for my mouth.

I have to remind myself to be gentle. For this first time, at the very least, I have to go easy on her. Get her good and ready for me.

"Do you trust me, Rosie?"

She nods, but I cover her throat with my hand again and lean in to press my lips to her ear.

"I need your words, Baby Girl. Do you trust me?"

"I trust you." Her throat works under my palm as she swallows hard and the pulse under my thumb is strong and fast. "More than anyone."

"Good. We're going to take this nice and slow."

"Or, we could hurry."

I smile against her skin as I make my way down her

body, kissing her *everywhere.* "No, I'm not about to rush this incredible moment. No way."

She arches her back as I take a nipple into my mouth, wanting more. Those hips are moving, her long legs scissoring, and I loop my thumbs in her little pink panties and pull them down her legs, tossing them onto her discarded dress.

"Gorgeous," I groan, but she moves her knees together almost shyly, and I shake my head. "Open those pretty thighs for me."

She takes a deep breath and lets it out slowly, but she does as I ask, letting her thighs fall to the side as her gorgeous eyes never leave mine.

I press my hand to her chest bone, then slowly drag it down. Her breath shudders when I reach her pubis, and I pause.

"You can stop this at any time."

"No stopping," she says breathlessly, her chest rising and falling. "Do not stop, Holden."

I grin, dragging my hand lower, and when I cup her already soaking pussy, she moans.

"I'm the first one to touch this pretty pussy?" I drag my fingertip through her already swollen lips, up around her hard clit, and back down again.

"Yes." Her hand dives into my hair as I shimmy down to nudge my shoulders between her thighs.

With one long stroke, I lick her from her glistening opening up to her clit, and her hips arch up off of the blanket.

"Holden!"

"Easy," I croon before licking her again. "Easy, baby."

She's fisted the blanket in her hands, her head moving back and forth.

"Look at me, Millie."

Instantly, she follows that command. My girl is good at taking orders, and it only makes me want her more. I want to pound into her and brand her as mine.

But first, I have to make sure I won't hurt her.

I press one finger inside of her, and she moans low in her throat. And when I fasten my lips to her clit and rub my fingertip over that spongy spot, she comes undone, bucking against me.

Not able to hold myself in check any longer, I find the condom in my wallet and toss it next to her hip, then strip out of my shirt and jeans, thankful that Millie and I both took off our boots when we got here. Her hands reach for me, gliding down my abs, and I grin at her.

"Like what you see?"

"You're so sexy."

She licks her lips again, and I grab the condom and slip it on, then kiss up her gorgeous body—Jesus, I've never seen anyone more beautiful—and kiss her hard as I lay the head of my cock against her.

"Inside me," she says, gripping onto my shoulders. "Please. Please, Holden."

"We'll go slow," I promise her, easing just the tip into her, and it takes all of my strength to hold back, to not just pound into her, taking what I've wanted for weeks.

"Oh, God." Her eyes close, and I grip onto her throat.

"Up here, baby. Eyes on me."

She complies, and I ease in more. One inch at a time, watching her face as she takes me.

"You're so fucking amazing." I kiss her lips lightly, breathing in her gasps. "You're so beautiful. And all mine."

"Yours," she agrees, and I push the rest of the way in until I'm buried to the root, and I pause here, as if I can freeze this moment in time.

"Mine," I say again as I begin to move. "God, Rosie, you're so snug. You're so fucking good."

And she's all mine. No other asshole has been here but *me*. And no one will be. I'll make fucking sure of that.

"Oh, God," she says, her eyes widening in alarm. "Oh, I can't. This is too much. It's too much."

"Baby," I whisper against her lips. She's starting to tremor, to contract around me. She's about to have her first orgasm, and I fucking love it. "It's okay. Let go, Mill."

She looks so worried. It's adorable.

"Trust me," I remind her, and then her whole body erupts under me as the orgasm moves through her.

It's the most amazing thing I've ever seen in my goddamn life.

And I can't hold back anymore. I follow her over into the most intense climax I've ever had.

Suddenly, she's giggling beneath me.

"You think that's funny, Wild Rose?"

She laughs again, and it makes me groan because her muscles pulse around me.

"Holy shit, we did it," she says, smiling up at me so big she could light the night sky. "I'd like to do it again."

"Give me a few to recover, and we'll see what we can do."

It's the best night of my life, lying out here under the stars on this hot summer night, making love to my girl.

My girl.

My Millie.

My little wild rose.

And when the sky begins to lighten with the promise of dawn, we get dressed, smiling softly at each other.

"I'll see you tonight?" she asks. "At the usual spot?"

"Of course." I take her wrist and tug her against me, kissing her hard. "Wouldn't miss it."

"Have a good day at work," she whispers against my lips. "I'll miss you."

With nothing but Millie and our amazing night together on my mind, I hop out of my truck and start toward the small cabin that I live in here on the Lexington ranch. I moved out of the family home years ago, but I want to be close by for my sisters.

"It won't happen again."

I stop short and scowl, my hands fisting, when I see my father sitting in the one chair on my porch.

"What are you doing here? We don't start morning chores for an hour."

"You won't be with her again," he repeats. His voice is hard and mean, just like it always is. "The fact that you've been fucking around with a *Wild* is not acceptable."

"Dad—"

"Shut the fuck up," he snaps as he stands to his full

height. He might be getting older, but he's still fit from ranch work, and he's tall. "Whatever the fuck you've been playing at is over. You won't see that whore again."

Hot blood rushes through my head. I want to fucking kill him.

"I'm an *adult,*" I remind him through clenched teeth. "There's not much you can do about it."

"Oh, no?" Now that sick, evil grin slides over his face. "If you don't stop seeing that cunt, I'll kill Charlie."

My heart stutters. My mind spins. Jesus Christ, he can't be serious.

"I know she's your favorite. There are a lot of places to hide a body on this ranch. Animals will take care of it for me. Girls get taken all the time."

"You're insane."

"I'm not fucking with you," he says, losing the smile. "No son of mine is going to so much as sniff at a Wild. You keep it up, and I'll kill everything you love, starting with that sister of yours. And then I'll see what kind of hellfire I can rain down on that little Wild bitch."

"Charlie's your *daughter.*"

"Who the fuck cares?"

He smirks and walks down the stairs to the truck that I didn't notice when I pulled up and drives away.

When he's out of sight, my knees give out, and I lower to the top step of the porch, covering my face with my hands.

He would do it. He's not bluffing.

God*damn* it.

Chapter One
Millie

"How many grandmas do you have?" I press my phone to my ear and scowl as I lean my hip against the counter and absently wipe a rag over it. "Because this is the *sixth* one that's died in the past six months, Shelly."

"Uh, well—"

"And don't forget that we live in the same small town, and I've known your family longer than *you* have."

"Millie—"

I roll my eyes, listening as the sixteen-year-old stammers through a bunch of excuses. Shelly is notorious for calling out, whether it's because she claims to be sick or because a mythical grandmother has sadly crossed to the other side.

And I'd have fired her sooner, but I'm short-staffed.

Looks like I'm even *more* shorthanded now than before.

"Shelly," I interrupt. "I'm too busy to do this with you. I get it. You're not coming in tomorrow."

My one and only day off.

"But," I continue, "you won't be coming in at all. This is the last straw for me. Good luck to you."

I hang up and sigh. I am *not* giving up my day off tomorrow. And since I no longer have the second staff member for the day, I'll have to close down the shop.

It's not my favorite solution, but damn it, *I'm fucking exhausted.* Not to mention, I have plans for the whole day that I can't shift.

"You okay, boss?"

I turn to Candy, the one employee that I can count on for literally anything, and sigh.

"Shelly's done. Which means I need to close down tomorrow."

"Cool, I can use the day off," she says with a smile. "But it sucks for you. I have a couple of friends who just moved to town and might need jobs."

"A *couple* of friends?" I ask her. Candy's in her mid-twenties and has worked here since she was in high school. She's a total ski bum in the winter and a sun goddess in the summer.

"Yeah, they want to be here for the summer, and they came early."

"But that means that they probably won't be here long term."

"Maybe they'll love working for you as much as I do, and they'll never want to leave." Candy bats her eyelashes at me, making me laugh. "At the very least, it'll get us through the summer rush."

"You have a point." I push my hand through my hair, remembering that I need to put it up in a ponytail. "Okay, have them come see me. They'll need references."

"No problem." Candy turns to take a customer's order.

"I'll be right back. I have to grab more medium cups."

Hurrying to the stockroom, I make a detour to pull a scrunchie out of my purse and throw my hair up into a high pony, then I grab some sleeves of cups before returning to the dining room, smiling at Beckett Blackwell, who happens to be placing an order right now.

"Hey, Beck," I say with a smile as I stow the cups away. "How's it going?"

"Can't complain," he says with that easygoing smile. Of all the Blackwell brothers, Beckett is the most laid-back. He's just a big ol' sexy-as-all-get-out teddy bear. "How are you, Mill?"

"All in all, things could be worse." I wink at him and turn to make his coffee.

I love it when my shop is bustling like it is right now. Not just because that means that I'll have a profitable day, but because I enjoy seeing the people from my town that I love so much. I know that Bitterroot Valley is growing, but the connections from my childhood are still here, too.

Just after I pass Beckett his cup, I turn and find Holden Lexington standing on the other side of the counter.

Jesus. Fucking. Christ. Warn a girl, will you?

It's been eight years, and still, every time I lay my eyes on this man, my entire being longs for him. And after the shit he put me through, that just pisses me right off.

"Hey." *Good, Millie. Keep your voice neutral. You've got this.* "What would you like today?"

"My usual."

"And that is?" I know exactly what it is. Medium roast, black, one sugar. But I'll never let him know that I remember his drink. He doesn't get even that much from me.

He narrows those blue eyes, and my stomach flutters.

Stop it.

"Coffee. Black. One sugar." I hate it when he watches me with those eyes that see too fucking much. Eyes that used to look at me as if he loved me. As if he couldn't get enough of me. As if I hung the goddamn moon.

Of course, that's ancient history.

"Ah, yes, that's right." I tap his order onto the screen of the computer. I always feel so awkward with him. So, I try to fill the silence with small talk. "What are you up to today?"

"Headed to the lawyer's office." He taps his card on the screen, paying for his coffee, and I can't help but watch his hands as he pushes the card back into his wallet. I know from experience that Holden has *really good* hands. "Will reading."

That brings my gaze back up to his, and I can't help but soften toward him just a bit. I can't imagine losing my own dad. I know that Holden's not as close to his father, but still, I'm not a complete ice witch. "I'm sorry, Holden."

"Yeah, well. Have to get it over with." He shrugs, as if it's nothing, but I know it's not nothing by the way his whole body just tensed up.

I might despise this man, and the wounds still ache, even though it's been so many years since he broke my heart—or, you know, tore it out of my chest and set it on fire—but I still know him.

And that's its own special, horrible hurt.

"I was sorry to hear about your dad." My voice is softer, and I can tell by the way Holden's muscles relax a bit that he believes me. He simply nods again, and I take that as my cue to turn and get his coffee ready.

I know *exactly* how he likes it. He doesn't just want one sugar. It's more like one and a half. After stirring it, I snap on the lid and turn to give it to him.

"Thanks."

"You're welcome. Good luck."

He turns away and walks out, and I have to take a long, deep breath to get my body to calm the fuck down.

He doesn't want you, you idiot. He made that crystal clear. You have got *to let this go.*

Thankfully, we're busy the entire day, and that makes the hours pass quickly. Before I know it, Candy has locked the door and we're cleaning up the espresso machine, mopping the floor, and I've counted the till and stowed the cash away in the safe.

"Well, boss, have a good day off tomorrow," Candy says, after looping her purse across her body. "I'll see you in a couple of days."

"Have fun," I reply with a grin and walk the short two blocks home to my apartment.

I like my place, and it totally suited my needs in the past, but lately, I've been feeling like I've outgrown it, so I've decided to move. I'm renting Polly's house just a few blocks over. I need tomorrow to get most of my stuff moved and settled in so I can clean the apartment for the next tenant.

I grew up on a ranch twenty minutes outside of town, and once I was old enough to make those kinds of decisions, I knew that I didn't want to stay that far away from civilization.

I'm a town girl. *Not* a ranch girl.

Don't get me wrong, I do love our family ranch. The mountains are spectacular, and I like helping with branding and vaccinations on the calves in the spring.

But I do not want to live out there.

"Hi, Hazel." I offer my elderly neighbor, Hazel Henderson, a wave as I unlock my door. That woman is *nosy* and always pokes her head out the door to see who's out here whenever I come home, and I'm going to miss her after I move.

"Hi, Millie. Did you have a good day, dear?"

"It was fine, thank you. How's the corn on your foot?"

I shouldn't know about Hazel's corn, but she likes to tell me about *all* of her ailments.

"What's that?"

She must have her hearing aid turned down, so I point to my own ear, and she hurries to adjust her volume.

"How's the corn on your foot?" I repeat.

"Oh, I went to the podiatrist yesterday. They took it out. It's sore today, but I'm fine. Thank you for asking."

"Well, you go take it easy, Hazel. I'll see you later."

I let myself inside and toss my keys and purse on the floor by the door, kick out of my shoes, and walk straight past all the packed boxes to my bedroom, where I strip out of the clothes I've worn all day, and then flop down on the bed, naked.

I like being naked. Not in a pervy, exhibitionist kind of way, but I don't like tight clothing, and when I'm at work, I have to wear jeans and T-shirts, and they feel like straitjackets. I can't wait for summer, when I can wear loose summer dresses on my days off.

If I get any days off.

After throwing my arm over my face, I start to feel guilty about closing up the shop tomorrow. It's a Friday, and I should stay open. It's not quite tourist season yet, so we're not swamped, but still.

It's not exactly a good business decision to just close up on a Friday. But damn it, I'm ready to move to the cute little house just a couple of blocks away.

I knew when I bought the coffee shop almost two years ago that it would be a big undertaking. That it would mean long hours and that it's not easy to keep workers year-round in a ski resort town. But man, I didn't realize that it would be *this* hard. I hope Candy's friends work out, because if they do, I'll be covered for the summer.

"Okay, no more work." I rub my hands over my face and blow out a breath. "You're taking the next thirty-six hours off. You're going to be productive. You're going to finish selling the rest of the furniture and get all the boxes moved over, and then you're going to clean the fridge."

I wrinkle my nose. I don't want to clean the fridge.

I must fall asleep because the next thing I know, I

open my eyes, and I'm *cold.* I have goose bumps all over my body because I didn't crawl under the covers after getting naked and throwing myself onto the mattress.

Deciding that I need a shower anyway, I pad into the bathroom and start the water. Thirty minutes later, I'm warmed up, my face is clean, and I'm no longer super tired.

I hate napping late in the day. I'll be up all night now.

"I need a drink." Staring at myself in the mirror, I brush on a little mascara and lip gloss, brush out my hair, and then I pull on a white blouse that I like along with a pair of dark wash denim.

I'm going out.

Typically, I wouldn't want to go alone, but I know that all four of my best friends, who happen to be married to my brothers, are busy tonight. They all have kids, and they can't just leave at the drop of a hat. Sure, my brothers wouldn't mind, but it's not considerate of me to just call them up and be like, *Come on, bitches, let's go get hammered.*

So, a night out alone it is.

I'll inevitably see someone that I know anyway, and we'll have a beer and chat, and then I'll walk home, and all will be well.

After sliding my feet into a new pair of Adidas and grabbing my bag and keys, I lock the door behind me and walk the couple of blocks to The Wolf Den.

Surprisingly, I recognize most of the faces here, and I can't help but grin when I belly up to the bar and Brenda, a gal I went to school with, waves at me excitedly.

"Hey, Mill," she says. "What can I getcha?"

"Tequila. Straight up. No training wheels."

Her eyebrows climb into her bleach-blonde hair. "It's like that, is it?"

"Oh, yeah. It's like that. Hook me up, Bren."

"You got it." She pours the drink and passes it to me, and I swallow it in one gulp, then pass the glass back to her. "Another. I'll sip this one."

She pours again, and I turn on the stool to look around the bar. The Wolf Den is the hot spot in town, where locals and tourists alike come to eat, drink, and socialize. I love it when the five of us girls come and order just about everything on the menu to help soak up our huckleberry margaritas.

We'll have to arrange for a girls' night out soon.

Suddenly, someone laughs to my left, and I'd know that laugh *anywhere.*

I turn my head, and sure enough. There he is. Holden, drinking a beer, and then laughing at something another guy has said. He nods and takes a pool cue to the table and takes a shot.

And misses.

He already looks a little drunk. He also looks delicious in a black Henley, sleeves pulled up his forearms, showing off tattoos on one muscled arm that he didn't used to have, and tight jeans.

Of course, he's wearing dark cowboy boots. The man is *always* in boots. And tonight, rather than a cowboy hat, he's in a backward baseball cap.

Fuck me.

Why does he have to be so...*beautiful*? Just why?

I set my untouched second drink aside, already deciding that I'll be helping Holden get home tonight. I would usually scoff at him. Call him an idiot for being out and acting like a moron.

But his dad recently died, and they had the reading of the will today. It was likely hard on all of them. And while the Lexingtons aren't my favorite family in town, I don't hold the ill will for them that my ancestors did.

The rivalry is just stupid, if you ask me.

Of course, Holden is my least favorite, but I don't wish anything *horrible* for him. Maybe he could lose his dick to a flesh-eating bacteria, or he could trip and fall and break his nose, ruining all that handsomeness, but I don't want anything *catastrophic* to happen.

I snort and turn back to Brenda. "You know what? Let's switch to Coke."

"You sure?" She lifts an eyebrow, and I nod.

"Yeah, a Coke will be fine. Thanks."

She fills a glass and passes it to me, and then I turn to watch Holden some more. He's pounding another full glass of beer, and in the past ten minutes, his steps have only gotten sloppier. It's almost as if getting hammered was his whole goal in life tonight.

Not that I can blame him. It was going to be my goal, too. No judgment here. And I *really* try to judge Holden Lexington as much as humanly possible.

Because he's a first-class ass.

And he *has* a first-class ass.

"For fuck's sake," I mutter before drinking my Coke.

With one ear on what's going on in Holden's corner, I turn back to the bar. I'll just sip my Coke and hang out until he's ready to go home. Because there's no way in hell that he's driving out to his ranch like this.

I would hope that he'd call a sister, but I want to make sure.

Why do I feel responsible for him? Why do I have this ridiculous soft spot for him?

Because I'm a masochist, apparently.

"Millie?" I turn and frown at the sight of Bridger Blackwell. Not because I don't like him, but because *what* is he doing here? "I thought that was you."

"You never come out," I say as he takes the stool next to me. "What are you up to? Where's Birdie?"

"My mom's with her," he says on an exhale, and when Brenda approaches, he orders a beer. "And I needed an hour away."

"I get it." I clink my glass to his when Brenda slides his drink to him. "How is she?"

Bridger's young daughter has had a lot of medical issues over the past year, and I know it's been really hard on him. For quite a long time, I helped him out by staying with her when he had to work at night.

"She's doing better. I'm not really sure that they've figured her out completely, but the new medication seems to be working."

"Good. I'm glad to hear that, for both of your sakes."

Bridger nods and swallows his beer. He and I have been friends for a long, long time. There's never been anything besides friendship between us, which is too bad because this man is hot as hell, and on top of that, he's the fire chief.

I mean, hello, hot man in uniform.

But it's just never been like that for us. He's one of my best friends.

"What are *you* doing out?" he asks, making me sigh.

"I just needed a drink and didn't want to be in my apartment alone. Which sounds really, *really* pathetic."

"No, it doesn't." He grins over at me and then nudges me with his shoulder. "It sounds pretty normal. Next time, call me. I'll go with you."

"You have a daughter. I'm surrounded by a bunch of parents." I sigh into my Coke and ignore the feeling of longing as my own biological clock lets out a little *gong*. "You're no fun."

"I will have you know that I'm a *lot* of fun," Bridger replies with a mock scowl. "Just ask my daughter."

I laugh at that, and then the hair on the back of my neck stands up when I feel eyes on me.

Not just any eyes.

Stark blue, intense, *Holden* eyes.

I glance over, and sure enough, he's watching us with his jaw clenched and his eyes hot, and it almost makes me laugh.

Instead, I let out a deep sigh.

This man is *so* damn confusing. He doesn't get to be territorial. He made it clear that he didn't want me.

But apparently, he doesn't want anyone else to want me, either.

For the next hour, Bridger and I chat and laugh, and finally, he tosses some bills onto the bar and stands up.

"I'd better get home," he says and leans in to hug me tight. Bridger gives the *best* hugs. "You okay?"

"Oh, yeah, I only had one drink, and you know I don't live far. I'm glad I got to see you."

"Same goes." He pats my shoulder and then leaves, and when the door closes behind him, I feel Holden standing next to me.

"What the *fuck* is going on between you two?"

And just like that, my back is up, and I regret not drinking more and feeling responsible for *him.*

Slowly, I turn on the stool and look up at him.

He's so...*broad.* Muscular. Tall. Strong.

And such a pain in my ass.

"Hello, Holden."

"Tell me," he says, bracing one hand on the bar, caging me in.

"No." I push my empty Coke glass away. "I don't think I will. Are you about done drinking for the night?"

"Why, baby? You want to go home with me?"

My heart stutters at that, and I feel the goddamn blush move over me, effectively embarrassing the shit out of me.

Fuck. This.

"I was trying to be nice," I grind out through clenched teeth. "Because you had a hard day, and you're drunk, and I was going to stay sober and help you home. But you know what? Shame on me for dropping my guard for even *one fucking minute*. You're such a piece of shit, Holden. Find your own way home."

"Shit, I'm sorry, Ro—"

"Don't you fucking dare." I get in his face now, glaring at him and ignoring the heat coming off of him. "You will *never* call me that again. Do you understand me?"

He swallows hard, clearly more sober than when he walked over here, and nods.

"Yeah. Got it."

Without another word, I turn away from him, hop off the stool, and stomp out of this fucking bar all the way home.

My heart is going to come flying out of my chest at any moment, it's beating so hard. I haven't heard that name roll off his tongue since that morning in the field, when I was ready to pledge my undying love to him and beg him to marry me.

He will *not* do that to me ever again.

Fuck Holden Lexington.

NEWSLETTER SIGN UP

I hope you enjoyed reading this story as much as I enjoyed writing it! For upcoming book news, be sure to join my newsletter! I promise I will only send you news-filled mail, and none of the spam. You can sign up here:

https://mailchi.mp/kristenproby.com/newsletter-sign-up

ALSO BY KRISTEN PROBY:

Other Books by Kristen Proby

The Wilds of Montana Series

Wild for You - Remington & Erin

Chasing Wild - Chase & Summer

Get more information on the series here: https://www.kristenprobyauthor.com/the-wilds-of-montana

Single in Seattle Series

The Secret - Vaughn & Olivia

The Scandal - Gray & Stella

The Score - Ike & Sophie

The Setup - Keaton & Sidney

The Stand-In - Drew & London

Check out the full series here: https://www.kristenprobyauthor.com/single-in-seattle

Huckleberry Bay Series

Lighthouse Way

Fernhill Lane

Chapel Bend

Cherry Lane

The With Me In Seattle Series

Come Away With Me - Luke & Natalie

Under The Mistletoe With Me - Isaac & Stacy

Fight With Me - Nate & Jules

Play With Me - Will & Meg

Rock With Me - Leo & Sam

Safe With Me - Caleb & Brynna

Tied With Me - Matt & Nic

Breathe With Me - Mark & Meredith

Forever With Me - Dominic & Alecia

Stay With Me - Wyatt & Amelia

Indulge With Me

Love With Me - Jace & Joy

Dance With Me Levi & Starla

You Belong With Me - Archer & Elena

Dream With Me - Kane & Anastasia

Imagine With Me - Shawn & Lexi

Escape With Me - Keegan & Isabella

Flirt With Me - Hunter & Maeve

Take a Chance With Me - Cameron & Maggie

Check out the full series here: https://www.

kristenprobyauthor.com/with-me-in-seattle

The Big Sky Universe

Love Under the Big Sky

Loving Cara

Seducing Lauren

Falling for Jillian

Saving Grace

The Big Sky

Charming Hannah

Kissing Jenna

Waiting for Willa

Soaring With Fallon

Big Sky Royal

Enchanting Sebastian

Enticing Liam

Taunting Callum

Heroes of Big Sky

Honor

Courage

Shelter

Check out the full Big Sky universe here: https://www.kristenprobyauthor.com/under-the-big-sky

Bayou Magic

Shadows

Spells

Serendipity

Check out the full series here: https://www.kristenprobyauthor.com/bayou-magic

The Curse of the Blood Moon Series

Hallows End

Cauldrons Call

Salems Song

The Romancing Manhattan Series

All the Way

All it Takes

After All

Check out the full series here: https://www.kristenprobyauthor.com/romancing-manhattan

The Boudreaux Series

Easy Love

Easy Charm

Easy Melody

Easy Kisses

Easy Magic

Easy Fortune

Easy Nights

Check out the full series here: https://www.kristenprobyauthor.com/boudreaux

The Fusion Series

Listen to Me

Close to You

Blush for Me

The Beauty of Us

Savor You

Check out the full series here: https://www.kristenprobyauthor.com/fusion

From 1001 Dark Nights

Easy With You

Easy For Keeps

No Reservations

Tempting Brooke

Wonder With Me

Shine With Me

Change With Me

The Scramble

Cherry Lane

Kristen Proby's Crossover Collection

Soaring with Fallon, A Big Sky Novel

Wicked Force: A Wicked Horse Vegas/Big Sky Novella
By Sawyer Bennett

All Stars Fall: A Seaside Pictures/Big Sky Novella
By Rachel Van Dyken

Hold On: A Play On/Big Sky Novella
By Samantha Young

Worth Fighting For: A Warrior Fight Club/Big Sky Novella
By Laura Kaye

Crazy Imperfect Love: A Dirty Dicks/Big Sky Novella
By K.L. Grayson

Nothing Without You: A Forever Yours/Big Sky Novella
By Monica Murphy

Check out the entire Crossover Collection here:
https://www.kristenprobyauthor.com/kristen-proby-crossover-collection

ABOUT THE AUTHOR

Kristen Proby has published more than sixty titles, many of which have hit the USA Today, New York Times and Wall Street Journal Bestsellers lists.

Kristen and her husband, John, make their home in her hometown of Whitefish, Montana with their two cats and dog.

Made in the USA
Middletown, DE
14 June 2025